HOT-BLOODED

"I think," Marcus said, stepping to the right just as Sydney did. "I think I deserve some kindness now."

"Oh, really?" She stepped to the left; he blocked her again. She moaned in annoyance then backed away as he stepped closer. "I'm going to bed."

"Not until I get some answers." Marcus grabbed her by the arm, pulling her to him. Her cotton bathrobe was an unwelcomed barrier between them.

"Let go of me." Sydney pulled away, the only result being her robe loosened, falling off her shoulders and revealing the satin spaghetti straps of her rose tank top.

Marcus's fire ignited at the sight of her soft, shining skin. "Tell me . . ."

"Let me go." She felt naked as his eyes raked over her.

"You're trying to change things here," he said, his other hand trailing her shoulder. "You've come in sheep's clothing, but you're really a wolf, out for blood."

Sydney felt her breath race. "Not this family. The blood here is too cold. Besides, you're all too busy sticking your fangs into each other."

He swung her around, bringing her body to his. "You're wrong at one point. My blood is warm, and right now its steaming hot, Ms. Tanner. So it's my turn. You turned your charms on Bree, Aunt May, and Keith. Even my father seems taken by you. A different brand of charm for each person. Now convince me."

Sydney twisted and turned, but there was no fighting. His mouth came down hard, encompassing hers.

She let him kiss her.

BOOK YOUR PLACE ON OUR WEBSITE AND MAKE THE ARABESQUE ROMANCE CONNECTION!

We've created a customized website just for our very special Arabesque readers, where you can get the inside scoop on everything that's going on with Arabesque romance novels.

When you come online, you'll have the exciting opportunity to:

- View covers of upcoming books

- Learn about our future publishing schedule (listed by publication month and author)

- Find out when your favorite authors will be visiting a city near you

- Search for and order backlist books

- Check out author bios and background information

- Send e-mail to your favorite authors

- Join us in weekly chats with authors, readers and other guests

- Get writing guidelines

- AND MUCH MORE!

Visit our website at
http://www.arabesquebooks.com

A FOREVER PASSION

Angela Winters

ARABESQUE
☆BET☆
BOOKS

BET PUBLICATIONS, LLC
WWW.MSBET.COM
WWW.ARABESQUEBOOKS.COM

ARABESQUE BOOKS are published by

BET Publications, LLC
c/o BET BOOKS
One BET Plaza
1900 W Place NE
Washington, D.C. 20018-1211

First Printing: February, 2000

10 9 8 7 6 5 4 3 2 1
Printed in the United States of America

This book is dedicated to my family, who, in trying times, reminded me that "everything works out eventually."

ONE

It was all falling apart.

Sydney Tanner's stomach was clenched tight. She felt cold on a warm, mid-May day. She couldn't hear anything, see anything. She could only focus internally on the disaster that was on its way. If she couldn't say it was here already. Her life's obsession—her one and only all-encompassing goal—was screeching to a halt and she didn't know what to do about it. Helplessness was worse than death.

Howard University Professor Maggie Shue pushed thin-rimmed reading glasses up her nose with her long mahogany-brown hand. Half a second later, they fell that half inch down again. She eyed the eight out of thirty remaining students. This was a wind-up class. Attendance was completely voluntary. Finals ended yesterday—any turnout was a good one.

"My point is," Professor Shue said in a hallowing voice, never leaving her podium, "genealogy is a double-edged sword. That's the point I've been trying to make all semester."

Sydney heard someone pop chewing gum in their mouth, and she blinked. Back to her surroundings, she wondered why she was even here. It wasn't as if she had time on her hands to sit in a class that had officially been over for over a week. Her world was crumbling down around her, and here she was, listening to parting comments from an elective class at that.

"Tracing a family tree," Professor Shue continued, her eyes not concentrating on any one student for more than two seconds, "the regathering of roots, linking the past to you. This can bring joy, pride . . . a sense of completeness. It can also bring grief, embarrassment, self-doubt, and more questions that can never be answered no matter how much you search."

Sydney heard the purest form of laughter in the hallway outside the Genealogy 101 classroom. Laughter backed by an intangible security. Not in reference to any particular problem, but the knowledge that everything, no matter what, would somehow work out. Sydney knew she'd never laughed like that. Too busy holding on, keeping the plan, the goal in sight. Proving *them* wrong.

And for what, this? She had no job, no money, no place to live, and no one to help her. Not that she'd ever ask. She'd never ask, but she would accept offers. One had to occasionally to survive. There was no one there to offer. Those she knew, she wasn't close to. They were business contacts to be revisited at a later point. Sydney needed those people to have confidence in her. She couldn't let them know she was desperate. Desperate was an understatement.

Only one year away and it was all disintegrating. Sydney's caramel-colored hand discreetly grabbed her nutmeg-brown french braid and pulled. She squeezed tight. Don't panic. Not yet.

"Are you okay?"

Sydney let go and turned toward the whisperer. She knew her only as Gabrielle. They had this one class together and had talked a few times. Really, the girl bugged her, but was likeable enough. Gabrielle was twenty-three, five years younger than Sydney, with very different tastes. Their relationship had never left discussions in this room and down the hallway.

"A little anxious," Sydney answered with her deep, raspy voice. She remembered Gabrielle wasn't the most regular attendee, making her curious as to why she was here today of all days. "What are you doing here?"

Gabrielle shrugged, smacking her gum. "All my friends have gone home. I'm getting picked up later today 'cause my car broke down. What a piece of . . . Anyway, I got tired of watching television, so I figured, why not."

Gabrielle was a beautiful milk-chocolate brown. Just over five feet with short black hair, she was nothing short of adorable. Restlessness was evident in her eyes. Sydney had the feeling the kid didn't even want to be in grad school. Her parents were probably making her go, wanting the best for her. That was something Sydney knew nothing about. She blamed *them* for that.

"A reward," Professor Shue said, this time a little loud to regather the girls' attention. "For those of you who chose to stick around, a moneymaking opportunity."

Sydney's ears perked up. She sat up straight. *Don't panic, not yet. Money!*

"The history department is planning a genealogy exhibit for next semester. Well, the fall semester. They're looking for a student from each class level to do a project for display. You pick a family, not your own, and go to work. As far back as you can. Preferably before slavery."

"How much?" A boy in the first row asked the question Sydney wanted to.

"Five hundred dollars." Professor Shue lifted her finger in caution. "Now listen. They're serious about this. It's not going on your mama's fridge. This has to be indepth, detailed, and documented. The leading genealogical societies from Maryland, D.C., and Virginia will be reviewing this project."

Sydney didn't care how hard it would be. She'd taken this class as an elective, padding whatever she could find to her MBA. Corporations like the well-rounded person, she'd been told. Somehow she'd found a way to enjoy it, thinking if things had been different she might have elected a softer degree like this. Now she was being rewarded with a chance to make money. She needed money more than anything right now.

"Pick up the instructions, rules, and procedures sheet on the chair at the door on your way out." Professor Shue stepped from behind her podium. She placed both hands on generous hips and looked around. "Deadline to enter is next Friday. Aren't you all happy you came?"

Sydney wasn't going to wait until Friday, or another second. She jumped up, her five-six, one-hundred-fifty-pound frame garnering a little attention as the chair thumped against the hard floor. Grabbing the paper, she rushed back to her seat. She looked it over as Professor Shue continued with salutations and words of wisdom and advice for the summer.

"You're such an overachiever." Gabrielle stuck her hands in her blue jean shorts pockets. She leaned over to catch a glimpse of the paper.

"I need the money." Sydney shrugged as she whispered. "It might not be that bad. God knows I've done a ton of research in my life. Every internship I've had over the past ten years has been some form of research or another."

"I'd do it," Gabrielle said with a nod that lacked confidence. "Yeah, 'cause I'd like to do it on my own family. Get at some of those secrets Mommy and Daddy love to keep."

"That'd be too simple." Sydney showed her the line

on the paper under Rules. "Has to be a family other than your own. Like a professional that was hired."

"Well, forget it then. Tomorrow I start vacation. I'm not working again until September."

Sydney paused, watching Gabrielle lean back in her chair. She was serious. She noticed Gabrielle's watch, her bracelet, saw the shoes. She refused to be jealous. A long time ago, she'd made that promise to herself. Still she was a little envious that Gabrielle didn't have a care in the world. Sydney couldn't remember a day when she hadn't worked. Not since she was fourteen. She had to work, to save so she could get out of that place, that hell. Away from *them*.

Sydney hadn't taken vacation from work or school for six years. A week in Maui with Brad Lewis. But then she fell in love, and it was downhill from there.

"So are you old or something?" Gabrielle spoke louder now that Professor Shue was finished and the other six students were talking, leaving.

"What?" Sydney stood up. She frowned at the question, her thick brows centering over her large black eyes.

"You said you've been interning for ten years. I'm thinking four for undergrad and you told me a while ago that you're a first-year MBA. How does ten fit in?"

Sydney laughed. Four for undergrad. Yeah, right. She wished. "I got my bachelor's degree at Chicago State. Took me six years."

"Slow learner?" Gabrielle smiled. She was joking. "Or else indecisive?"

"Broke." Sydney vowed years ago to never tell her sob story. Don't show your weakness. She wasn't unique. A lot of kids had Satan in human form for parents and were left on their own to make their way in this world. Some succeeded, some didn't. She was going to succeed. She'd show *them*. *They* were wrong.

"Broke? That's even worse." Gabrielle turned her tiny nose up and shook like she'd just gotten the chills.

"What are your plans for the summer, Sydney?"

Both women turned to face the professor, who had placed herself uncomfortably in a chair one row ahead of them.

"I'm making five hundred bucks." Sydney waved the sheet of paper detailing the project.

"I think you'd be good at it," Maggie said. "I know you said over and over again you wanted to be a corporate bigwig, Wall Street, right?"

"One of those," Sydney answered with an ambitious smile.

"Whichever." Maggie tipped her head, blinking her eyes. Her thickly braided hair moved with her. "I just think you've got a knack for this. So whose family are you going to trace?"

"She can't do her own, right?" Gabrielle added, appearing to dislike being left out of the conversation.

Sydney laughed at the thought. Even if it was allowed, she hadn't spoken to them in ten years.

"Go ahead and leave," Linda Williams said. Her hands were on her hips, her paisley housedress made her look sloppy and mean. She stared at her eighteen-year-old daughter with contempt-filled black eyes. "Do what you want, Syd. You'll fail anyway. And don't think you're coming back here when you do. I'm sick of seeing your father's face every time I look at you anyway, girl."

Sydney hadn't cried in years, but she'd wanted to. She hated her mother.

David Williams laughed out loud. He smiled at his wife. "I'm with you, baby. Shame, Syd. You gotta look like a man that ain't want nothing to do with you since you been born."

Sydney didn't even glance at her stepfather. The nights she'd spent praying for his death.

She didn't even say good-bye. She just turned around and walked out with two bags. Everything she wanted. Everything she owned. She stepped onto Austin Avenue. Chicago was ugly and unforgiving in January, but she'd prefer to take her chances in the cold, cruel city than that ugliness she'd just come from.

She stood at the bus stop with no idea where she was going, but she was going there. She'd show them.

"You'll have to pick a family," the professor said. "Pick wisely. Don't choose someone who's never met anyone past a first cousin."

Sydney laughed. Another challenge. "Okay. I'll figure it out."

"Sydney." Professor Shue leaned closer, making the wrinkles around her fifty-year-old eyes more prominent. "Besides making five hundred bucks, what are your plans for next year?"

"I couldn't say right now." Sydney liked Maggie. She tended to be a little nosy, but was helpful and seemed genuine. "The money thing isn't hittin' too good."

"What about an internship?" Gabrielle asked. "You said something about an intern a few weeks ago."

"Didn't work out." Sydney felt her stomach turn just thinking about it. It had been set. It paid only eight dollars an hour, but a major marketing firm in D.C. hired her for the summer. She had the job. It would look great on her resume. "Right after they made me the offer, they lost their biggest client, a major airline. They had to lay off folks and make all their internships unpaid. I can't afford to work for free. My job in the school's business office was over last week and they'd already hired someone for the summer. It's there for me when I get back, but not before then."

Maggie laid a comforting hand on Sydney's knee for a moment. "You're so sharp. You'll find something else for the summer. Regarding your job in the business office, I want to talk to you about the fall. If you do this project, you can win the five hundred dollars. But even if you don't win, you can be my assistant for a semester."

"Me?" Sydney was surprised. After all, she was an MBA student, not a regular grad student.

"I need someone." She looked at Gabrielle, who was more than attentive. She curved her lips in a smile. "No offense, Gabrielle, but I need someone a little more mature than the average grad student. Sydney, you've worked in the real world before, beyond internships. From what I've observed, you show professionalism in everything you do."

Sydney took in the praise. It was praise she'd never gotten as a child at home. She'd gotten it from teachers, she'd felt it from her own conversations with God, but not at home.

"This is paid, right?" Sydney asked. Professionalism and gratitude aside, she needed money.

"Wouldn't waste your time if it was any other way," Maggie said. "And it'll get you a break in your tuition."

Sydney tried to hide her excitement. She saw light again. Possibly. Maybe. She knew something good would come of this. That's why she'd shown up on a day when it made the least sense.

"I'm doing the project." Sydney slid the sheet of paper in her notebook.

"Do my family!" Gabrielle hopped up and down in her seat, gripping the edges of the desk as Maggie left to address a waiting student.

Sydney wondered if Maggie had any idea how much

hope she had given her. Maybe it wasn't all falling apart. Maybe next semester was a possibility. Only there was still a summer to deal with. Sydney hated weakness and dependence, but right now she needed Darrin. She needed his listening ear, his comforting arms. Too bad he dumped her three days ago.

"Hey, Sydney!" Gabrielle snapped her fingers, returning Sydney to reality. "You space out more than anyone I know."

"I got a lot on my mind, kid." Sydney grabbed her notebook and threw her purse over her shoulder. She knew Gabrielle was right behind. Sometimes they'd walk halfway down the hall together before departing for the next class.

"Did you hear me?" Gabrielle asked. "I said, do my family."

"For my project?" Sydney shook her head. Her options were limited. She knew so few people. "You live here in D.C.?"

Gabrielle pouted. "No, I live in Baltimore, but it's only an hour from here. Really."

"I'm in D.C. I need someone close."

"Where do you live in D.C.?" she asked as they entered the campus courtyard. "Because I have family in Georgetown."

Sydney laughed. As if she could afford to live in Georgetown. Gabrielle was oblivious to her world. "To be honest, I really don't live anywhere."

Gabrielle stopped dead in her tracks. Her mouth was wide open. "Oh, my God! You're homeless! You're a homeless college student. I've read about kids like you."

"I'm not homeless." Sydney grabbed her by the arm, dragging her behind a tree. People were staring now that Gabrielle was providing the drama. "Would you keep it down?"

"Do you have a home or don't you?" Gabrielle's eyes danced. She was intrigued.

Sydney couldn't imagine leading such a sheltered life that something this simple, this ordinary, would excite her so much.

"I have an apartment right off campus. I'm being evicted because my landlord sold our building to a company that wants to build condos."

"Aren't they supposed to give you time to get out?" Gabrielle was obviously disappointed in the simple explanation.

"He gave everyone time. I tried to find a new place. It's hard to find a reasonable one-bedroom in a safe area close enough to campus."

"What about a roomie?"

"No." Sydney shook her head defiantly. "No roommates. No attachments. No sharing. No arguing over the phone bills. None of that."

"Are you so full of choices?" Gabrielle raised one brow.

The twenty-three-year-old was sharper than Sydney gave her credit for. "Look, loudmouth. The point is, I didn't have enough time or enough money. I needed a security deposit, first month's rent. All of that. I'm paying for everything here."

"What about financial aid?"

"It doesn't cover everything." Sydney knew Gabrielle wouldn't ever understand. She was from a different world. "Besides, every time I got a little something, another bill came. To make a long story short, I'm not homeless now, but I will be in one week."

"What about your family?"

"I don't have a family." Sydney felt her chest tighten. What a fool. Ten years since she'd left, after eighteen years of abuse, and she still caught herself getting emotional about it. It was worse when the obligatory *Oh, I'm so sorry* inevitably came.

"You're an orphan?" Gabrielle asked. "I'm sorry."

Sydney had dreams of what it would've been like to get away from *them*. She'd go to an orphanage. Sleeping in a room with twenty other kids she'd never met wasn't so horrible. Maybe they wouldn't have called her stupid, fat, worthless. At least if they had, it wouldn't hurt as much. They weren't supposed to love her.

"I'm not an orphan," she said. "I'll just say I'm estranged from my parents. Haven't talked to them in a decade." Why was she telling this girl she barely knew so much? Why not? What did she have to lose?

Gabrielle shook her head. "What's your man doing for you?"

Sydney didn't answer. Her look said it all. Darrin had moved on. He'd wanted a commitment she couldn't give. He refused anything less.

"Wow." Gabrielle leaned against the oak tree. She shook her head. "No man. No home. No job. No money. No family."

"Thanks for the repetition." Sydney turned and headed toward the main student building. There were jobs posted there. Most were filled, but there was always a chance.

"I can solve all your problems." Gabrielle ran after her, her tiny figure keeping up with Sydney's brisk pace.

"Teasing is not appreciated." Sydney wondered if this girl had ever had a real problem.

"You can come live with me." Gabrielle's smile widened as Sydney stopped and turned to face her. "Hear me out first."

"No." Sydney laughed at herself for that one second she thought to say yes. "Look, I don't have time to—"

Gabrielle's hands were firmly on her hips. "It looks to me like you're about to have nothing but time."

There was that sharpness again. There was more to Gabrielle than met the eye.

"I don't even know your last name," Sydney said. She sat down on a wooden bench only a few feet away from them.

Gabrielle sat across from her. "It's Hart. My friends call me Bree. I already know your last name is Tanner. Aside from the weekly small talk, you don't pay much attention to me, but I've been paying a lot of attention to you. To put it plainly, girl, you need to loosen up."

"Appreciate the advice." Sydney lifted a finger. "But you have no idea of my life. It isn't anything like yours. I don't have the freedom to loosen up. I have to fight."

"Fight who?" Gabrielle looked around. "Who's attacking you? It's just me here."

Them! Sydney wanted to scream the word, but she kept it inside. *They told me I'd never amount to anything. Born a mistake, always a mistake. I was trying to be bourgeois black or trying to be white.*

"I'm gonna run down your list," Gabrielle said. "And don't interrupt me."

"Knock yourself out." Sydney crossed her legs and leaned back. She liked this persistently annoying sister.

"You need a place to live. You can come live with me at my parents' house in Baltimore." She saw Sydney begin to protest, but thwarted it immediately. "Don't interrupt! Now we have a huge, huge house. We have two empty bedrooms that are always filled with either my friends or my brother's friends or girlfriends. Family in town, visiting bigwigs, whatever. It's a gigantic place. I barely even run into Mom and Dad—thank God. My parents love it when we bring people home. You look at me like I'm crazy, but

I'm not lying. We do it all the time. They like to show off what we have."

What a world, Sydney thought. She never asked why she wasn't born into a family like that. She accepted the cruel hand she'd been dealt. Still.

"My parents wouldn't let you pay rent," Gabrielle continued. "They'd be insulted. They'd throw you out. Which leads to number two on the list. You need money. If you stay with me, you'll save whatever you were gonna pay in rent all summer wherever you were going to live, which is nowhere a week from now. Then you need a job. My brother is a hotshot lawyer at a big-time Baltimore firm. They need interns for this big lawsuit that's coming to a head this summer. It's paying eleven bucks an hour."

Sydney leaned in closer. The pros and cons were running through her mind a million miles a second. She knew what she knew. She had to get money, she needed a place to live. She had to be back here next fall and get her MBA.

"So next you have this project." Gabrielle's youthful face held accomplishment at every angle. "You can do my family. If you need characters, we're the ones you want to be around. This class has really got me interested in my past. When I tried to do that midsemester project, tracing my own family tree, my mom had a fit. We must have some skeletons in my closet. They've always been so secretive. You know, appearances. I love 'em, but they're extremely snobbish. I think they're ashamed of being descendants of slaves."

"There are worse things parents could be." Sydney sighed. "You seem to have an answer for everything."

"About that family problem"—she threw her arms in the air—"you can have mine. I've got more family than I can deal with."

"I'm not a leech," Sydney said, gathering herself together.

"Fine. Just stay with us until you get a sublet. My family's got connections. Take the job, do the project on my folks. Everyone wins."

Am I crazy, Sydney asked herself. *Throwing myself at these people?* This family knew nothing of her, and she was going to revolve her life around them for a summer. It seemed ridiculous, too impetuous, but then she thought . . . she knew no one. No one knew her. Sydney felt so alone, but that was okay. She could deal with alone. When she got that MBA and that big-time corporate job in New York, she'd have plenty of time to find love, close friends, and plant roots. What she couldn't deal with was more time wasted. The goal was in clear sight. No more blinking.

"How much time do I have?" She wasn't crazy, but she was desperate. Very similar.

Gabrielle clapped her hands and kicked her feet. "Someone's picking me up at three."

"Someone?"

"Mother said someone would be here. It might be my big brother, Marcus. You'll like him. He's as close to perfect as it gets."

Sydney knew she was getting herself into something that could be bad, but she was getting out of the worst possible thing. The risk was worth it even if she did have to do something as foreign as sitting down to dinner with a loving family.

They exchanged information, agreeing that Sydney would be picked up at three-thirty.

"Why are you doing this for me?" Sydney called after Gabrielle as she started to walk away. She'd debated asking the question, but couldn't help it. "Besides some friendly banter in class, I'm not important to you. Why would you go out of your way, open your home to me?"

Gabrielle frowned, confused. She tilted her head to the side. "You need help. I can help you. Why wouldn't I?"

It was that simple. Sydney smiled, pretending for a moment that she had no worries, that her past wasn't her past. In that moment, with that life, she could see it being that simple. She hated *them* for robbing her of that.

"What are you doing, girl?" Linda Williams burst into her daughter's bedroom. "You heard me calling you."

"I'm studying." Sydney was already closing her books. She knew it was about to start.

Linda laughed, strutting slowly to the bed. It was a twin-size mattress on the floor, but that was the only bed Sydney had ever known, living in the same apartment on the worst side of Chicago all her life.

"You always studying," Linda said. She made a smacking sound with her lips. "Like it's gonna get you somewhere. S-A-T. What class is that?"

Sydney's stomach was tightening. She'd learned her lesson the last time she'd mentioned college. She thought she'd never hear the last of it. "It's just a test."

"You'll probably fail, Syd. So don't waste your time." Linda grabbed the book and tossed it across the room that was as small as a closet. It slammed against the broken-down drawer and hit the dark wooden floor.

Sydney did nothing, she knew it would only make things worse. She had learned that—if she'd learned anything in sixteen years.

"What the hell is going on in here!" David appeared in the doorway. He had on nothing but his boxers, as usual. "Linda, get that girl up. I'm hungry."

"She was studying." Linda could barely get the words out through her laughter.

David leaned against the wall and smiled. He looked at Sydney, but she kept her eyes on her hands. "What else she gonna do? Ain't got no friends. She's too fat. Ain't got no boyfriend."

"I'm keeping it that way." Linda sashayed over to her husband, leaning up against him. "She ain't getting knocked up. I'll be damned if I got to take care of her and a stupid baby."

"My stomach." David grabbed his protruding belly. "Syd, get up and start dinner."

Her determination was building. Sydney hated them both so much, but they weren't going to destroy her. She'd show them. Nothing else mattered to her as she headed for the kitchen.

"Is that it?"

Gabrielle's face showed surprise as she stood in the doorway to Sydney's tiny basement studio apartment.

"What did you expect?" Sydney asked. She had two suitcases, one large with a strap, one small with a pull, and a larger than usual backpack. "My purse makes four."

"This is everything you own?" Gabrielle grabbed the larger suitcase.

"Thanks." Sydney closed the door and followed her down the steps. "Yeah, it is. I can move easily without a lot of attachments. The apartment owns the furniture."

"What about plates and stuff like that?"

"Paper. Plastic. Toss and use."

Sydney didn't believe in attachments. She had no time for them: travel light, bring as little as possible. Besides, she was always broke. The few times she actually spent money on something big, she eventually had to pawn it.

"I'm extremely perceptive," Gabrielle said as they stepped outside. "I'm thinking you've got some serious issues about something."

Sydney ignored her. Not a day went by when she didn't think maybe she wasn't all together in the head over what had happened to her. But in reality, who didn't have some issue or another? At least her issue urged her to achieve and do better for herself.

"You've got to be kidding me." Sydney stood frozen in place as right outside her door was a white limo.

Gabrielle never broke stride. She handed a suitcase to the driver and headed for the backseat.

"This is someone coming to pick you up?" she asked. The driver smiled as he approached and accepted her bags.

"Would you stop looking ghetto and get in here?" Gabrielle slid all the way in.

Sydney did as she was told. "I just didn't expect—"

"My stupid brother is already in Baltimore." Gabrielle pouted as she reached into the fridge and grabbed a soda. She offered one to Sydney, who refused. "Left last night. He said he forgot. Yeah, right."

"This is the same brother that you described as the closest thing to perfect just this morning?" Sydney leaned back. The walls of the limo were jet black, the windows tinted. The seats, navy blue, were as soft as a feather.

Gabrielle shrugged. "Yeah, well, Marcus is perfect. Except when he's being a jerk. All the better. He'd only ask a million questions. My family has been on me a lot lately."

Sydney had mixed feelings about having siblings. She would've loved someone to share her life with growing up, but she'd never wish her worst enemy being brought up in that house. Maybe a brother or sister would've taken some of the abuse, making it a little easier on her. Only then there would be two people full of hate and anger instead of one. That wouldn't solve anything.

"You're kind of weird," Gabrielle said. She leaned over and flicked on the television. "A good weird though."

"Thanks," Sydney said, "I think."

"You haven't even asked me any questions."

Because I don't have a choice, Sydney thought. *It's you or the streets.* "About what?"

"My family." Gabrielle took a gulp. "You probably know all about them already."

"Would I be offending you if I said I don't?"

Gabrielle's expression mixed confusion with surprise. "No. I guess there are a few out there. You don't read the papers, watch the news?"

"I only read the business section," Sydney said. "Don't own a television."

"Not owning a television has got to be the weirdest thing I've ever heard." Another swig, another gulp. "What do you do in your spare time?"

"Work." Sydney didn't know the meaning of spare time. "Until two weeks ago I worked at the university business office between classes and at the university grill evenings and weekends."

Gabrielle frowned like she'd just tasted something awful.

"So," Sydney said, wanting to change the subject. "Tell me about this family tree I'll be tracing."

Gabrielle sat up straight and cleared her throat. "Mother will tell you we are one of Baltimore's finest families, but her snobbish crap is so through. Appearances, appearances—that's how I'd describe my mom, Victoria."

"What does she do?" Sydney sensed a problem here. If Victoria Hart was hung up on appearances, how would she take to a no-name, broke-as-sin girl from the Chicago inner city?

"Mother is a society woman." Gabrielle batted her eyelashes. "I could say she's a housewife, but she's actually out pretty often with society functions: associations and stuff like that. She's pristine, a little difficult, but you seem tough. You'll handle her."

"What did she say about my coming?" Sydney asked.

Gabrielle blinked. "Don't worry. They'll all love you. Next, my dad. Anthony works for the Prez. His office is actually in the White House, which is kind of cool. He runs Public Affairs."

"I think I do recognize his name." Sydney thought back. She'd remembered reading in *Ebony* about the record number of African Americans holding positions of power in the President's closest circle.

"I thought so. He speaks at Howard a lot. Marcus has as well, but he's a big Georgetown guy. Spends most of his time there."

"This is the perfect one?" Sydney followed Gabrielle's lead and lay across the seat. They were both sideways, facing each other.

"So everyone says." Gabrielle shrugged. "He's a congressman. He spends most of his time in D.C., but I never see him. He's always working, pounding the pavement or entertaining the ladies."

"An unmarried congressman." Sydney found that interesting. "I thought the voters liked their leaders settled. Must be young."

Gabrielle laughed. "No, he's old. Thirty-five. Many women have tried to latch on to that Hart name. One came close, but none got him to the church."

"Who else?" Sydney asked.

"My other brother, Keith. Now Keith is cool. He's thirty—closer to you. He's a junior partner at some high-powered law firm with a bunch of guys' last names."

"He's the one we're working for, right?" Sydney smiled to herself. Eleven bucks an hour. Scrimping and saving, she'd make it into tuition money if she spent the whole summer eating tuna and noodles out of a Styrofoam cup.

Gabrielle nodded. "He hooks me up every summer. I hardly do anything, but he said he's got too much work this time to let me slack off. Watch—I'm smart . . . I'm not working. Marcus has been Mother's favorite forever, but Keith is pushing him off the podium."

Sydney wasn't interested in hearing about the internal conflicts. She wasn't getting involved in this family's lives. "Then there's you."

"No . . ." Gabrielle paused, placing the empty can in a holder. "Keith has a twin, Kelly. Kelly's cool. She went to Cornell. Big deal. She's a consultant for one of those big strategy firms in Alexandria, Virginia. She lives there with her husband, Mike. He used to be a pro-football player in Denver. He owns this huge real estate company now. They have everyone's little love, Jordan. He's four and the cutest thing you'll ever want to see."

Sydney watched the smile on Gabrielle's face permeate every inch. It took everything to keep from being jealous. Sydney's instincts urged her to love, despite all the hate and indifference she'd experienced in her life. She couldn't help but envy the Harts. They didn't only have money, but they were a family. All the kids were prosperous, no doubt from years of encouragement and support.

Sydney considered the idea that being around this family, witnessing their love and support of each other, might be more difficult than she'd imagined. It might just be too foreign, too much of a reminder of what she never got.

"Who wants to take your fat self to the prom?" David Williams spoke between burps as he popped the top off his fourth beer can.

Standing in the middle of the kitchen, preparing her

lunch, Sydney didn't answer him. She rarely answered him. He'd threaten to hit her, but never would. Coward, she'd called him under her breath.

"This fool down the street," Linda said.

She had a pack of cigarettes in her hand. Yesterday was the twentieth time she'd decided to quit. David brought home a pack that afternoon to drive her crazy.

"What fool?" he asked.

"Billy Kel . . . something." She tossed the cigarettes in the trash can. "Quit calling her fat. Syd's not fat."

Sydney blinked. Her mother rarely defended her.

"She's as big as you," David said, laughing. He went to retrieve the cigarettes.

"She needs to lose ten, maybe fifteen." Linda shrugged. "Aw, hell, she got asked to the stupid prom. Somebody wants her."

David tossed the cigarettes back at his wife. "If somebody wants her so bad, then let her go live with him. I ain't paying for no damn dress."

Sydney had never known anything different, but she'd always known this wasn't right.

Two

Sydney's eyes ballooned as the driver made a left turn around plush, enveloping trees.

Gabrielle rubbed her eyes. She'd taken a short nap and was just awakening. "This is Victoria Hart's castle. And don't be mistaken. She is king and queen."

As the car came upon the short, brick entrance columns connected by a wooden gate made of three thin logs, the enormous circle drive welcomed one to the colonial-style, three-story home with three-car garage. Redbrick, with a white roof, it was long with a dip in the middle, giving only a peek at the acres behind. Windows were everywhere, tempting with a calm luxury inside. The seven-step concrete entrance was welcoming, but subconsciously judgmental at the same time. "Know you're stepping into money before you come here," it said.

"I'm impressed," Sydney admitted.

"Told you we had room." Gabrielle eased out of the car and headed straight for the door. She tossed back her head. "He'll get your bags. Come on."

Sydney could see the difference in Gabrielle right away. She was home now and her every move spoke of authority and confidence.

Sydney followed as Gabrielle opened the large, intimidating white door with the shiny brass handle. They walked into a large foyer with sanded, glossy hardwood floors, marble statues, and a large grandfather clock. Don't let this intimidate you, Sydney told herself.

Linda Williams leaned over the kitchen table and stared into her daughter's eyes. "What do you think is gonna happen? You go to college, hang out with all those bourgeois black folks, but they won't want nothing to do with you. You're what they want to get away from. Syd, you're reaching for something you ain't never gonna get. Try all you want, you'll end up right back here.

Sydney squeezed the spoon in her hand. She didn't say a word. She just kept her eyes on her corn flakes. She'd show her.

"Excuse me, ma'am."

"Excuse me."

"Sydney, move." Gabrielle pulled Sydney out of the way of the chauffeur as he placed the bags on the floor.

"Sorry," she said. "I—"

"It's just a house." Gabrielle knocked on the wall beside her. "Not that special."

"Don't let Mother hear you say that," he said, walking toward them, his face holding a friendly, unthreatening smile. He was attractive and thin, almost six feet with skin like Gabrielle's, light eyes, and fine features. In smooth, khaki pants and a midnight-blue striped button-down, nothing was out of place.

"Where is she?" Gabrielle asked as she hugged him and kissed him on the cheek.

"Right on the other side of this wall," he said, turning his attention to Sydney.

"Sydney." Gabrielle wrapped her arms around his waist and squeezed. "This is my brother, Keith. Keith, this is Sydney Tanner. She's MBA at Howard."

They said hellos, shook hands. Sydney found him charming, his grip strong and professional. He winked at her flirtatiously.

"I don't remember hearing about you." Keith's smile was wide, pleased. "I know I'd remember if I'd seen you around here."

Sydney smiled. He was cute, friendly, and harmless. "Thanks for the hidden compliment."

"Get your boots out," Gabrielle said. "My brother is full of it."

Keith pushed her aside and headed for Sydney. "You live in Baltimore, Sydney?"

Sydney blinked. Confusion set in. Didn't he know? She turned to Gabrielle. "No."

Gabrielle cleared her throat, avoiding eye contact with Sydney. "Sydney is staying with us for the summer. She's staying in Kelly's old room."

"Oh." Keith didn't appear fazed. He gently took her arm and began leading her around the corner.

"You didn't tell anyone I was coming, did you?" Sydney poked Gabrielle in the side. She'd just assumed, unlike her usual self. Possibly in her desperation, she'd let normal qualifiers fall to the side.

"Wasn't necessary." Gabrielle shrugged.

"How do you figure?" Sydney questioned her rationalization. Everything probably always worked out for Gabrielle.

"I've done this before." She winked. "Trust me."

Sydney realized she didn't have much of a choice.

They passed through the hallway, generously decorated with paintings of beautiful black people and exotic scenery. They approached carpeted steps that led to a sunken living room with large columns. It was full of elegant furniture, Italian sofas, sleepers, marble tables and more. It was expansive, with a decorative style that hinted at classic European.

In the middle of the room stood a woman Sydney knew could only be Victoria Hart. She was tall, milk-chocolate brown with fine auburn hair tied tightly in a bun. Her features, like Keith's, were small. Everything. Eyes, nose, lips. She wore a silk pant suit the color of primrose and it hung on her with style and class.

"Bree, darling." She held her arms out to her daughter, who hugged her before stepping away. "You're late. You should've been home an hour ago."

"I was picking Sydney up." Gabrielle rolled her eyes.

Victoria had scanned Sydney the second she'd entered the room. Sydney noticed that. She hadn't attempted to hide it. It was her home, after all. She had that look, Sydney saw as she was scanned again. King and queen, just like Gabrielle said.

"So we have company for dinner?" Victoria's voice was high and extremely polite as she stepped to Sydney, holding a jeweled hand out to her. "I'm Victoria. What's your last name, Cindy?"

"It's Sydney," she corrected, thinking for a second that Victoria misworded her name on purpose. "Sydney Tanner."

"Sydney's staying here," Keith added. He'd already started for the small glass bar in the corner. "In Kelly's room for the summer."

Victoria never blinked. She slowly removed her hand from its shake with Sydney. She laughed so quietly, it really couldn't be heard.

"Another one?" she asked, turning to Gabrielle. "Bree, I'm starting to think you don't want to be home unless you can bring someone other than a family member to talk to."

Sydney felt the clear rejection as Victoria turned her back to her and stepped away.

Gabrielle shrugged. "She's interning for Keith."

Sydney's eyes darted to Keith. Just as she expected, he'd had no clue. There was an uncomfortable silence for a few seconds. Sydney wasn't sure what she'd do, besides strangle Gabrielle, if she didn't get this job.

"Sure," Keith finally said. He winked at Sydney. "We need the help."

"Thanks," Sydney exhaled. "I've worked at law firms before. I've done a ton of research. I—"

"You've got the job, babe." Gabrielle patted her on the back. "No need for an interview. Besides, I can tell he likes you."

Sydney smiled, a little embarrassed. Victoria sighed as if annoyed.

Keith poured. "You do look better than any of the girls she's brought home before."

"Keith"—Victoria's tone was sharp—"that's enough. No drinking before dinner. We'll have wine."

Victoria didn't like her, wouldn't accept her. Sydney could tell that, but she wasn't too concerned. She wasn't trying to be a part of this family.

"Bree"—Victoria's eyes set on Sydney for a moment before turning to her youngest—"show Sydney her room and get ready for dinner. Five sharp."

"Whatever." Gabrielle grabbed Sydney by the arm and guided her out of the living room. She whispered, "You'll learn to ignore her. We all do. These things like dinner mean so much to her."

"Where are my bags?" Sydney asked as they passed the foyer.

"In your room. Laura probably took them up. Don't worry."

Sydney was led to a deeply carpeted marble-railed staircase that expanded until separating and leading in opposite directions.

"This is yours." Gabrielle swung open the door and stepped aside.

The room was large, but bare. It had a summer-on-the-beach look with sand-brown carpeting, white walls, and white-painted pine furniture. The closet ran along one entire wall. The bed was full, set with final posts at all four sides, creating a symmetrical style. The dresser and armoire stood out, with wider than usual drawers.

"This is nice." Sydney noticed the bathroom. "I get my own bathroom?"

"We share. I'm on the other side." Gabrielle stood in the doorway to the bathroom. "This used to be Kelly's room. We'd fight like cats and dogs over this bathroom."

Sydney peeked in. It was the biggest bathroom she'd ever seen.

"Dinner is in the dining room at five," Gabrielle said. "Give me a holler. We'll go down together."

As Gabrielle headed out, Sydney fell backward on the bed, looking up at the sandy-white ceiling. So far, so good. No disasters yet. Gabrielle was going to be a handful, but Sydney also figured she'd be fun.

She sat up. Her eyes focused on the tiny balcony. Her own balcony. This was too much. She opened the doors, closing her eyes as the fresh breeze hit her face.

The backyard was expansive, with a big garden placed uniquely to the right, underneath the rooms, growing wild and without restraint. There was an extended porch, perfect for party hosting. A large swimming pool, a perfect circle, was to the left. To the right a walkway lined with stucco tiles dug in the ground leading to a gondola and . . .

Sydney's eyes focused on him and only one word described him: sexy. She couldn't even remember what she'd been thinking before. Vigorously sanding a wooden rocking chair by hand, his muscles flexed and glistened. Dark, tall, and lean, he was wet with sweat and wearing only a pair of perfectly fitting blue jean shorts. Sydney took in a full view of his arms, his chest, his back, and thighs. She couldn't have imagined it better.

He stopped for a moment to pet a black Labrador retriever that ran in circles around him. Lucky dog, Sydney thought.

"So maybe a summer at the Hart estate won't be so boring after all." She leaned over the railing, biting her lower lip.

Sydney thought he was probably a handyman, a rent-a-servant the Hart family looked down on or didn't even notice at all. Well, she noticed him, and in all this luxury and high class, she was looking for something familiar to calm her nerves. It took a while, but Sydney eventually found her way to the back of the house and outside, past a maze of gorgeous, spacious rooms.

He was tired, but he didn't want to finish his sanding. He loved this work, zoning out while he fixed anything and everything. He didn't have to think about the problems. There were always problems, distractions. When he worked, worked with his hands, there were no distractions.

At least not until he saw her coming from the house down the walkway. Distraction didn't even describe it.

She was voluptuous, shapely, just like he liked a woman to be. She was youthfully seductive in a thin blue denim short jumper over a peach tank top. Her caramel-colored skin was beautifully tanned and held a healthy glow. Her light hair was glossy, with careless strands falling around her face, the rest in a childish braid down her back.

"Hi." He wiped his forehead with the back of his hand. He didn't want any sweat from his brow blocking his view.

As she stopped only a few feet from him, he took in the contours of her face. Her eyes were dark and large, her lips full and sexy. The hot May sun seemed focused on her, but she looked cool and collected, as if she wasn't concerned about a thing. He was intrigued.

"Hi," Sydney said. "Saw you working out here."

She hadn't seen his face from the balcony. He was gorgeous: piercing dark eyes, a hard jawline, broad nose, and persuasive lips. Not a pushover, but no sign of abrasiveness. His face held honesty and promise.

"Where did you come from?" He wiped his hand on his shorts before presenting it to her. He threw the sander to the ground.

Sydney tried to focus on his face, which was distracting enough, to avoid staring at his chest. It was hard. She accepted his hand and was startled by his strong, quick grip. She felt herself tense, become uncomfortable, as if at any moment he would pull her to him. Would she resist it?

"I'm . . ." She searched for the words, pulling her hand away. "I'm a friend of Gabrielle's from Howard."

"So she's home?" He stepped closer. Her eyes were secretive, seductive without meaning to be. Or maybe that's exactly what they meant to be, he thought.

"Yeah." Sydney stuck her hands inside her jumper. They felt awkward, like they were missing something. "That might not be good news for you."

"What do you mean?"

"Another one." She rolled her eyes. "I'm sure the less Harts here, the better for you."

"I don't mind, really." He folded his arms across his chest. He was smart and he caught on quick. "They're not so bad."

"Don't hold back on my account," Sydney said. "I really know only Gabrielle and she's pretty cool. But the others, well, you tell me."

"Well, you're right. Gabrielle is pretty okay. A little temperamental, indecisive."

"That's excusable due to youth." Sydney shrugged. He was so serene, so cool. She wanted to appear the same, but he was so attractive, she was losing her calm. "I guess I'm wondering how to act—you know, around people this rich. They're probably pretentious."

"Probably." He wondered what her name was. It was probably cute, unique. She had a stubborn little nose.

"That Victoria." Sydney's eyes caught a bead of sweat. She watched it trail his cheek and fall onto his chest—his bare, dark, shining, glistening, muscled chest. What was she doing? She tried to snap out of it.

"What about Victoria?" So, he thought, Gabrielle brought another buddy home. He was never a fan of this practice, but he'd have to make an exception in this case. He wondered how close she was to Gabrielle and if she had anything to do with her recent unusual behavior. He imagined this friend sitting out by the pool, sipping drinks, and regretted not living here.

"I'm sure she's a mess." Sydney reached down and patted the dog that had run up to her after a lap around the yard. "She had her nose in the air from the first second she saw me."

"She can be a little difficult," he added, assuming she was a little older than Gabrielle. That was a good thing.

"She must be hard on you."

"I just do what she tells me to." At least he wasn't lying. "Grin and bear it while I'm here. I get to go home eventually."

"You're lucky." Sydney could tell this man could handle himself. Not even a queen like Victoria could really control him, affect him. He might be her hired hand, but he was his own man. "Do all the servants . . . I mean workers . . . get to go home?"

Should he end this now? he wondered. No, he was having too much fun. Besides, she had a lot of nerve and deserved pie in her face. "Laura stays. She lives here. She's always been here. I assume she always will be."

Sydney stared, not knowing what to say next. He was too fine to be out anywhere working hard without a shirt on. That smile on his face was enough to make her feet feel a few inches off the ground.

Men had always been a particular challenge for Sydney. When she was younger, her weight problem solved that issue. They were nowhere to be found. Now she was still what they called a little big-boned, but she carried it well—like only a black woman could. Now it wasn't the weight, it was the attachments. No attachments. Settling, planting roots, were only distractions from the ultimate goal. She had to fight herself sometimes, but so far the goal had prevailed. It wasn't getting easier, but she knew one day, when all was achieved, she wouldn't have to fight anymore.

"You must be Sydney."

Sydney turned around, coming waist to face with an elderly woman in a motorized wheelchair. She was dark and glowing with her smile, with hair as white as snow in a bun on her head.

"That's me." Sydney felt a pleasant warmth as the woman took her hand in a welcoming, honest gesture.

"Bree told me about you." Her eyes were tender, having shown love and understanding for decades. "I'm May. Forget what you hear, child. I'm really running things here."

"You've got that right," he said.

"I don't doubt it." Sydney already knew she'd like her, but wasn't so sure that was a good thing. No attachments.

"I'm Anthony's aunt," she continued, leaning back. She placed her hands comfortably on her lap. She looked right out of a storybook with her paisley dress and sensible shoes. The all-wise elderly woman. "Glad to have you for the summer. I hope my grandnephew isn't boring you with his handyman talk."

Sydney froze. She couldn't breathe. She looked at him. The smile on his face was so smug, so satisfied. It said everything. She felt her blood begin to boil and her cheeks turn hot like fire. He acted as if . . .

May had never stopped talking. "He loves doing work on anything. Always talks about how it clears his head, keeps that Washington nonsense from getting to him."

Marcus Hart didn't blink. Sydney, as he knew her name now, stared at him with anger and fury, but he wouldn't back down. He just smiled. She had some nerve, but then again so did he. He knew she wanted to slap him for letting her dig a hole for herself, but she was embarrassed at the same time. He should've been angry at her, but all he saw was the fire in her eyes and he liked it. He liked it very much.

"I was just talking to Bree," May continued. She seemed oblivious to the heightened tension. "She was looking for you. Told me everything. Seems my other grandnephew has taken quite a liking to you."

"Is that so?" Marcus asked, still holding Sydney's eyes with his own. His smile was gone. He wasn't amused by that news. When had Keith gotten a chance to meet her? "Keith has grown fond of our new houseguest so soon?"

"Don't act like you haven't." May's tone was playfully scolding as she rolled her eyes. "I'm old, but I'm not blind."

The embarrassment was becoming more than Sydney could bear. How dare he?

"It seems like everyone is fond of Ms. . . ." Marcus paused, raising an inquisitive brow.

"Tanner." Sydney said her last name as curtly as she could. He was teasing her now, she knew that much—making it worse. "Sydney Tanner."

"Sydney's a nice name," he said. "Unique."

That's Ms. Tanner to you. She said the words to herself, but her eyes translated every word. He knew.

Sydney rolled her eyes before turning again to May with a smile. "It's nice to meet you, May."

"Well"—Marcus threw his arms in the air and stretched the kinks out—"I guess I'd better get ready for dinner. Want to look nice for our guest."

"We all should," May said.

He reached over and kissed his great-aunt on the forehead. Glancing back at Sydney, he said, "See you at dinner, Sydney."

She nodded with a snarling smile. *Jerk.*

Marcus knew Keith could never handle a woman like this. He, on the other hand . . .

Sydney felt her blood boil to overflow as his eyes slid down her body. He was quick and discreet, but the effect was like he'd spent the last ten minutes soaking in every inch of her. She couldn't even calm down as he turned and walked toward the house with confidence, his strides quick, his head up high. Yeah, he was a Hart all right. Just like his mother.

"Don't you let little Marcus get to you, honey." May smiled at Sydney.

Sydney wondered how obvious she'd been. Growing up as she had, she'd become gifted at hiding her emotions. One show of those and Linda and David Williams were all over her.

"Look, Linda." David laughed. *He leaned back so far in his tattered chair he almost fell backward on the back porch of the apartment. "Syd is angry. Little Syd is angry."*

Linda came out from the kitchen and looked tersely at her ten-year-old daughter. "What's wrong with you, girl?"

Sydney tried to hold it in, but she was fuming. She hated David. He was a drunk, a cheat, a liar, and anything else she knew was bad. Now he was staying.

"I just told her we was getting married." David slapped his ringless fiancée on the rear. "Syd ain't too happy 'bout that."

"Get that frown off your face, girl." Linda pointed her finger, placing it only inches from Sydney's nose. "Don't nobody care 'bout your feelings."

"I don't want him!" Sydney spat out. David wouldn't stop laughing. When he wasn't laughing, he was cursing or screaming.

Why him? Of all the men her mother had been with since Sydney's father left, and there had been many, David was one of the worst.

Linda was angry now. "Who gives a damn what you want, girl? You don't pay bills around here. You have no say."

Linda rolled her eyes and returned to the kitchen. She mumbled, "I don't want him. Ha! Is that what you said? Hell, I don't want you, but guess what?"

David laughed so hard this time, he did fall off his chair and cursed out loud when he hit the ground.

"You don't have to try and hide it, dear." May's words jolted Sydney back to the present. "Marcus can be a bit difficult, stubborn, and hardheaded. Makes him a fighter. Makes him a good congressman."

"Don't worry about me," Sydney said. "I can handle it."

May's smile was wry as she squinted one eye. She looked Sydney up and down. "I get that about you."

Sydney could look into this woman's eyes and trust her. She was a nurturer, a giver, the kind of mother Sydney always wished she had.

"Now you go get ready for dinner." May pointed to the garden. "You be sure to get a good look at my garden soon."

"That's yours?" Sydney followed May toward the house. "It's beautiful."

"Sure is." May spoke with a youthful, quick enthusiasm. If you weren't looking at her, you wouldn't believe she was her age. "Sweat and tears. Don't let the wheelchair fool you. I use it 'cause I don't like walking all over this goliath of a house, but I'm the most nimble eighty-two-year-old you'll ever meet."

"I don't doubt you." Sydney heard a voice warn her she'd grow to love this woman. No attachments.

They headed together to the stairs, where May left her wheelchair. Sydney helped her up the stairs, noticing she really didn't need it just as she'd said. Before parting ways, May placed a careful hand on Sydney's shoulders.

"I see something in you," she said in almost a whisper. "I'm a good judge of character. Good at predictions too. You're going to toss things up around here."

Sydney shook her head. "I . . . I would never. No, I wouldn't—"

May hushed her. "No, Sydney. Don't get me wrong. I know you don't intend to do anything. Still, I know you will. Don't worry. You're a tough girl and this family needs a little tossing."

Did it? Sydney wondered. Everything seemed fine in the Hart household. With the exception of an arrogant congressman of a son and a snobbish mother. Sydney expected a problem-free summer. She was going to make money, do this genealogy project, and then finish her MBA. Then on to New York and corporate America.

No, she repeated to herself. She wouldn't be tossing anything around. She was going to play it safe and keep her eyes on her one and only goal. She'd show *them.*

THREE

"Nice of you two to join us."

Victoria seemed sure to paint her words with extreme sarcasm.

Sydney didn't pay much attention to the elegant design of the sparkling dining room, with the table prepared like a party feast. Her eyes fixed on Marcus sitting at the head of the table. He was devastating in a purple cotton button-down. The fact that she noticed this made Sydney angrier at him.

"It was my fault," Gabrielle said, pointing to a chair next to hers for Sydney. "Sydney was ready a long time ago. I asked her to wait for me. It's no big deal."

"Watch your mouth." Marcus eyed his little sister sharply.

She was only a momentary distraction. He was surprised at himself for having anticipated Sydney's arrival to dinner. As he expected, he only got a roll of her eyes as she sat down, placing her hands on the lap of her innocently sexy butterfly-yellow sundress.

"So you've finally taken his place," Gabrielle said, filling her plate with the ham, potatoes, salad, and corn bread perfectly laid out for them.

Sydney could tell that Gabrielle had touched a button

with Marcus as the casual, controlled charm was erased. She focused on her food, not wanting any part of this.

"What the hell does that mean?" Marcus tried to control his temper. She was a kid, twenty-three. *Remember that.* "Because I'm sitting in Dad's seat?"

"You said it yourself." Gabrielle's voice hinted at regret for bringing the topic up, and stubbornness.

Keith coughed and reached for his drink. Victoria sighed and leaned back in her seat.

"You've got a problem with my sitting here?" Marcus couldn't lie and say his sitting there meant nothing. He knew only that when he'd walked into the room tonight, he'd wanted to sit in this seat left empty most of his life. Dinner seemed to last for years when his father wasn't there.

"Never mind." Gabrielle moved restlessly in her seat.

Sydney focused on her corn bread, feeling uncomfortable in this family setting. She couldn't remember eating dinner at home in any way but alone as a child.

"Look, Bree." Marcus sighed, not letting it pass that the tension was affecting Sydney. "If it bothers you, I'll move."

"No, you won't," Victoria interjected. She exaggerated the movement as she reached for her glass of wine. "Anthony is in D.C. for a political dinner. His seat is empty. Marcus is the oldest. He can sit there. Bree doesn't have a problem with it."

Gabrielle's eyes were like fire darts to her mother. "Thanks for answering for me."

"So Sydney"—Keith's eyes widened, his voice high pitched—"ever been to Baltimore before?"

Sydney looked up. She wanted to focus on Keith, but her eyes would dart to Marcus. Still she knew Victoria's eyes remained steady on her.

"Only once," she answered, thinking of Darrin. She

wanted to miss him, but couldn't afford to. "My ex-boy-friend and I visited the harbor for a weekend."

"How romantic," Marcus sneered before stuffing ham in his mouth.

Sydney threw him a contemptuous look.

"Did I hear ex?" Keith asked. "Some guy was stupid enough to let you go?"

"Keith." Victoria shifted in her seat, becoming notice-ably uncomfortable.

"Something like that." Sydney forced a smile. She wished Marcus would quit staring.

He wouldn't. Marcus surprised himself with his preoc-cupation with this distant woman. She couldn't stand him, he was certain of that. He was a good judge of character, his job forcing him to be so. What he really wanted to know was what influence Sydney had on Gabrielle.

"Well, I'll be happy to show you around town," Keith said. "Baltimore has as many neighborhoods as streets, and they're all unique."

Victoria wiped the edges of her mouth with her napkin. "Keith, I'm sure Sydney has other things to do in her spare time."

Sydney decided Victoria's intention was to keep her high-class sons away from Gabrielle's low-class friend.

"A lot of exciting sites in Baltimore." Marcus spoke only to get Sydney's attention. She was purposefully avoid-ing eye contact with him and he found himself a little agitated by that. "Not just the harbor."

Sydney knew something in that last comment was insult-ing, but couldn't put her finger on it. Thank God, Marcus didn't live in this house. He'd be leaving eventually.

"There's the famous Blacks in Wax Museum," Gabrielle added. "And Baltimore's Black America Museum on Car-swell Street."

"Sounds great," Sydney said, not so comfortable with all the attention on her. She sent Keith a warm smile.

What was this? Marcus noticed the smile. How had Keith been able to form something with Sydney in mere hours? Maybe he underestimated his kid brother.

"Don't let Keith drag you around," he said. "Unless you like the bar scene."

Keith made an annoyed expression and Sydney sensed the competitive tension between the brothers. Well, she wasn't interested in either man, so she wasn't about to feed that fire. She focused on her food, saying nothing.

"I'm not a bar-hopper," Keith protested, his fork hitting the plate a little louder than necessary. "You're one to speak anyway. How long is your list?"

"Boys." Victoria eyed them both.

"Comedy, young man," Marcus said. "You must have left your sense of humor in your room."

"Where is Laura?" Victoria lifted her chin, looking around the corner. "She's supposed to make a plate for Aunt May."

"Comedy, my rear end," Keith said. "You always try to insult me in front of people and turn it around to a joke, so I look like the heel."

"Why isn't Aunt May at dinner?" Gabrielle asked. "Is she okay?"

Sydney felt the tension rise, the family chaos beginning, and could see that everyone at the table besides her was used to it. Were Victoria and Gabrielle going to ignore the men and let them duke it out?

"I give up." Marcus held his frustration in check. Since the lawsuit, Keith didn't want to hear anything from him. "Forget I said it."

"She's fine, dear." Victoria took a sip of wine. "She mentioned something about a television program she didn't want to miss."

"Don't tell me to forget it." Keith seemed ready to go. "Don't brush me off."

Sydney felt her stomach tense. Keith was angry, but even she could tell he was no match for Marcus. He was obviously more affected by the exchange than his older brother.

"Boys." Victoria's impatience was showing. "Such disruption."

"Let it go, Keith." Marcus was more than aware of Sydney's nervous preoccupation. He felt bad for causing this. "I'm sorry."

Keith leaned back in his chair. "You always get to end it. You sit in Dad's chair and you think your word is final."

Marcus thought twice about responding for the women's sake. This lawsuit was causing a wedge between the two of them that made things impossible.

"Boys," Victoria said again, a little louder this time. "We have company."

"Look," Gabrielle spat out. "Sydney's hanging with me anyway. Besides, she's got a school project that's going to take up her free time. You're fighting over nothing."

"What project?" Marcus asked.

None of your business! Sydney swallowed. "It's a genealogy project."

"I thought you were an MBA?" Keith was a little calmer now, returning to his food.

How did Keith know so much? Marcus wondered. An MBA? Yeah. He could see Sydney handling herself in a boardroom. Straight facts, no small talk.

"It's an elective." Gabrielle spoke before Sydney could. "Genealogy 101. If she wins, she gets five hundred bucks."

"Genealogy?" Lines of concern formed on Victoria's forehead. "Not that nonsense you were doing earlier this year?"

Gabrielle sighed and looked away, with cold eyes. "Thanks Mother."

"I'm tracing the Hart family tree," Sydney said. She sensed the apprehension as Victoria made no attempt to hide her disapproval. "Gabrielle said it was okay."

"She does that a lot." Victoria jammed her fork into a slice of baked ham.

"What's the big deal?" Gabrielle pushed away her plate.

"Keep it calm, Bree," Marcus said.

"I won't!" Gabrielle folded her arms across her chest. "What's she gonna find? That we came from slaves? Don't ninety-five percent of us black folks in America today come from slaves? I'm not ashamed of it. You're so hung up on—"

"Don't you attempt to tell me about myself, little girl." Victoria's words were harsh, but she didn't move. Not even a blink.

"Look," Sydney said. This was more than she intended. "I don't want to cause trouble."

"Don't worry," Marcus said. "You're not causing anything."

Sydney looked at him. Was he cleverly insulting her again? That was the trick, right? Say it just so, and you couldn't tell. Or was she getting antsy?

"What is it?" Gabrielle asked. "Do we have child molesters in our family?"

"Watch your mouth!" Victoria seemed frazzled for the first time tonight. "To say such—"

"Can we change the subject?" Keith asked.

Sydney could see the differences in the Hart brothers begin to emerge. Marcus was stronger, more independent. They both chose to avoid conflict, but for different reasons. One to keep the peace, one out of fear? It didn't make sense, with Keith being a lawyer.

"Family is a private issue," Victoria said. "Wouldn't you agree, Sydney?"

Sydney knew she was being baited and wasn't sure how to respond. She looked Victoria in the eye. "Family issues are, but who and what . . . I guess that would depend."

Marcus was impressed. Mother was on her game, just getting started. Most people would've quickly agreed or been stopped cold.

"What about yours, dear?" Victoria carefully dotted the edges of her pursed lips with the cloth napkin. "Your family."

King and queen, Sydney reminded herself. No wonder Mr. Hart wasn't a regular at dinner. This woman was a hard pill to swallow.

"What about them?" Sydney smiled as wide a smile as she could. She had manners. She had no intention of openly disrespecting this woman in her home.

"Would you care to throw your family tree out to the world?" she asked. "To strangers."

What family tree? "I think it's an interesting project. If it was helping Howard University or the—"

"You didn't answer my question." Victoria's words came quick, her stare subtly threatening.

Sydney was a little startled by the interruption, but she caught herself before letting it show. "No, Mrs. Hart. I wouldn't mind."

"Mom." Marcus knew this was a bad thing. Victoria had expected Sydney to crumple—shut up or stutter her agreement—but she didn't flinch. He was enjoying the sight of someone standing up to Victoria, but it was time to intercede.

"Then why don't you share some with us now?" Victoria shifted again in her seat. Her eyes set on Sydney, ready for combat. "Let's start with your parents. Your father."

"Mom." Gabrielle sighed loudly. "What is—"

"Quiet, Bree." She didn't look at her daughter as she silenced her. Only Sydney.

Sydney's blood was beginning to boil. Victoria didn't know her family situation, but she knew it wasn't as squeaky-clean as her own probably was, and was determined to make Sydney point that out to herself and everyone else here.

"Mother!" Marcus caught Victoria's stare. He startled her and everyone else at the table. All eyes were on him. He was used to that.

"Mother," he said. "It's obvious Sydney isn't interested in going into this. We can talk about her school project later."

School project? Sydney suddenly felt like she was five years old. Even when defending her, Marcus found a way to make her feel insulted.

"I apologize," Victoria said, followed by a quick, saccharine laugh. "I hope you weren't offended. That wasn't my intention of course."

"Of course." Sydney paused a second before looking away. *Liar.*

There was a silent pause at the table before Gabrielle spoke, barely loud enough for everyone to hear. "Another lovely evening at the Hart home."

Keith laughed, but only for a second after noticing no one else did.

"Sydney, I hope you make your way to D.C. this summer," Marcus said. Despite her obvious aversion to him, he found her attractive and enticing and he wanted her attention, even if it was in the form of a scowl. "I know some of the students like to get away in the summer, but Bree likes to pay me a visit every now and then."

"You can get excited about the Capitol Building only so many times," Gabrielle said, "but Georgetown is an awesome area."

"I enjoy Georgetown," Sydney added, trying to seem conversational. "I love the beautiful brownstones."

Marcus smiled and Sydney was forced to admit again how attractive he was. She'd never seen a politician's smile as sexy as this one.

"The brownstones are our pride and joy," he said. He read people well and could see that Sydney had just fought the urge to smile back. "Wild horses couldn't drive me from mine. You should come by. I could take you and Bree—"

Victoria coughed loudly. It was the fakest cough Sydney had ever heard. Her eyes darted at Marcus, then returned to her plate.

"Sydney knows Georgetown," Keith said. "She needs a tour of Baltimore. Besides, she's working with me. I'll show her around."

"So the battle for the fair maiden begins." Gabrielle laughed.

"Don't be silly, Bree." Victoria's eyes blinked. "Your brothers are only being courteous."

Sydney wondered who Victoria was trying to convince. Her last words sounded more like a question than a statement of opinion.

"It's about time, Laura." Victoria sighed, raising a thin hand to fix a strand of hair that was just about to fall out of place. "Where have you been?"

Laura, a medium-height, rosewood-brown-colored woman with an athletic build and short, curly raven-black hair stood in the archway to the dining room. She didn't seem sure if she should respond. Looking about forty, with tired light brown eyes and no makeup, she smiled before answering and coming in.

"I was with May," she answered in a very southern voice while clearing dishes from the table.

"Why didn't you tell me?" Victoria asked. "Imagine my

state, sitting here thinking my aunt has not gotten her dinner."

Imagine my state? Sydney had to bite her lip to keep from laughing. So she was a drama queen too. If she was worried, she could've gotten up, couldn't she?

"How is Aunt May, Laura?" Marcus asked.

"She's fine, sir." Laura smiled tenderly at the younger man. She was obviously fond of him. "Just tired. Spent too much time in that garden, reaching over."

"You're supposed to watch for that," Victoria said as if she were speaking to a five-year-old. "Looking after her is part of your job, isn't it?"

Sydney watched as Laura paused again, never taking her eyes from the plates she collected. "Yes, ma'am."

"Nice, Mother." Gabrielle shook her head. "Hey, Laura, this is my friend, Sydney Tanner. Sydney, this is Laura Wright."

"Nice to meet you." Sydney held out her hand, but pulled it back as she saw Laura's reluctance to shake it. Maybe that wasn't done. How would she know?

"Nice to meet you, Ms. Tanner." She nodded almost obediently and stepped away. "I hope you enjoyed your dinner."

"Actually I loved it." A life of packaged noodles and canned pasta made a well-cooked meal something like paradise. "The ham especially. Did you make this?"

Laura smiled proudly, wiping one hand on the thin blue apron she wore. "That's my great-grandmother's recipe. The key is to—"

"Sydney," Victoria interrupted. "Laura is very busy now. We don't want to keep her."

Gabrielle leaned over to whisper. "That's her not so subtle way of saying don't include the help in dinner conversation."

Sydney nodded. This was getting better every second.

The incorrigible older son and the impossible mother. Would she last the whole summer?

Keith cleared his throat. "Sydney will be staying with us for the summer. She's in Kelly's old room."

"Glad to have you Ms. Tanner." Laura nodded obediently again. Sydney didn't like that.

"We're all glad to have her here," Marcus said with a sideways smile. He held his last bite only inches from his mouth as Sydney's eyes met his. She was ticked. He'd never admit to meaning anything but politeness by his words.

Victoria's fork hit her plate and she reached for her glass of wine. Her eyes closed for a moment, then opened, as if she was barely tolerating the conversation. "Laura," she said. "You can bring dessert to my room. I'm suddenly tired myself."

Sydney noticed a vast amount of tension disappear with Victoria. Now if only she could rid the room of Marcus. She couldn't wait for him to leave. Unfortunately Keith was the first to leave as they ate dessert. A phone call from a partner at the firm had him up and running. As soon as he was out of earshot, Gabrielle started in on Marcus.

"Great job, bro," she said. "Why don't you lay off Keith?"

Marcus sighed. He wasn't hungry for dessert, but needed the excuse to stick around Sydney. He wasn't ready to say good night. "What did I do now?"

"It's not so much what you do." She pushed her chair away from the table. "It's just . . . this lawsuit."

"Not now, Bree." Marcus could sense Sydney's discomfort. "We don't want to bore our guest with family conflicts."

Sydney smiled, trying to make it seem genuine. She'd had two glasses of wine at dinner and blamed them for her preoccupation with his deep, dark eyes. She needed to get away from him.

Gabrielle grinned as she stood up. "You're right. I'll leave it up to you to entertain her. I gotta go."

Sydney felt her stomach tighten. Gabrielle wasn't actually leaving her alone with him, was she? "Where?"

"I'm tired. Going to bed." She placed her hand on Sydney's shoulder and lightly pushed her down just as Sydney started to rise. "No, you stay. Finish your cobbler. Marcus will keep you company."

"With pleasure." He leaned forward. Her eyes were so wide and open, but still mysterious. She was putting out a good effort to appear uninterested. Still, he wasn't buying it.

"I'm done with—"

Gabrielle was gone before Sydney could finish her sentence.

Dead silence.

She felt his eyes on her. The cobbler was good, but her appetite was gone. She felt fat and uncertain. This was his fault.

"Don't you need to start heading home?" she asked. "It's a good hour to Georgetown, isn't it?"

He laughed. "Forty-five minutes if you drive it right."

"That's an interesting headline." She turned to him. Maybe she'd had three glasses of wine. "Local congressman pulled over for speeding. A Hart at that. What would your constituents say?"

"Excellent point." He leaned back, placing his hands behind his head. "Irrelevant for tonight's purposes. You can't get rid of me yet. I'm spending the night."

Sydney let out an unconvincing laugh. "I'm not trying to get rid of you."

"Let's not play games, Sydney."

She backed away from the table, astonishment on her

face. "Games? You think I'm playing with you? Don't flatter yourself. That I would care—"

"You cared enough to send icy stares my way all evening." He followed as she got up and left the room.

"What are you doing?" She stopped, looking him up and down.

"Walking you to your room." He met her hands on her hips by doing the same, mocking her.

"I don't need you to." She walked faster, but his long legs kept up in an effortless stride. "I know my way."

"Feisty, feisty." He liked the way her braid bounced as she walked.

She swung around, fumingly mad. "Feisty? That's the most sexist term any man can use. I thought politicians at least made an effort to be politically correct." She rolled her eyes and turned away, walking faster this time.

"I'd apologize, but what good would it do? You've already decided to hate me."

Sydney sped up the stairs. One more second and she'd slap him. "What do you expect? If you want to apologize, why not start with that little game you played out back earlier?"

"Game I played?" She had her nerve. She was going to try and make him the bad guy in this.

"Letting me go on and on, knowing I had no idea who you were."

Marcus laughed out loud as they reached the door to her room. "No one forced you to say what you said to someone you didn't know. You never even gave me a chance to introduce myself."

"You should have stopped me." She felt so short standing across from him. His stance was like a brick wall.

"You should watch what you say." Marcus squinted his eyes, leaning forward. *"You* owe *me* the apology."

Sydney inhaled in anger. She balled her hands in fists at her side. "You were having fun at my expense."

"How rude of me. I should've stopped you to say, 'Wait a second, I'm Marcus Hart.' Okay, continue insulting my family!"

"I wasn't—" She bit her lip. He was right and she wanted to kill him for it. "Just get out of my way. I want to go to bed."

"Never go to bed angry, right?" He stepped aside. Her anger was like fire, and it only served to excite him.

"That's only for people going to bed together," she said, swinging open the door. "Since that doesn't apply to us, and I stress that it never will, good night!"

"Okay." He reached for her, grabbing her arm. Her skin was soft and supple and his awareness of that struck him mildly.

Sydney let him pull her to him, shocked by his behavior, and even more that she felt a sharp hit in the depths of her belly by his touch. Must have definitely been three glasses of wine.

"Let me go!" She pulled, twisted. No game. He was much stronger.

"A truce." He held up his index finger. "For one moment, listen to me."

"Let go." When he did, Sydney tried to calm down. She could feel herself breathing heavily.

"I'll admit I should've said something." He humbly placed a hand to his chest. "I can apologize if you do the same. We both give."

Sydney averted her eyes, looking down the dimly lit hallway. She shrugged her shoulders.

"I'll go first," he said. "I'm sorry."

Sydney blinked a few times, took a deep breath, and looked him in the eye. "I'm sorry too."

"I apologize for my mother as well." Marcus realized

how difficult that apology must have been for Sydney. It was more than stubbornness. "Victoria can be . . . I like to call her amusing in a particular way."

"No sweat," she lied. Sydney had another name in mind, but this was the woman's home.

He turned to leave, but stopped. Turning halfway back, he was unreasonably pleased to see she was still standing there and hadn't started farther into the room.

"And Keith," he said. "Well, Keith is easily smitten."

"What does that mean to me?"

He shrugged. "Probably nothing. Just thought you should know."

"You thought wrong." She wasn't a fool. He thought he was charming her with that sexy half turn, his hands so casually stuffed in his pockets.

"That's for the best." So Keith wasn't a factor. Marcus found a little pleasure in that. The tension between him and his brother was bad enough.

Sydney's anger returned. There he went again. So he didn't think she was good enough for his brother? And this, after apologizing for his mother.

Sydney slammed the door behind her.

Marcus blinked. What had just happened? Everything seemed fine, then suddenly her eyes turned to fire and *slam.*

"Women." He sighed and headed for his room.

With the lawsuit and Gabrielle's recent irrational behavior, Marcus had originally anticipated a difficult summer. Now he saw a spark in the form of a curvaceous Sydney Tanner.

Sydney didn't bother to unpack her clothes. She changed into her pajamas, washed her face, and fell into bed. Between Victoria and Marcus Hart, she was wound

in knots. Sleeping in a strange bed in a strange house
didn't help matters.

"I don't even know these people," she said to herself
in the dark, tossing and turning. "They could be devil
worshipers or gun fanatics."

Trust came hard for Sydney, but her choices were slim
and something told her that the Harts, no matter how
unpleasant some of them might be, were her only chance.
She felt confident in her assessment of Gabrielle as a
good person from their limited interactions throughout
the school year, especially after this gesture of help in her
time of need. So she jumped, and here she was at the
mercy of trust.

*"Life is full of disappointments, little girl." Linda Wil-
liams stood behind her sixteen-year-old daughter as she
stared into the bathroom mirror. "You need to get used to
it."*

*Sydney tried to stop crying, but she couldn't. She had
learned not to cry at home. They always pounced on her
when she did. Only now she couldn't help it. Justin Reid
had stood her up. She was deeply, deeply infatuated with
him and thought he'd never notice her. He noticed her and
asked her out. She waited two hours before she couldn't
take it anymore.*

*"Especially men," Linda went on. "I told you not to
get your hopes up. I saw you gettin' ready. Putting makeup
on. Wearing black so you can hide your weight. Now look
at you. You're to blame in a way."*

Sydney's eyes squeezed shut. "Go away!"

*"You keep hoping you can be something you can't. Let
it go, girl." She pointed to the mirror. "You'll always be
this. Nothing more and no such thing as less."*

After she left, Sydney slammed the door and fell to her

knees, sobbing. She could hear the two of them laughing,
watching television into the night.

Sydney felt a chill run through her. She threw off her
covers and jumped from the bed. She hated herself for
always remembering, needing to remember. They invaded
her awake, asleep, and she needed it that way, as sick as
it made her.

Air. She needed air. Stepping out onto the balcony, Sydney took a deep breath. She looked around. There was
a soft light illuminating May's garden. The chair Marcus
was working on when she'd first seen him was swinging
back and forth in the wind. She heard a cracking sound
to her left. A movement out the corner of her eye made
Sydney turn and lean forward.

Gabrielle had changed her clothes, but these were no
pajamas. She threw her purse over the balcony and followed right behind. The sturdy white vine ladder against
the wall of the home held her fine. She jumped to the
ground from close up, grabbed her purse, and ran
around the side of the house.

"I'm not even going to touch that one," Sydney said
to herself as she turned and went inside.

FOUR

"Looking for anything in particular, ma'am?"

Sydney jumped, alarmed. She swung around to face Laura looking at her with a cup of smoking coffee in her hand.

"Sorry to alarm you." Laura took a seat on one of the tall onyx stools surrounding the sparkling white kitchen island.

"It's okay." Sydney closed the door to a large pristine white, state-of-the-art refrigerator. "And please, don't call me ma'am. I'm Sydney."

"Mrs. Hart would have a fit if I called a guest by their first name." She tightened the belt on her fashionless, matronly gray dress. "Don't worry. It's just work."

"How do you deal with"—Sydney took a seat next to her, grabbing a fresh bagel from an assortment platter on the island—"the Harts."

Laura laughed. "Child, don't sweat it. They're more bark than bite. Mr. Hart is a fine, fine man."

Sydney could see from the expression on Laura's face that she held the absent Mr. Hart in high esteem. "What's he like?"

"Busy." She narrowed her eyes. "Some of the family don't appreciate the burden on him. You know the Hart name carries responsibility. Anthony is a great man. I enjoy working for him."

Laura leaned forward. "Mrs. Hart . . . Just stay out of her way. She's a holy terror sometimes, driving these kids crazy. If she locks her horns on you, grin and bear it. It never lasts too long."

Sydney took note of that. She'd lived through worse than she imagined Victoria could ever give.

"Now Marcus," Laura went on. "He's not here too often, but when he is, he's always a pleasure. I sure wish he would try to reconcile with Mr. Hart. I . . . You have something to say?"

"Who, me?" Sydney supposed her expression was betraying her again.

"When I mentioned Marcus," she said, "you got an unusual look on your face. Like you have a comment."

Sydney shrugged and tore at her bagel. She had a comment all right. "Just morning face."

Laura smiled knowingly. "You two didn't hit it off?"

Sydney paused, thinking. "That's the nicest way of putting it. When does he usually come down for breakfast? I don't want to run into him."

"Don't worry." Laura stretched, yawning. "He left early this morning. He should be home now."

"Oh," was all Sydney could say. Why wasn't she relieved?

"You seem . . . disappointed."

"Me?" Sydney laughed nervously. She was relieved. She had to be. Her eyes shifted around the kitchen to the all-white countertops. She'd never seen so much new stuff.

"Bree is a handful when she's here," Laura continued. "She provides entertainment and unnecessary drama. Keith is simple. Not here much but for dinner. Loves his mama. Loves the ladies. Then there's Ms. May."

Sydney couldn't help but smile at the wide grin on Laura's face.

"I get that about her," Sydney said. "A gem, huh?"

"Pure gold." Laura put down her cup, stood up and reached for the refrigerator. "Look, if you're worried about getting on in this house, don't be. You'll do fine."

"Victoria isn't happy about the genealogy project," Sydney said.

"What genealogy project?"

Sydney summarized the project and Victoria's response at dinner last night. She was surprised at Laura's amusement.

"You find this funny?" she asked.

"I'm not laughing at you," Laura said. She offered Sydney a plate of cream cheese and a knife, putting it back after she declined. "I'm just looking forward to this summer. It's going to be interesting."

"I would prefer a less interesting summer," Sydney said. "Only I need this money and assistantship next semester. Besides, I'm a little curious about the Hart family."

"The Harts have a long, prestigious history in Baltimore." Laura shrugged. "Don't know what Mrs. Hart's problem is. She loves to throw around that name she was so lucky to marry into."

"Like it was hers all along," Gabrielle said as she sauntered lazily into the kitchen.

"After thirty-six years of marriage, I suppose she's earned it." Laura went to the coffeemaker, grabbing the container. "Earl Grey this morning?"

"No, Laura." Gabrielle smoothed out her primrose satin tank and short pajamas. "Something with apple and cinnamon."

"You know your mother prefers you wear a robe." Laura handed the girl her cup of tea.

"Nag, nag, nag." Gabrielle surveyed the bagels. "No donuts, muffins?"

"Mrs. Hart says no more sweets." Laura leaned against the counter. "We've gone over this."

"Sorry I left you last night, Sydney," Gabrielle said. "I was tired. I hope Marcus wasn't too difficult."

"I left right after you." Sydney wasn't going to mention the balcony scene from last night. It wasn't any of her business where the girl went.

"Did Marcus put the moves on you?"

Sydney felt her cheeks heat up. "No. He only annoyed me, then left me alone."

"He's available, you know." She gave an exaggerated wink.

"Not exactly," Laura interjected, lightly smacking Gabrielle on the arm.

Gabrielle waved her away. "Lindsay, the snot-nosed pig lady. Yeah, right. He's single."

Sydney fought an overwhelming urge to ask who Lindsay was. She knew she shouldn't care.

"Shouldn't we get going?" Sydney glanced at her watch.

"We'll stop by Mickey D's first." Gabrielle hopped off the stool. "I want something greasy. Look at you."

Sydney was wearing a business casual gray pantsuit with a white GAP T-shirt underneath and black flats. Her hair was in a neat french braid down her back. No jewelry, only lipstick.

"You're gonna make me look bad," Gabrielle said. "Come with me. I just need to get dressed. It'll take ten minutes."

"Beware of her ten minutes," Laura called after them.

"Nag, nag, nag." Gabrielle blew a kiss to the maid. "Is my car fixed?"

"It's fixed," Laura said, "but still in D.C. Your rental is in the driveway. Keys in the car."

"You're a gem!" Gabrielle started a sprint.

"Ms. Tanner," Laura called after her.

"Yes?" Sydney enjoyed the frantic pace of the house. People fulfilled with busy lives, all interchanging with each other. It was unfamiliar to her.

"You were looking in the refrigerator like you needed something," she said. "Would you like me to get you something from the store?"

Sydney hesitated. She blinked and smiled. She wanted to say no, hating to be a bother.

Laura seemed to sense her hesitation. "Now, young lady. You're going to have quite a time at this house over the summer. You'll need whatever comfort you can get."

Sydney smiled. "One thing."

"Name it."

"Chocolate for milk."

Laura laughed. "Chocolate syrup?"

"I like to have chocolate milk at night before I go to bed. Sometimes regular, sometimes hot."

"Then you'll have it." Laura smiled, tightening the belt on her robe again and headed back for the kitchen.

Linda and David Williams were horrible parents. They barely gave Sydney what she needed, never giving more. She would get days of grief for asking for a toy or ice cream. She stopped asking.

Only there was one thing. There was always chocolate syrup or hot cocoa packets in the house. Sydney would make a cup at night before bed, except when David or Linda was in the kitchen. It wasn't worth it then. She'd made it her little treat. The fact that it was always there made her feel good. She tried to make herself believe her mother was trying to say she did care some by providing the chocolate. It was something at least.

* * *

"Congressman Hart?" The voice paused. "Congressman Hart, are you there? Marcus!"

Marcus jolted out of his imagined diversion at the sound of Ellen Austin's impatient voice over the speaker phone. How long had she been calling him?

"I'm sorry, Ellen." He leaned over, pressing the speaker button. "What can I do for you?"

"Are you all right?" she asked. "Do I need to come in? You've been acting a little—"

"It's nothing," he said, even though he knew he was lying.

Ellen knew, too. She was a career congressional secretary. The best there was, in Marcus's opinion—pulling in fifty grand after thirty years of raises. She was a steal.

"David Long is on line one for you."

Marcus felt heavy in his chest. He was thirty-five, but felt like fifty right now. David was his best friend since they were young boys, but he wanted nothing to do with him right now. It was out of his own shame.

"Take a message, please," he said.

"You're in a committee meeting? Seeing a constituent?"

"No, Ellen. David is a friend. We won't lie to him. Just tell him I can't talk now and take a message."

There was short silence. "Yes, sir. And remember your meeting with Senator Jemens in ten minutes. His office."

"Yes," he said. "Thank you."

Marcus leaned back, glancing around his small office at the Capitol. There was a lot of work to do, voters to call about complaints. There were countless bills up for vote, of which each had at least one hundred pages of definition he needed to read. He couldn't think of them, and wasn't prepared for his meeting with the senator.

It was *her* fault! All he could think of was Sydney Tanner. He was intrigued by the young woman and at the same time annoyed with her. She was mysterious and guarded, but her eyes said she was capable of loving completely. He couldn't get her natural beauty and nothing less than dangerous body out of his mind.

His attraction to Sydney wasn't the only reason she was on his mind. Marcus knew Gabrielle had left home last night after saying she was going to bed. He'd been on his way downstairs for a late snack when he heard noise while passing Gabrielle's bedroom. The door had been locked. He'd knocked quietly. No answer. He'd called her name. No answer. He'd gone downstairs to get a master key he knew was hidden in the kitchen. It was then he'd heard a small car or motorcycle slowly drive off.

Marcus had a feeling Sydney was a part of this. She had a secretive aura about her, and this new friendship with Gabrielle came with the unusual behavior told to him by his brother and mother.

Gabrielle. Sydney. The lawsuit driving a wedge between him and Keith. Lindsay. Oh, yeah, Lindsay. Marcus promised himself to call her tonight. Unlike the last time, but he would finish what he had to say this time.

Sydney Tanner. Who was she, and what gave her the right to occupy his mind at a time and in a way he least needed a woman to?

"Thanks for showing up on time your first day!"

Keith grabbed Gabrielle's arm, pulling her into his office. Sydney followed behind.

"We're sorry, Keith." Sydney felt awful. They were a half hour late. Laura had been right. Gabrielle's ten minutes turned out to be forty-five.

"Don't apologize, Sydney." He eyed his sister with contempt. "I know who's to blame here. I told you how important this lawsuit is to me, Bree. The partners are watching me like hawks."

Gabrielle plopped her petite figure into the leather chair behind the desk. "Oh, please. Like there's a question they'll make you partner. You're a Hart."

He pulled her out of the chair. "I want to earn it. Just like you're gonna earn your money this summer. None of last summer's nonsense."

Sydney couldn't help but laugh at the look of disgust on Gabrielle's face.

"Yeah, I mean it," Keith said. "You'd better be here at eight every morning. Now go to the research center and talk to Hillary about time cards."

"Keith . . ." Sydney wanted to apologize again, but Keith was already on the phone, asking his secretary to come in.

"You said the day started at eight-thirty." Sydney followed Gabrielle through the office. "We're an hour late."

"My day does start at eight-thirty." Gabrielle winked. "Eight in the morning? I don't think so. I didn't get in until . . ."

Gabrielle caught herself as soon as she seemed to realize what she'd done. Sydney's expression never changed.

"You didn't give anything up," she said. "I was out on the balcony last night getting a breath of air. I saw you."

Gabrielle stopped and grabbed her. Desperation was in her eyes. "You can't tell! You can't tell!"

"Chill out, kid." Sydney pulled her arm from Gabrielle's grip. "I'm not trying to get caught up in any drama."

Gabrielle sighed and paused before resuming walking. "I'm waiting for you to ask what was up."

"I have an idea," Sydney said. "But it's none of my business."

Gabrielle opened a door to a large library with rows of books. The design was classically legal. "His name is Gary Odum. He's the most perfect thing in the world."

They came to an elderly woman with white, shoulder-length hair and old lady glasses covering eyes as blue as the sky. In her sensible gray business suit, she held up an impatient hand to the girls as she spoke on the phone.

Sydney looked around. Every inch of this office said money. If it wasn't marble, it was cherry wood or brass. Everything was shiny, polished, refined.

"I'm glad you're happy," she said, realizing Gabrielle wasn't going to let the issue go.

"Well, it's not all great. No one can know we're dating."

"Why not?" Sydney continued to indulge the girl. They were just waiting anyway.

"Mother and Daddy." Gabrielle shook her head. "They're such snots. They'd give me a hard time. They'd make our lives hell."

Sydney felt for her. "Don't tell me. He's poor."

"A mail clerk. He works here at the firm." She smiled mischievously. "Right under Keith's nose and he doesn't have a clue."

"You're playing with fire with this kind of stuff," Sydney said. "It never works."

"Well, it's getting close. I know they're suspicious, but now I have you."

"Me?" Sydney shook her head vigorously. "No way. I don't want anything to do with this."

"I just might need a cover every now and then." Gabrielle batted her eyes and entwined her hands at her chest. "Please."

"You're twenty-three, Gabrielle. Do what you want."

"It's not that simple," she whispered with a frown. "You don't know Victoria. She's another kind of mom."

Try your hand at the Linda Williams's model, Sydney thought. "You'll never be your own woman if you don't stand your ground with her."

Gabrielle blinked, her long lashes pleading. Sydney didn't want to do this. The last thing she needed was to get entangled in this family's secrets and deceptions. Still it made her angry to think of Victoria trying to control the girl's life.

Defeated, Sydney sighed and Gabrielle hugged her.

"I promise I won't take advantage of you," she said. "Just maybe an alibi or two."

"Did I hear the word *alibi?*" the woman behind the desk asked as she replaced the receiver. "Starting lawyer talk already?"

"Hi, Ms. Green." Gabrielle smiled and blinked innocently. "This is Sydney Tanner. She's interning this summer, too."

"I wasn't aware of this." Ms. Green spoke with a strong German accent as she glanced at her clipboard. "I don't see . . ."

"She's a friend of the family," Gabrielle interrupted. "Keith approved everything."

Ms. Green appeared satisfied with this explanation. "In that case, welcome, Sydney." She held out her hand. "I'm Hillary Green, director of research. Do you know anything about researching lawsuits?"

"Plenty." Sydney reached in her bag and pulled out a copy of her resumé. "I've been doing research of some kind for years. I interned at a D.C. law firm two summers ago. Much bigger than this."

"Yes," she said as she read. "Well, Panka, McDaniel, and Wagner is a small firm with select clientele. We aren't about volume. We're about quality."

"She means we defend only people and corporations that are as rich as sin," Gabrielle said.

Ms. Green slipped Gabrielle an annoyed grin. "I'd forgotten how much I missed your sense of humor. You can go to the research room. There is plenty of work waiting for you at your usual desk. The others started an hour ago. As usual."

"Cool." Gabrielle seemed to pay no mind to the condemnation in Hillary's last words. "I'll show you where it is, Sydney."

"Not so fast." Hillary shook her head. "Sydney is going upstairs. Your resumé says you're a better fit for the advanced research. Our legal assistants are overloaded. Come with me."

"What?" Gabrielle pouted.

"That's all, Ms. Hart." Hillary lowered her head, her glasses slipping down her nose a bit. "Thank you."

Sydney waved an apologetic good-bye and followed along. She returned to the tenth floor of Baltimore's twenty-seven-floor World Trade Center Building and was given a desk that was connected to five others in a jagged circle. At the desk were women, varying in age and personal style. They were all busy on the phone.

Hillary grabbed a couple of manila folders from each desk and piled them on Sydney's.

"These are yours," she said. "To your left is Melinda, next Francis, Amy, Keisha, and Jennifer. Melinda will fill you in on what you're doing as soon as she's off. I'll tag your time card for nine. It will be at my desk. Need anything, I'm extension 7-9-1-1."

With that, Hillary was gone. Sydney sat down, returning smiles to the women who took a second to look in her direction. She grabbed the files, sifting through them. Each sheet was similar, each titled Appointments to be Made.

APPOINTMENTS TO BE MADE
Mr. and Mrs. Ernie Bay, 1234 Central Street. Mr.
Bay is opposed to selling. Mrs. Bay (Presia) is
wavering. Last offer $80,000.

APPOINTMENTS TO BE MADE
Mrs. Alice Covert, 1799 Christian Walkway. Last
offer $75,000. Not wavering. Filed a complaint
with police in March. Alleges harassing
phone calls.

"You're a godsend." Melinda reached over and shook
Sydney's hand. "Melinda Donaldson."

She was a pretty, thin redhead with dark green eyes
and freckles everywhere. With no makeup, she wore a
white T-shirt and schoolgirl plaid skirt. Sydney wasn't sure
how old she really was, but she didn't look a day over
eighteen.

"Sydney Tanner." She shook her hand. "Ms. Green says
I'm supposed to be here and you'll tell me why."

"We weren't expecting you," Keisha said as she hung
up her phone. "You're a temp?"

Sydney explained her relationship with Gabrielle, noticing the expressions on the girls' faces change. Even
the three girls still on the phone paid attention after hearing the name Hart.

"You must be smack in the middle of the family fire,"
Keisha said, her brows raised. Her tawny-brown skin was
shining and flawless. She had tight, small braids that
stopped at her shoulders. Her eyes were almost hazel.

Melinda blushed. "Keith's hot, but that Marcus. Have
you met him yet?"

"Yes." Sydney was sure Marcus got that reaction from
women often. "What do you mean, family fire?"

"The whole reason you're here," Keisha said. She

seemed confused. "The lawsuit pitting bachelor brother against brother, making or breaking their careers."

"How well do you know the Harts?" Amy was ready to join in. She was about thirty, with a biracial makeup. Her golden-brown skin matched perfectly with her almost sandy-blond hair. Apparently she liked bright colors and large earrings. Today they were dangling mini-figures of the African continent: red, black, and green.

"Not too well," Sydney said. "Just Gabrielle from school."

"They're black royalty in Baltimore, girl." Keisha lifted her chin. "I'd call them the black Kennedys, but they're more like *Dynasty* than *Camelot.*"

"They get VIP treatment all over town," Amy said. "Must be nice."

Sydney shrugged. She couldn't imagine such a life. "Keisha, what did you mean when you said the family fire was the reason I'm here?"

"Has Bree or Keith said anything about the lawsuit?" Melinda asked.

Sydney recalled the comments here and there. "A few references. It has something to do with Marcus and Keith."

Amy laughed, looking around the office. "Keep an eye out for a lawyer. They don't like us gossiping."

"All these files on our desks," Melinda said, pointing, "are regarding a lawsuit filed by the people of the Fairview Hills neighborhood against our client, Preston Corporation."

Sydney's business knowledge kicked in. "They're a multi-million-dollar real estate company in Baltimore."

Keisha nodded. "They want to build a bunch of high-priced condos in Fairview Hills."

"Some of the residents say Preston went too far in their

efforts to get the residents to sell their homes. They're suing for harassment."

Sydney's interest was piqued. "What kind of neighborhood is Fairview Hills?"

"Poor," Keisha said. "Working class at best, and predominately African American. The thing is, it's part of District 17, which includes some of the richest, nicest neighborhoods in Baltimore. The people that live in Fairview Hills clean up after their neighbors."

Sydney was putting two and two together. "District 17 also happens to be represented by none other than the honorable Congressman Marcus Hart."

"You're quick." Melinda winked.

"His reputation as a congressman," Amy said, "his future political hopes, could depend on his efforts for these people."

"The same for Keith," Sydney said. "His legal career could be made or broken by this case."

"This is the big-time chance for both of them," Keisha said. "All I care about is for whoever loses to know they can cry on my shoulder. Either one is a catch."

Sydney could see a disaster in the making. The boys were already competitive "What do we do?"

"We document complaints," Melinda answered. "We track them and conduct interviews in the neighborhoods to see if we can find some folks on our side. If we can get them on our side. Interviews start next week."

As the girls explained the process, Sydney dug into her work. She wasn't looking forward to visiting a strange neighborhood that Amy described as less than great, to put it nicely. Besides, she had no idea why these people weren't eager to sell homes no one else wanted to buy to move someplace better. She developed an image of Fairview Hills in her mind and it reminded her of her home. Home. She called it that only because she couldn't think of a more appropriate word for it.

"So how was your first day?" Gabrielle met Sydney at Hillary's desk at six that evening, just as they had agreed at lunch.

"The quickest first day I've ever had." Sydney enjoyed the hectic, fast pace of a law firm. "A little tired, but looking forward to starting the project tonight."

"We're gonna have to reschedule that." Gabrielle grabbed her arm and pulled her behind a rolling shelf of books. "I need an alibi."

"You're taking advantage of this pretty early."

"I beg you, plead of you." Gabrielle slapped her flattened hands in front of her chest. "I need to see him."

"What do I say?" Sydney sighed, shaking her head. This was a huge mistake. It was going to end in a mess.

FIVE

Keith frowned, looking confused. "Seems rude to me. Bree gets invited for drinks with her fellow researchers, and doesn't invite you?"

"She did actually." Sydney cleared her throat to lie clearly. "I passed. I don't want her to feel obligated to entertain me. Besides, they were all her age. That crowd can be too young for me sometimes."

Keith signed several sheets of paper on top of each other. He checked his watch. "To answer your question, of course I'll give you a ride home. I'll have Ana order a rental for you to use for the rest of the summer."

"Thanks." Her own car? That was easy.

"One thing." He grabbed his jacket, slipping it on. He signed, pausing to flash a charming smile. "You don't mind having dinner with me, do you?"

Sydney blushed. She could tell he wasn't coming on to her. She thought him a nice guy and wished Marcus was more like him. "Dinner sounds fine."

"Good," he said. "It'll be a foursome. We're meeting Richard McDaniel and Michael Wagner."

"As in two of the three names on the door to this place?"

Keith jokingly faked a frightened shiver. "Those indeed."

"Do I look okay?"

Sydney wanted to impress. If she'd learned anything in one day, it was that this was a top-notch law firm. She needed to take advantage of her fortune and develop contacts for the future, but she wasn't in her best corporate getup.

Keith laughed as he wrapped his arm around her and side by side they walked out of his office.

"You're a knockout and you don't know it," he said. "You'll fit in perfectly at the Sierra. You didn't get enough compliments as a child."

If you only knew, Sydney thought.

Marcus straightened his tie before accepting the drinks. The female bartender was a beautiful Latino woman in her early twenties. Her soft olive skin was highlighted by her curly, lustrous black hair. She winked at him as she accepted his twenty dollar bill.

"Keep the change," he said.

Turning around, he handed Lindsay Price her gin and tonic.

"Thank you, dear." She smiled appreciatively. "Looks like you aren't the only congressman here tonight. Senator Busse is right outside the cigar lounge."

He followed her pointing finger. The Bethesda Country Club, located in the Maryland town of its name, was frequented by the political crowd. Congressmen, senators, and other influentials were regulars. It wasn't more than twenty minutes from D.C. Marcus hadn't wanted to come here tonight. He'd prefer somewhere more anonymous. He had a job to do and knew it wouldn't be pretty. He looked back at Lindsay. She would be livid.

"Of course," she said, flipping back her long, thick auburn hair. Her light brown eyes sparkled. She was a beautiful woman. "None of them is as popular as you."

Lindsay was always forthcoming with the compliments. Marcus smiled, chiding himself for his rare cowardice. He'd always been one to do what had to be done regardless. The temporary pain wouldn't compare to that of the long term.

"We should step out a bit," she said. "Let him see you. Let him come to you."

"I've had enough political banter for the day," Marcus said. Lindsay was always giving him helpful suggestions for his career advancement.

So helpful, complimenting. She was beautiful, sexy, smart, and successful as a public relations executive. She was a gem for his ego and crazy about him. They'd been dating for four months.

Lindsay sighed. "All right. At least let's take a seat. I know we don't have reservations, but you're a Hart. They'll make an exception."

Marcus shook his head. She made no protest. Lindsay never did, she was so obliging. Too obliging. This wasn't right. He knew this and had to handle it. He hated himself for thinking of Sydney Tanner—for wishing Lindsay had Sydney's spice and mystery.

"Lindsay," he said. "We have to talk. Let's go out on the balcony."

He didn't wait for her agreement. He knew it would come as it did only seconds later. Taking her arm gently, he led the tall, thin beauty out of the darkened cocktail lounge and through the waiting area for the dining room.

"Hey, Congressman," someone said. He smiled and waved.

"Mr. Hart," a young woman called out flirtatiously, "keep up the good work."

He raised his head in appreciation, intending to guide Lindsay along. Just then, he saw her and thought he was hallucinating a vision as a result of thinking about her all day. He stood frozen as he watched her laugh and touch the shoulder of the man next to her. When he saw who it was, a wave of uninvited jealousy rolled over him.

Keith hadn't informed Sydney that the Sierra was inside the Bethesda Country Club. It was opulent, decadent, and packed with people who dressed well and carried themselves with the assurance of money. If you were at this club, you had made it.

"That was Michael." Keith flipped his cell phone and put it back in his coat jacket. "They'll be a few minutes late. Caught in bad traffic. That outerloop is always ugly."

Sydney let in the sounds of the diverse, but mostly white, club. No one looked at her as if she didn't belong as she was sure they would. She felt relaxation set in, and it was such an unfamiliar feeling.

"What are you looking at?" Keith asked. His smile showed amusement.

"Just this place," Sydney said, looking around. "This is nice. Come here often?"

"My father is a lifetime member," he answered. "Has been for almost a decade. Marcus has an honorary membership."

A waiter arrived and took drink orders. Sydney sat back in her chair, relaxing even more. She and Keith engaged in small talk. He was an incredibly intelligent young man with a cynical sense of humor, hinting at a little insecurity. He was flirtatious and charming.

Sydney enjoyed the company of men, although it wasn't a frequent occurrence in her life. From time to time, when things got a little hard, the goal on shaky ground, she had to keep extra complications at arm's length. So then, men were a no-go. Other times she'd been tempted and let a relationship form. She answered her loneliness and her desire, but never to a point where she let it take prominence in her life and priority over her goal. It was hard to fight those emotional tugs. After all, she was a woman. Just like every woman, she wanted love and felt the urge to nurture.

"Great." Linda Williams crossed her arms with a disgusted look on her face. Her thirteen-year-old daughter sat in her bed, huddled over. "Just great."

"It's not my fault." Sydney's stomach hurt and she wanted to sleep. She only wished her mother would leave.

"Well, congratulations," Linda said with extreme sarcasm. "You're a woman now. I hope you know you can get pregnant now. And boys love to prey on pitiful girls like you."

"I don't do that, Mama." Sydney was determined to defend her honor, no matter who questioned it.

"Better not. If you get pregnant, you're out. Remember that. And to answer your question—no, I don't have any aspirin. Take the pain like a woman."

". . . but Mother asked Marcus to do it instead." Keith had continued talking as Sydney's mind wandered. "So you know, whatever."

Sydney nodded in agreement to a comment she knew nothing of. What she had noticed was that Keith's conversations seemed to veer toward the same topic: Marcus. As much as she disliked the man, Sydney had to admit he'd made an impressive success of himself and had great presence. She imagined that was hard to live up to.

"Speak of the devil," Keith said as he removed his coat jacket and wrapped it around his chair. He stood up to greet the oncomers.

Expecting stuffed-shirt lawyers, Sydney was surprised to see Marcus walking toward them, companion in hand.

He was looking dead at her, not his brother, and the feeling of comfort that Sydney had immediately disappeared.

He looked dashing in a sleek, tailored navy-blue suit. His strides were quick and demanding of attention. He was a leader, Sydney had to give him that. She'd give him nothing else.

"Pleasant surprise," he said, as they approached. "What are you two doing here?"

"Having dinner," Keith answered defensively. "What does it look like?"

Marcus winked and laughed, mocking amusement. "Mr. Stand-up Comedian. I mean, together. Are we witnessing a romantic bloom?"

Sydney's eyes turned flat, guarding as he looked down at her. She felt too warm and uncomfortable with him standing right next to her. His hand hung only inches from her upper arm, which was bare.

"Why do you care?" Keith asked. He smiled at the frown on Marcus's face, then turned to Lindsay. "Hey, Lindsay. How are you, tonight?"

"Just beautiful." She smiled wide and squeezed her way between Marcus and Sydney. "A little tired, but Marcus insisted we have dinner."

"So demanding, my brother."

Marcus wanted an answer to his question. He was angry. Hadn't Sydney told him Keith's easy tendency toward infatuation wasn't an issue for her?

"Where's Bree?" he asked.

"Out with friends," Keith answered, taking his seat. "We're waiting for—"

"What friends?" He turned to Sydney. "Sydney, do you know something about this?"

"She's allowed, isn't she?" Sydney was certain he was accusing her of something.

"Who are these friends?" Marcus just knew she knew

something about Gabrielle's mysterious behavior. He wanted answers.

"From work," Sydney answered, accepting her drink from the waiter.

"Can we discuss this another time?" Keith asked, sounding irritated.

"Who are they?" Marcus persisted. "How well does she know them? What are their names?"

"You ask that like you'd know them if I told you," Sydney said. "You know you wouldn't, so why ask? Look, she's an adult. If she wants you to know this, she'll tell you. I'm not her guardian."

He mumbled angrily, turning to his brother. "Keith, you know Mother said—"

"How would I know what Mother said?" Keith asked. "She talks to you, not me."

"Boys." Lindsay laughed nervously, rubbing a calming hand down Marcus's arm. "Save it for the sandbox. Keith, you know Marcus is only concerned about little Bree."

"Lindsay." Marcus didn't care for her interference on this topic. Sydney had made him angry now. What was this dinner about anyway?

"Excuse my brother's rudeness, Sydney." Keith folded his arms across the chest. "You haven't met Lindsay Price, Marcus's girlfriend."

"Hello." Lindsay held out her hand with reluctance as if she were debating whether or not she wanted Sydney to touch her. "You are . . . ?"

"Sydney Tanner."

The woman's hand was moist, her shake very tepid. She was very pretty. Sydney expected no less for the congressman. She assumed Victoria would greatly approve.

"Tanner?" Lindsay coyly bit her lower lip. "Any relationship to the Falls Church, Virginia, Tanners? Samuel and Christina?"

"No, I'm sorry." Sydney forced a polite smile. *I'm from the Chicago Tanners. I only know my father's name: Edward. Last I heard, he was in Cook County for armed robbery. That was seventeen years ago.*

"Where are you from, dear?" The voice was so politely condescending.

"Chicago," Sydney answered. *Marcus, go away and take your arm candy with you.*

"Is this a working dinner?" Marcus asked, his frustration building, feeling ignored.

"I love Chicago." Lindsay laughed, her head tipping to the side. "The symphony. Bloomingdale's. The Ritz Carlton. I always have fun when I'm there. Marcus, we should go before it freezes up. A romantic weekend. Father knows the mayor. You should meet him. He should meet you."

Sydney thought her lunch would come back up.

Marcus felt a headache coming on. He had to end this with Lindsay tonight, but not now. Now he wanted to talk to Sydney. Alone.

"See now!" Keith stood up, exasperated. He looked behind his brother. "Can you leave? The last thing I need is—"

"What are you talking about?" Marcus asked.

"Just . . ." Keith smirked. "Excuse me for a moment."

They watched as Keith walked past them and into a crowd along the wall, away from the table. Sydney was perplexed. He was leaving her alone with them? Where was the ladies' room?

"Lindsay," Marcus said. "Can you wait for me on the balcony by the entrance?"

Lindsay's eyes widened. "Why?"

"I need to speak to Sydney alone." He noticed her apprehension, but wasn't in the mood to console it. "Family business."

"Marcus, I . . ." Sydney shook her head.

"Family?" Lindsay asked. "What family is she? How do you know her so well?"

"Lindsay, now." Marcus knew she'd listen, and after a rebellious sigh, she retreated.

"Marcus," Sydney said right off. "I am not family. Don't include me in your family business."

"You include yourself when you cover up lies." He harshly grabbed the chair next to her and sat down. "Where is Bree?"

Sydney became red-hot. This man. His nerve. "How dare you?"

"Easily, young woman." He scooted closer. He tried to ignore her beauty, the shine her skin set off, the way rebellious strands of hair fell around her face. "Answer me."

"Are you under the impression I take orders from you?" Sydney didn't like him this close, but she wouldn't back her chair away. He'd think she was intimidated.

"Answer me?" she questioned, mocking his demand. "What kind of fool are you?"

He fought the smile that wanted to curve his lips. He liked her comeback. She wasn't a pushover. Still he was angry and no woman was going to back him down. "So you aren't lying to me about Bree?"

Sydney turned away, her eyes focusing on the elderly man playing the piano twenty or so yards away. She was lying, but that fact only made her angrier at him.

"Then what about this dinner?" he asked.

"You don't quit, do you?" She pursed her lips to catch herself. "You think your last name gives you a right to know other people's private business."

"So this *is* private?" he asked, his anger regathering its steam.

Sydney smiled, realizing he was at his wit's end with her. She spoke with a calm, slow tone. "It's none of your business, Congressman Hart. Don't you have a girlfriend waiting for—"

"He's my brother," Marcus interrupted. She was toying with him and it infuriated him—at the same time exciting him. "My family *is* my business."

"And I'm not good enough to have dinner with your brother, is that it?" She leaned forward. She wouldn't let this pompous, arrogant snob get away with this. "Well, you're wrong. I am having dinner with your brother and it's because *he* asked me to."

"I wasn't suggesting—"

"Furthermore," she continued, visions of her mother's criticisms dancing in her head. "I'm still good enough for your country club even though I don't come from the Tanners of Falls Church and my daddy doesn't know the mayor of Chicago."

"Leave Lindsay out of this." He'd touched a nerve with her, he could see her eyes glossing. He felt guilty for making her feel this way. "Look, I'm sor—"

"I'll leave Lindsay out of this," she said, "if you get out of my face. Don't leave her waiting much longer. I'm sure she's dying without you near. I, on the other hand, am dying because you *are* near."

Quickly he stood up. He knew she'd hurt his feelings, but wouldn't let it show. He'd come over with no plan in mind, which was unusual for him. He was a politician and had learned to always think before speaking, or it would come back to slap him in the face. Sydney had just verbally slapped him in the face. He'd made a mess of this and had no one to blame but himself. Now something about her rebuke made him feel like a rejected teenager.

He headed for the balcony, smiling to another constituent, a well-wisher. Why had he come here? Lindsay begged and begged. She loved to be seen. If he had put his foot down, she'd have given in, but he hadn't. Now thoughts and images of Keith and Sydney were branded in his mind, and he was more than ticked.

He couldn't show it. He was a Hart and a congressman. He couldn't show anything in public. Appearances. Confidence. He was sick of some of this, but he'd made his choices. He refused to feel sorry for himself—he was a man, not a boy.

Lindsay turned with a mixture of concern and impatience on her face. She tried to hide it with a beautiful smile, but it wasn't working. Marcus sighed. He was— tired, and the worst was yet to come.

Sydney tightened her robe and tiptoed through the dimly lit house. It was eleven and there was total silence. Gabrielle's car was in the driveway and it appeared that everyone was asleep. She and Keith had gotten home only ten minutes ago. Sydney tried to enjoy herself, but her encounter with Marcus had set the tone for the evening. Keith had left them alone to retrieve his bosses. When they returned, the rest of the night was spent discussing the lawsuit.

She'd let her mind wander and her eyes follow as she kept alert for Marcus's return, but it never happened. She wasn't certain she could stand a summer of Marcus. He irked her to death and she could tell he felt the same about her. Still she found him attractive and hated herself for it. She wanted to believe she was just lonely. It came in handy. After all, she'd been with Darrin for six months and had gotten used to the comfort of a man's arms around her.

"Chocolate," she mumbled as she reached the kitchen and searched for a light. Finding one, the kitchen was illuminated.

Two doe-like eyes stared up at her, and Sydney jumped with a strong breath. The black Lab's head tipped to the side, his tongue hanging out of his mouth.

"Hey . . . doggy." She stood still, gauging the threat. Realizing there was none, she patted the dog on his head and moved on.

"His name is McKenzie."

Laura stood in the opposite doorway that apparently led to her bedroom. "I'm sorry. He's supposed to be outside, but he hid from me."

"I don't mind." Sydney reached into the refrigerator for the chocolate milk. She pointed to the cutlery tray atop the kitchen island. "Can I grab a pot?"

Laura laughed. "You don't have to ask for anything, ma'am. Not anything."

"I'm just not . . ."

"Not used to this," she finished for Sydney. "I can tell. You feel like you don't belong. Why is that?"

Sydney shrugged, hating that she was so obvious. "I feel like I'm getting a free ride. I'm not comfortable with it."

"You're working, aren't you?" Laura attached the leash to McKenzie.

"Yes." Sydney took a seat at the island, waiting for the milk to boil. "It's just all this. I should pay rent or help clean up, or . . ."

"Mr. Hart wouldn't stand for it. Besides, putting up with Mrs. Hart is a payment in itself."

"I haven't run into her much," Sydney said. "I'm grateful for that."

"You probably won't, except for dinner. And as for everyone else . . ." She paused. "They're happy to have you."

"What do you think Mr. Hart will say?" Sydney found

Laura to be easy to talk to and she relished the opportunity to divert her mind from Marcus.

Laura smiled a warm smile, her eyes softening. "Mr. Hart is a welcoming soul. Good people. He's not here very often, but he's responsible for so much. He is dignified and respectful. He'll have no problem with you here and he'll treat you right."

"How long have you known him?" Sydney heard the personal tone in Laura's voice, speaking of Anthony.

"My mother worked for Kenneth Hart, Mr. Hart's father. I've known him my whole life. The Harts have been very good to my family for a long time."

As they said their good nights, Sydney could tell Laura would be a loyal servant to Anthony Hart as long as either of them was alive.

Sydney took her drink into the sitting room, turning on a soft lamp near the wall to look at the myriad of photos that she and Gabrielle were supposed to have spent this night going over for the genealogy project.

Each picture showed a practice in privilege. Most were recent, within the last twenty years or so. Sydney found it interesting how many more pictures there were of Marcus than any of the other children. She noticed a pretty young woman she suspected to be Kelly, Keith's twin sister. Formal events, family getaways, dinners in a formal dining room. Every place was luxurious, high glamour, and high class. The Harts were a very attractive family, used to having their picture taken. They were never caught off guard—always ready with a smile, exuding family unity, hands entwined.

Sydney could count on two fingers how many childhood pictures she had. She didn't care. She wanted to forget all of it anyway.

"Marcus is a handsome devil, isn't he?"

Sydney almost spilled her drink as she swung around.

Coming face to face with him for the first time, Anthony Hart looked even more dashing than his picture in various African-American magazines.

"Didn't mean to startle you." He entwined his hands behind his back and smiled. "You must be Sydney."

Sydney shook his hand with a nod. He was very attractive, looking younger than the sixty years she knew he was. He was a dark, deep brown, a mixture of Marcus and Keith. The lines formed on his face, lines of responsibility and burden, were perfectly placed at the edges of his lips and eyes. Along with the gray temples of his jet-black hair, they made him look distinguished, trustworthy. Powerful.

"I noticed your concentrating on this picture." He pointed to the oval-shaped, pine-wood framed photo. "He was sworn into office for the first time. He was thirty-three. A very proud day for the Hart family."

"You want him to follow in your footsteps?" Sydney asked. She appreciated that he didn't make her qualify her presence in his home. Laura was right. "Entering the political realm."

Anthony turned to her. His proud smile vanished. He frowned for only a moment, then looked void of emotion. "Marcus would leave politics if I considered his track a follow-up to mine. Besides, I'm still a private-sector guy. He'll be a senator soon. Then governor. Then . . . well, I expect he'll be much more important than I ever was or am."

"I'd love to hear more about it, Mr. Hart," Sydney said. She knew Anthony Hart was an absent father, but his occasional absence would have been preferred to her own father's desertion and his replacement, David Williams's, constant presence.

His brow raised. "Should I be flattered, or is there an alternative motive to your interest?"

"How much do you know about why I'm here?" she asked.

Anthony shoved his hands in his pockets. "I spoke with my maid, Laura. She said you were a schoolmate of Bree's. You're working at Keith's firm and living here for the summer. I trust Bree's taste in associates, although I hear her recent behavior has been questionable."

"How do you know that?" Sydney asked. "I mean, I'm sorry for intruding, but Gabrielle has been home for only two days. Why does everyone already suspect her of something?"

Anthony nodded in resignation. "Bree is a Hart. Her behavior reflects on the whole family. No offense to you, but college kids . . . well, my wife monitors her closely."

Sydney wasn't happy to hear that. Would she be monitored now that she was living here? She wondered if Gabrielle knew this.

"And yes," Anthony said, "Bree knows her mother has spies. Our family knows many people in D.C. as you might know yourself."

Sydney nodded. "I guess I should be off to bed. It was nice to finally meet you."

"You didn't finish earlier," Anthony said. "There's more to your stay? You were focusing on Marcus's picture. Does it have something to do with him?"

"No." Sydney resisted sighing. Lord, no. "I'm doing a genealogy project for my class. The Hart family is my subject."

Anthony was silent. He blinked, looked away, and shrugged. He looked back at her. "Bree talk you into this?"

Sydney shook her head. She was intimidated. He wasn't pleased. "She offered her family since I'd be here. I was hoping—"

"There are plenty of good Baltimore families to trace," he said, pulling at the cuffs of his tailored white button-down. "Bree has already made an attempt with ours. Her mother and I discouraged it because there are forces out there that aren't happy to see such a successful black family. They'd love to find dirt, even if it happened ten, twenty, or even one hundred years ago. Besides, I don't see the purpose."

"What do you mean by that?" Sydney asked. He hadn't looked at her for some time, and Sydney was feeling uncomfortable. "The purpose of genealogy? I think it's great for black people. I don't think we focus on our family roots enough."

"What do we find?" he asked, looking sternly at her now. "That we were slaves? If we're lucky enough to go that far. Our families were broken up, sold, names stolen. We were lied to about our origins, taught to be ashamed of them, so we chose to forget. It's painful. Why go back to it?"

"To take back what was stolen from us," Sydney urged. "Learning our past, regaining our origins no matter how painful. We need it to save our fleeting families. Not every black family is like yours, Mr. Hart. So many of us are torn apart, still lost."

"Call me Anthony." His eyes softened. "Sounds like you're speaking from experience."

Sydney looked away. "I am. Martin Luther King once said that when we were brought to this country, we were robbed of our names. We lost our religion, our culture, our God. Then he said, by the way some of us act, we even lost our minds. That's what is still destroying our families. It all goes back to that."

"You think we can reclaim our families by being reminded we were slaves? We've never forgotten that."

"We weren't always slaves," she said. "Genealogy is about the family, not just the family in America. Going

back to a time when we were strong can help us regain
it again. In Africa. . . ."

"Good luck with that." Anthony laughed. "Even the
best can't go that far. What's your major?"

Sydney was taken back by the quick change of topic.
"MBA General."

"You're wasting your time with genealogy projects," he
said. "You should spend your summer studying business.
Keith's law firm is as good as any place to start. Focus
your efforts there. Don't waste your summers—like Bree
does."

Sydney nodded. She wasn't going to tell him that she
was desperate for the five hundred dollars and the assistantship next semester. Her choice was already made. She
had to do this.

"If you'll excuse me," he said. "I need to go to bed.
Please, Sydney, feel like you're home this summer. Everything in the house is just as much yours as ours. If you
need anything . . . anything, Laura will see to it that you
get it."

Left alone in the large room, Sydney took the last sip
of hot chocolate. Marcus took after his father. Both men
had presence and left a profound effect without effort,
even though on opposite ends of the spectrum.

Sydney suspected this would be an interesting summer.
She had no idea of what was to come.

SIX

Sydney settled into life at the Hart residence as the week went on. Anthony was always in D.C., Victoria mostly ignored her, and Gabrielle avoided the topic of genealogy, spending time creating new ways to see Gary without being found out. Keith was consumed with the lawsuit and Sydney was busy researching. She had her own car now, but rarely ventured out. She spent her free time covering for Gabrielle and getting to know Laura and May, who she found herself liking more and more every day.

When she was supposed to be with Gabrielle, Sydney was by herself mostly at Inner Harbor. She visited the National Aquarium, the Renaissance at Harborplace Mall, the Baltimore Museum of Art, and the Maryland Science Center. With it all in mind, Sydney found the Inner Harbor to be the most charming section of the city.

She tried her best to forget about Marcus, but it wasn't working. She hadn't seen him much. He was advising fellow representatives, who were up for reelection in November, on strategy and reviewing several bills up for vote before Congress adjourned for the summer recess. He hadn't called the house to speak with anyone, although he generally called every few nights when he knew Anthony wasn't home. Sydney couldn't convince herself she'd forgotten their encounters, but she had almost convinced herself that she hated him—that was, until Gabrielle entered her room before dinner on Saturday to tell her Marcus was here.

"And you're telling me because . . . ?" Sydney did her best imitation of carelessness, although she knew her whole body was tense. She sensed the tinge of excitement. Could it be? She wasn't at all ready to believe she could actually be excited to see him. No, not after almost a week of hoping she'd never see him again.

"Oh, I don't know." Gabrielle, in only a peach-colored full slip, lay on the bed as Sydney ironed her shirts. "It's just . . . well, I mean he usually comes home once or twice a month. He's already fulfilled his quota for June."

"Stop it now." Sydney stared her down. "There may be something, but it's not me."

"Laura will do that for you, you know."

"I can iron my own clothes."

Gabrielle laughed. "You have this martyr quality about you. Maybe that's what Marcus likes."

"Gabrielle!" Sydney hung her shirt in the closet and moved on to the next one.

"I'll leave the issue alone if you do one thing for me."

Sydney sighed, shaking her head before Gabrielle finished. "I'm not covering for you tonight. I'm tired of touring this city alone while you have a romantic tryst with Gary."

"Not that. Something else."

"Your mother doesn't mind your walking around here in your underwear?"

"She hates it." Gabrielle smiled. "That's why I do it. Stop trying to change the subject."

"Fine." Sydney plopped on the bed. "What deal are you proposing?"

"I won't tease you about Marcus or Keith ever again."

"I'll do it."

"I haven't told you what you have to do yet."

"It doesn't matter," Sydney said. "To avoid that, I'll do anything."

Gabrielle smiled with accomplishment and sat up. "You're easy. Get undressed."

Gabrielle's deal wasn't as scary as Sydney had imagined. Get undressed, she'd said. Sydney was stunned, frozen in place. Gabrielle laughed at her for three minutes straight.

Tonight was the annual formal for the Maryland Historical Society at the grand Baltimore Museum of Art. Victoria was a member of the board and the Hart family went every year. Five thousand a couple, twenty grand for a table. Proceeds went to several art programs at the local public schools from kindergarten through college.

Gabrielle would rather die than go alone with her family. She needed backup, she'd said, and Sydney would be it. Sydney protested, knowing Marcus would be there, but a deal was a deal, and Gabrielle was prepared to throw a fit that threatened to be worse than a night in Marcus's company.

Gabrielle was already throwing dresses out of Kelly's old closet and onto the bed.

"Pick a dress," she said. "Any dress."

"What are these?" Sydney hadn't even opened that end of the closet. The one side she used was larger than she'd ever need.

"Some of Kelly's old dresses," Gabrielle answered. "She leaves a few here because she usually gets dragged somewhere she never intended to go when she visits. Although she hasn't been here in the longest. Trust me, she doesn't miss them. She has a ton."

"Is she my size?" Sydney noticed the dresses were beautiful, but looked smaller in the hip area than she needed.

"What size are you?"

"I don't know you that well yet." Sydney smiled. "What size is Kelly?"

"She's a ten."

"I'm not."

Gabrielle smiled. "Understood. What's the saying? I'm a size ten, but eleven fits so good, I wear a twelve."

"Something like that." Sydney said, laughing.

Gabrielle picked out a thin black dress, long sleeved with gold speckles trailing down the front and back to the ground. There was a long slit up the left leg and thigh. "This one will do."

"How do you know?"

"Kelly was in her second trimester with Jordan when she wore this."

Sydney stepped back with a gasp. "You're giving me a maternity dress?"

"No." Gabrielle bit her lip to hold back the laugh. "It's just a larger size. The stomach isn't out or anything."

Sydney snatched the dress. "Just give it to me. I'd better have a good time."

"Well, you'll be with my family, so no chance of that. But a deal is a deal, so hurry it up."

"What are you, deaf?" Keith asked his older brother. "I've told you twice already she's getting dressed."

Marcus ignored Keith's irritated tone. So what if that was the second time he'd asked where Sydney was. He wouldn't do it again. Not because he wasn't anxious to see her, but because both times he had, his mother looked as if she were going to pass out.

"I find this amusing," Victoria said as she flicked away

an imaginary piece of lint from her Donna Karan dress. She looked stunning in the crimson, spaghetti-strap beaded gown.

"What is *this*, Mother?" Keith asked, after he seemed to realize no one else would.

Marcus had done a lot of rearranging to be home this weekend. Since his last encounter with Sydney, when she handily dismissed him, he'd been able to think of nothing but her. He'd been in a half daze all week, which professionally and personally, he had no time for.

He hadn't been able to completely end things with Lindsay. He'd tried, but Sydney consumed his thoughts, interfering with his resolve. The result was his agreeing to slow things down. It was the first time he'd really seen Lindsay aggressive with him, and he was embarrassed to admit he gave in to it.

He had to see Sydney. He didn't know why or what he'd do once he saw her, but knew he had to. There was something . . .

"The fact," Victoria answered, "that the only way my daughter wants to spend time with her family is if this Sydney is along."

"This Sydney?" Marcus was irritated by his mother's cold references to the guest.

Victoria got his meaning, as could be detected from the look on her face. "So she's got both you and Bree under her spell."

"Mother," Keith cautioned. He looked at his father, who lit his cigar and leaned back in his favorite chair in the sitting room.

"She doesn't have me under anything," Marcus said. He leaned back, thinking he'd heard something. "Keith, you said . . ."

"Don't ask me again." Keith sipped his wine. "I was

on my way down, stopped by Bree's room. She said they'd be down after they were dressed."

"So Bree just invited her?" Victoria asked. "Shouldn't she have checked with me or Anthony?"

Anthony said nothing. No one expected him to.

"We'll have the whole table," Keith said. "She can be my date."

"We don't know if she's bad for Bree either," Marcus added, not believing his own words.

"Where is this change coming from?" Victoria's eyes widened as she turned and leaned against the bookcase. "A month ago she starts coming home all the time, but spends less than a second of that time at this house or with this family. We all know she's been acting unusual lately. Sydney is the newest thing in her life. You agreed with me when we had our talk that she might have—"

"When was this?" Keith asked. He came from behind his father's chair, seemingly upset at not being included in some family conversation. "What did you agree on? When did you talk?"

"Nothing, Keith." Marcus held his hand up to calm him down. Keith was getting more and more possessive of their mother's attention. "Mother, I know what I agreed to, but we—"

"Where is Lindsay anyway?" Victoria asked, without looking at her son. "She's the woman you should be concerned with. Why isn't she here?"

"Lindsay will meet us." Marcus eyed his father, who was interested only in his cigar. Lindsay was Anthony's favorite, but Marcus still didn't care. Marcus found he wasn't concerned with his father's cares anymore.

"You couldn't bring her?" Keith said. "Never mind. Don't answer that. I think I can see why."

"No, you can't." Marcus sent him a glaring stare. "I had to pick up some papers I left in my room last week."

Keith wasn't satisfied, his brow still raised.

"Lindsay had to work late." He was lying, and he knew the more he spoke, the more obvious it was. What was he supposed to say? *I had to see Sydney and I didn't want Lindsay around when I did.* "It worked best this way."

"What papers?" Keith asked. "I don't see any papers."

Marcus's eyes tore into his brother, who got the message and let it go. There were no papers. He'd told the same lie to Lindsay, and wasn't proud of any of this. He didn't need Keith making it worse.

"Whatever the case," Victoria said. "Lindsay is the woman who should be holding your attention."

"Why is that?" Marcus asked. "Is Lindsay more appropriate—better breeding—good for appearances? Not like Sydney. Not like Celeste?"

A hush fell over the room. Even Anthony looked up. Silence, thick and heavy, filled the room.

"I'm sorry." Marcus pulled at the bottom of his tuxedo jacket. "I'm a little stressed."

"What's the problem with this young girl anyway?" Anthony asked.

Everyone turned to him, surprised that he even spoke. The past couple of years, Anthony Hart was hardly ever home and when he was, could only be forced to engage in social conversation with his family.

"I mean," he continued, "she seems like a nice kid."

"How would you know?" Victoria's tone left no question about her attitude.

Anthony ignored his wife's sarcasm. "I met her earlier last weekend. For only a moment, but she seemed fine. My point here is, Marcus isn't interested in the girl. He's very happy with Lindsay."

Marcus shook his head, throwing his father a look of contempt. The man had no clue as to any of his kids' lives.

"What about Bree?" Victoria asked.

"She might be a good influence on her," Anthony answered. "She seems smart, self-sufficient."

"She's definitely smart." Victoria laughed, her voice edged with contempt. "She's got all the Hart men wrapped around her finger."

"I like her." Keith's smile lasted only a minute as he endured ugly stares from everyone. "She's here just for the summer anyway."

"But she's going back to school with Bree," Victoria said. "They have their little genealogy project. That must be stopped."

"What's the big deal?" Keith asked. "It's a school project."

"Keith." Marcus didn't see the point to his mother's overprotection of their family business, but this was her hot button and Keith would only upset her if he continued.

"Quit trying to shut me up," Keith snapped. "Mother understands that I support her completely. It's just a question."

"She's not doing that anymore," Anthony interjected. "I talked to her about the uselessness of this genealogy thing and she seemed to agree. Don't worry about it."

Saying nothing, Victoria held her head up high. It was as if she felt she had to fight a look of appreciation to the man she'd been married to for thirty-six years.

"Good." Keith put down his empty glass and slapped his hands together. He headed out of the room. "That's settled. So no more problems with . . ."

Marcus turned, instinctively knowing what had silenced his brother.

Relief followed by desire swept over him at the sight of her coming down the stairs. Stopping at the bottom of the steps, Sydney was all woman, and the fitted, though not too much, black dress said so. It wrapped around her hourglass figure, teasing and refreshing. Her hair was up, revealing the shine of her glowing, flawless bronze skin. Her makeup transformed her natural beauty to one of confident sophistication.

There was no doubt about it, Marcus told himself. He knew now the reason why he'd been wanting, needing nothing more than to see her again. That's what this whole week of personal torment and constant confusion had been about. He wanted Sydney Tanner, even though he had no intention or right to act on it. She couldn't stand him. They weren't able to get along for five minutes, but that had nothing to do with physical attraction, sexual attraction.

"Put your tongue back in your mouth, Marcus." Gabrielle bumped him with her hip as she walked by and whispered, "If you can't take it, look away."

Sydney felt her face on fire. All eyes were on her, but none as intensely as Marcus's. She'd been caught up in Gabrielle's excitement of hurried preparation, herself having not dressed up in as long as she could remember. In it all, she'd been able to ignore the buildup of her own excitement. She'd wanted to fit in with the formal crowd, let Victoria Hart know she could be just as glamorous as the rest of them. But more than that, she wanted Marcus to salivate at what he'd never get—whether he wanted it or not.

Thoughts and questions swirled in her head as fast as light and cruel satisfaction wasn't there. In that moment she just wanted him to think she was beautiful. Good enough for him. Why did she care about this arrogant jerk's opinion? Why was she even here? Hadn't she vowed not to get involved in the life of this family. Here they were, waiting for her, staring at her. This was all a mistake.

So how did it go?"

Sydney's stomach clenched. She was almost to her room when the figure stepped from the darkness into the tight hallway. Her mother stood there with curlers in her hair, an unlit cigarette in her hand.

"Fine," Sydney answered. Why couldn't she have been asleep? She braced herself for whatever would come.

"Your charade lasted another day," she said. "Honors club dinner. Thought you fit right in?"

"I did," Sydney said. "I'm on the honor roll. I was invited."

"Dress up all you want, girl," she snickered. "You're a kid now, only sixteen. They like to fill your heads with dreams. It works on wannabes like you. But when the real world comes, the only way you'll be at a formal is if you're serving food or checking coats."

Linda disappeared into the darkness in a second, leaving Sydney in the hallway. She had belonged there. They had wanted her there. The world wasn't as ugly as Linda Williams. She'd show her.

"You both look exquisite," Anthony said, breaking the silence as he headed for the door. "Laura will keep Aunt May company. We have to get going."

Victoria took hold of the legs of her dress and walked past everyone. She paused at Sydney, still at the bottom of the steps, and forced a weak smile.

"You look very appropriate tonight, Sydney."

Sydney never broke her smile as the woman walked past her. Victoria Hart thought she was something. The woman had no idea how much Sydney had dealt with.

"Sydney, you—" Marcus stepped to her, feeling a fire in the pit of his stomach.

Sydney stepped back, conflicted by her attraction to this tall, dark magnetic man in a tailored tuxedo and her repulsion to what was inside of this sexy package. She tore her eyes from him and walked away, right into the outstretched arms of Keith.

"I'm the only guy here without a date," Keith said, taking her arm. "So I hope you don't find me too presumptuous."

"Not at all," Sydney said. Anything to keep away from Marcus.

Gabrielle smoothed out the contours of her short, purple velvet dress and scurried alongside Marcus.

Marcus felt his anger and searched for its justification. He was certain now something was going on with Keith, even though Sydney had said it wouldn't happen.

"Marcus, a loser?" Gabrielle whispered as she entwined her arm with his. They followed Keith and Sydney out of the house and to the waiting limo. "Say it ain't so."

"Shut up, Bree." Marcus knew he was a sore loser and he avoided that by making sure he did not lose.

"There's a first time for anything," she added.

He looked down into her childish eyes. He loved the kid, despite her mouth. "I wouldn't count on it, smart mouth."

He smiled, seeing his sister's eyes light up with hopeful anticipation. Bree was a drama queen.

The chauffeur closed the door behind him as he stared at Sydney. She stared back. She wanted to kill herself for being unable to turn away. He made her feel uncertain, self-conscious, not in control. She could tell he sensed this and got a particular joy from it. Charity or not, Sydney knew this was a huge mistake. Marcus Hart was going to be a thorn in her side. At the least.

It took Sydney only moments to get caught up in the beauty and privilege of the evening. She got away from

Marcus and his insistent gaze as Lindsay descended on him the second they arrived. Gabrielle led her around, introducing her to the cultural, political, and business powerhouses of Baltimore and its surrounding neighborhoods.

Sydney imagined herself being formally invited to an event like this, not tagging along at the last minute. She wasn't sure if she'd come, but she'd be invited. She'd show *them*.

Marcus sat at the table, watching Sydney as Gabrielle led her around. She seemed freer than he'd seen her before. The well-developed guard wasn't all the way down, but it was lowered and her charm touched everyone she passed. He was jealous of all of them. They were getting smiles she would never give him. He wasn't too pleased with the good number of stares she was getting from the men in the room either.

"Marcus. Marcus, please."

Lindsay cupped his chin with her hand and turned his head to face her. "Are you listening to me?"

He turned to her and saw the hint of desperation in her eyes. He hated putting it there. This trying to take it slow didn't make sense. It only prolonged the inevitable. It was wrong and cowardly of him to blame Sydney for his preoccupations. This wasn't going to go on any longer.

"Lindsay wants to come to our luncheon next month." Kelly Hart Jorman excluded any idea of enthusiasm from her voice.

Marcus smiled at his younger sister. He never saw the pretty, dark-complexioned woman anymore. He missed her petite, joyful character. She'd left home to get married and rarely came back. Kelly had never gotten along with their parents.

"I don't know," he answered. He looked at Lindsay.

She was trying to tie them together, knowing if he'd agreed to something, he'd stick with it. She'd be assuring herself another month at least.

"You always come to this luncheon, Marcus," Mike Jorman said. He wrapped his large arm around Kelly, his ex-football player body was still tight and almost busting out of his tuxedo. "These society things. You know me. I hate them, but I get my best clients at them. Come on, man."

"Marcus will be there," Victoria said, placing her silverware perfectly around a plate that was yet to come. "He knows some very important Virginia families will be there. Keith will be there too."

"There gonna be some available sisters there?" Keith asked.

Marcus didn't hear him, his attention solely reserved for Sydney as she and Gabrielle made their way to the table.

Victoria began in on them before they could even sit down. "Girls, you will notice that socializing is after the dinner and award presentation."

"Ya, ya, ya." Gabrielle intercepted Sydney's attempt to sit next to Kelly at the round, elegantly adorned table. The only other seat was between the Hart brothers.

Sydney hesitated before sitting down. She didn't look at him, refused to. She could feel his eyes on her, searing into her. She sensed anger, and it bothered her—not that he was angry, but that she cared so much.

"You were working the room well," Marcus said, getting an intoxicating whiff of her perfume. She smelled fresh, vibrant. He felt a sudden urge to touch her.

"I wasn't working anything." She whispered her words, neatly unfolding her napkin and placing it on her lap. He was too close. Her hands were shaking as she reached for the bread basket. She prayed no one would notice.

Marcus intercepted her, grabbing the basket and handing it to her. He wanted her to look at him. "I'm only trying to be polite. The way we left things . . ."

"Was for the best." She nodded. He leaned in closer to her and Sydney noticed her pulse quicken. She had to put an end to it now. "I know where you stand, you know where I stand. Now shouldn't you be leaning to your right? There's nothing for you over here."

He gritted his teeth. Why did she hate him so much? Why was she able to make him feel so rejected? "Whoever it was that made you build that wall, Sydney Tanner, must have been an expert."

Sydney ignored him. She swallowed hard, hating him for seeing so clearly. Yes, they did a bang-up job, but so would she. She'd show *them*, and all the people who didn't think she was good enough, including the man sitting next to her.

The dinner was less than pleasant, but Sydney bore through. She kept her attention with Gabrielle, Keith, and Kelly, who she'd just met and took a liking to. She found her grounded and intelligent, not so touched by growing up rich. She'd built a life, a family of her own. The fact that she made no comment, nor gave any peculiar looks regarding Sydney wearing an old dress of hers, made Sydney certain she'd be all right. Marcus was preoccupied with Lindsay, who clung to him, begging for his constant attention. Sydney was annoyed with her pretentious, needy behavior, but tried to see the lighter side. At least he was leaving her alone. Still she was irritated.

Victoria and Lindsay did most of the talking as Sydney became more aware of how imperfect the Hart family was. Anthony barely engaged in any conversation of meaning, but turned on all the charm when a well-wisher, the local elite, or an associate stopped by to greet him.

Sydney never thought she'd find compassion for Victo-

ria, but could see why the woman was so cold. She had
no marriage, but her life's purpose was to make it seem
as if she had the perfect marriage: the perfect marriage
and family. This was something almost pitiful as Victoria
and Anthony sat next to each other, seeming miles apart.
Sydney thought of her own parents. David and Linda
were the farthest from romantic, but in their own crazy
way, they loved each other. It was just that they never
loved her.

Keith gave his mother the most attention, keeping a
tension-filled table light with jokes and uncontroversial,
generic topics. He and Marcus barely said a word.
Gabrielle virtually shut off from her family, speaking only
to Kelly and Sydney. She rolled her eyes in response to
any questions from either parent.

Still Sydney envied them. They were a family, although
dysfunctional at best. She would have preferred this to
what she'd had. She'd have preferred almost anything.

"You and me," Keith said, grabbing Sydney's hand.
"Let's go."

Sydney resisted. The dance floor had been cleared and
the music was playing.

"I can't," she said. "There aren't enough people."

Marcus watched as Keith's hand took hold of Sydney's.
He'd gotten sick of Keith's endless flirtations with her
tonight.

"I won't accept no." He pushed his chair back, still
holding on. "You look too beautiful to stay stuck in a
chair."

"Keith." Victoria appeared concerned. "Leave Sydney
alone. There are plenty of unattached women here waiting to dance with a Hart."

Sydney smiled at Victoria, as Keith took her other hand and said, "They'll all have to wait."

"She said no," Marcus interjected, feeling himself heat up as his brother continued.

"On the other hand," Sydney said as she slid her chair back. She shared a stubborn gaze between Victoria and Marcus. "I think I do feel like dancing."

"Let's hit it." He led her to the dance floor.

"What's the scowl for, Marcus?" Gabrielle asked. "So unlike you."

Marcus eyed his baby sister at the same time as Kelly punched her in the arm. Lindsay bit her lower lip, flipped her hair back, and wrapped her arms around Marcus.

"Let's dance dear," Lindsay said.

"Yes, Marcus," Gabrielle mocked. "You and your girl-friend should dance."

"Bree," Victoria scolded. She looked at her husband, whose attention was owned by a twenty-something cocktail waitress working the room. She sighed helplessly. "That's enough, Bree."

"Excuse me." Marcus freed himself from Lindsay's grasp. "I see Congressman Bryant. I need to discuss the judiciary committee appointments."

"You're a shoo-in," Lindsay said, inviting herself along. "They need younger members. If he doesn't know, you'll explain it to him."

"I'm sure you're glad to get away from that mess." Keith was a smooth dancer, seeming a natural to the fast music with its seductive base.

"I wasn't going to say anything." Sydney moved in closer. "Is it always like that?"

"Things are a little rough right now," he answered.

"Aunt May usually keeps the peace, but she was too tired to come. It's not always this bad, but Marcus . . ."

"You blame this on him?"

Keith's enthusiasm waned. "Not all of it, but he's . . . well, its all of us . . . Dad mostly."

"He doesn't seem very involved."

"He's not. It's like we have only one parent."

Sydney felt compassion for Keith. Anthony's distance had damaged the young man. Victoria obviously preferred her eldest son, whom he would always be compared to. Keith didn't have it so easy.

She touched his arm gently. "Don't worry, Keith. Trust me. You have it better than so many."

"Speaking of yourself?" He grabbed her, jokingly dipping her and causing her to laugh loudly.

"Yes," she answered. "We'll leave it at that. Besides, you're an attractive, successful guy. Your future is going to be great."

He spun her around, garnering stares from others. "Yeah, but Marcus is more attractive, more successful, and more charismatic. His future is—"

"Keith," she interrupted. "Don't talk that way. It's not always about Marcus."

"You don't know." The smiles were all gone as he wrapped his arm around her. "Mother raves about Marcus to everyone, all the time. What he's done, what he'll do, what he means to the Hart family name. I guess anyone could be a partner at a law firm, but it takes a real Hart to become a senator."

"He hasn't made senator yet," Sydney added, "and you will make partner. You know this. And it's not that easy to make partner at a firm like yours. Besides, you won't have to deal with as much of the outside stuff like Marcus. You'll appreciate it."

Keith smiled and swung her around again. When she faced him, she noticed a dejected look on his face.

"Even you prefer him," Keith whispered, his eyes looking defeated.

"Keith." Sydney sighed. "I don't prefer either. I'm not in the market for romance. I just ended a relationship. Understand—"

"Still," he said, "if you were in the market. I mean, assuming you could deal with the psychotic family drama, you'd prefer Marcus. Every woman does."

"The right one won't." Sydney touched his cheek. She felt for him.

She also hated that he spoke the truth. She was attracted to Marcus, although she despised him. She felt nothing comparable to the more pleasing brother.

Sydney inhaled as she felt a hand on her shoulder. Keith's expression told her who it was.

"Just as I said," he told her as they stopped dancing. "Here to interrupt, I assume?"

"Not by choice," Marcus's deep voice spoke.

Sydney felt a chill run down her spine as Marcus's arm slid around her waist. She felt helpless to resist, feeling a pull at the pit of her stomach. She couldn't move.

"Your boss is here." Marcus pointed to Richard McDaniel, standing at the edge of the dance floor, looking eager.

With some hesitation and a spiteful look at his brother, Keith excused himself and headed off. Marcus took control of Sydney and jumped into the lead.

"We can stop now." Sydney felt too aware of his hand holding hers, his other around her waist. She was only inches from him. He was large, so strong. She felt a little dizzy.

"On the contrary," Marcus said, holding on to her as

she attempted to break away. He recognized his arousal at being so close to her.

As soon as Lindsay excused herself to go to the ladies' room, he'd headed for the dance floor. His jealousy attacked him as he watched Keith twirl Sydney, dip her, wrap his arms around her. They laughed. She touched him over and over again. He had to stop it.

Luck came in the form of Richard McDaniel, who never passed up an opportunity to kiss up to Marcus. His motivation was to get Marcus on the good side of the Preston Corporation, knowing his influence in the community. It took Marcus only a second to convince Richard that it was Keith who had some news on the issue and he needed to speak to him now.

"You said you wanted to dance." He pulled her closer, feeling the effect. He ordered himself to keep control. *Don't let her send your mind to pieces again. You can handle this woman.*

"Not with you." She averted his gaze, pushing away. His hand slid down her back. She was lightheaded and the room felt humid.

"What would people say?" he asked. "You're representing the Harts now. Appearances, remember?"

"I don't give a damn about your appearances." Sydney tried to control her breathing. "And I'm not a part of your family. I've told you this before."

"I was only teasing," he said, becoming intoxicated by the blossomy scent of her hair. Her soft cheek was so inviting. "But since you want to get serious, I'd say it sure looks like you're trying to be part of this family. You don't appear to be the twirling, dipping type, but I see you're making exceptions."

"Cut it out with the innuendos." She gave in to her fate and allowed Marcus's body closer to hers. She wasn't getting away. It could last only so long.

"I plead ignorant," he lied. He wanted the truth, and was determined to get it.

"You're a lot of things, Marcus, but not ignorant." She lifted her head, looking into his eyes. She paused, straining to remember what she wanted to say. He was too gorgeous for her. She swallowed. "You're suggesting I'm making the moves on Keith."

"I told you he was easily smitten." Marcus saw resistance in her eyes. He yearned to melt it away. "You suggested it wasn't an issue for you."

"I also told you it wasn't any of your business." She was locked on his face, hating him and wanting to kiss him at the same time.

"You're encouraging him," he said. If he could hold her closer, he would. Even still it wouldn't be enough. "He's very vulnerable right now."

"I'm doing nothing like that." Sydney had to think before she spoke. "Why don't you run off to your girlfriend? I'm sure it's killing her, not being able to fawn over you absolutely every second."

"Jealous?" He smiled.

"You should be so lucky." Sydney thought this song was lasting two hours.

He smiled wider, his eyes closing to a seductive halfway. "Lucky indeed."

Sydney felt her knees weaken. She had to get away. She was getting in trouble.

"Lindsay is not an issue anymore," he said, having already resolved to end it tonight.

Sydney recognized a sense of relief at his suggestion and was angry at herself for it. She refused to care about him, this family, anyone, right now.

"Let me go." She pushed against him.

"Sydney." He whispered her name. He'd thought he

was making progress, her resolve wasting away. Then suddenly, this.

"I don't care about you or your brother," she said. His lips were so enticing. "Leave me alone and let me go."

He obliged, confused and insulted by her comments. He watched her walk away, wanting to go after her. He had to get his head straight and figure out this woman. He had to use the gift of perception that thirty-five years gave him to find out what was behind that brick, double-concrete-enforced wall.

"I have to ask." Lindsay obstructed his view of Sydney. She was very displeased. "Is she why you deserted me? Very ungentlemanly of you. I can't imagine, but is she the reason you suggested we—"

"No, Lindsay." He shook his head, knowing it wasn't the full truth. Sydney was the reason he'd been unable to end it completely. She'd invaded his mind, his every thought.

"I hope not." She rolled her well-adorned eyes. "After all, she's not your type. A bit large, not well polished. Victoria and Anthony would never—"

Lindsay shut up quickly in response to the vehement stare Marcus sent her.

"Don't you dare insult her," he said.

Lindsay stood openmouthed, speechless.

"We need to talk, Lindsay." Marcus took her arm gently. "We need to talk now. Come with me."

"You're freaking over something," Gabrielle said as she offered Sydney a spoon to help finish off her pint of ice cream.

Sydney shook her head, content with her hot chocolate. "Just tired."

They sat together in the kitchen back at the house.

Everyone had gone to bed. The girls, dressed for bed, had retreated to the kitchen for a late snack. No one had seen either Marcus or Lindsay after he'd led her out of the museum hall. Sydney fought images in her mind of them going off together. She knew she shouldn't, didn't, care.

"Is it Marcus?" Gabrielle was persistent.

"No," she lied. The truth was too scary for her to even admit. It was all about Marcus.

"Then it's Keith," Gabrielle said. "I mean, I thought it was Marcus, but maybe I'm wrong."

"Can we change the subject?" Sydney asked. "What about this project? You were supposed to help me get started."

"Let's make a deal," Gabrielle said, nodding. "I'll get you the family pictures tomorrow. Show you everyone, give you names, the whole start-up. That is, if you tell me what your deal is with men."

Sydney resisted the girlish urge to dish her drama. "I've made too many deals with you already. I'm getting the short end of the stick each time."

"Then I'm busy tomorrow." Gabrielle pouted after stuffing a spoonful of ice cream into her mouth.

"What do you want from me?" Sydney said, mock-strangling her.

"I sense this *thing* between you and Marcus," she said. "But you're giving the off-limits signal."

"There is no *thing* between Marcus and I," Sydney said.

"Why not?"

"It's the summer. I want a break from drama."

"What kind of woman are you? I love drama."

"I've noticed." Sydney rolled her eyes. "Darrin and I just broke up. I'm not ready—"

"Why?" Gabrielle interrupted. "Why did you break up?"

Sydney wasn't comfortable talking about it. "I'm not going into detail, but he wanted a commitment I wasn't ready to give. He wasn't interested in any alternatives, so he broke it off."

Gabrielle sat for a moment, a confused expression on her face.

"It's complicated," Sydney said.

"You let things end with him because he wanted a commitment? That jerk. You were right to get rid of him!"

"Thank you for making fun of me," Sydney said. "Appreciate it. Would you like to slap me while you're here? Or cut my skin and pour lemon juice in."

Gabrielle laughed. "I'm sorry, but I just don't get it. You're saying you can't commit to a guy because a relationship isn't synonymous with pursuing business success?"

"Not always." Sydney wasn't about to explain her mother's constant insults and warnings. "Sometimes it's fine. But when you see a woman get caught up with a guy, sometimes the relationship—the results of the relationship—divert them and they end up—"

"Would you rather end up short on the business tip or short on the love tip?"

"I can have both," Sydney argued. "Just not now. I just have to get the business thing off and running before I let myself fall in love. Then I'll have both."

"Let yourself?" Gabrielle laughed heartily. "You're a trip. Please, girl. You're too smart for that."

"Maybe I won't hold my resolve forever," Sydney said. "But I'll hold it for this summer."

Gabrielle shook her head as she dumped her spoon in the sink. "Not with the attention my brothers are giving you. Marcus and Keith are super charming and they love to compete. Marcus usually wins, but you've got to give it to Keith for not giving up."

"Not happening."

Gabrielle shrugged. "Probably for the best. You don't want to marry into the Hart family. Kelly got out as soon as she could. Marcus, well he's his own man now, so he keeps a good distance. As soon as I get out of school, I'm making my own way no matter how hard it is. Really, Keith is the only one that really wants to be here."

"Why is that?" Sydney asked.

"I think he was dropped on his head as a baby." She headed out. "Otherwise I'd say he's a mama's boy, even though his mama's boy has always been Marcus. That's the end of today's episode of the Hart chronicles. I'm going to bed."

"I'm gonna finish this," Sydney said, holding up her cup. "Go ahead."

Sydney sat in silence for several minutes. She wasn't happy, but refused to feel sorry for herself. To get out of a worse mess, this was a mess she'd gotten herself in. Her life was one mess after another. She refused to let Marcus Hart be her biggest mess of all. She'd just have to get him off her mind.

"Enticing. Exciting. Tantalizing."

Sydney jumped in her seat, turning around to Marcus leaning in the doorway to the kitchen. His shirt was out, his cummerbund missing.

"I'm trying to figure out your middle name," he said. "You know how they say. Your middle name is what you are. Seductive. Enticing."

"You already said enticing." Sydney felt her heart race. She noticed the slight slur of his speech. "You're drunk."

"No." He put forth an effort to stand up straight and walked towards her with surprising agility. "I'm not drunk. Halfway there."

"You drove here?" She backed away, placing her cup in the sink.

"That would be illegal," he said, desire replacing the anger he'd felt only moments before setting eyes on her. "I caught a cab. Not that it's any of your business."

"You're right." She lifted up her hands. "I'm off to bed."

He ran to the island, heading her off. "No, no. You have to wait. Extraordinary. That's your middle name."

"No, my middle name is tired." She felt a rush at his closeness, but knew this was dangerous. "Step aside."

"I think," he said, stepping to the right just as she did, "I think I deserve some kindness now."

"Oh, really?" She placed her hands on her hips. "Is the poor little rich boy suffering? Well, this is a job for Ms. Price, not me."

She stepped to the left, he blocked her again. She moaned in annoyance.

"Shows what you know, Ms. Tanner." He waved an unstable finger at her. "Lindsay is the past now. As of nine-thirty this evening, we are old news."

Sydney believed him. She could see past the alcohol and into the pain in his eyes. Ending it had been hard for him. She hated that she wanted to console him.

"Lindsay's gone," Marcus said. He wished for once that he didn't care about all the disappointment this would cause. He wished he could give in and make everyone else happy. He just wasn't that type of man. He wanted, needed, to be happy and Lindsay wasn't going to make him that way. After Celeste, he wasn't sure any woman could.

"And Mother," he continued, "is never satisfied. She'll be angry. I'll have to console her, reassure her."

Sydney backed away as he stepped closer. "We all make choices. It's none of my business. Now step aside. I'm going to bed."

"Not until I get some answers." He grabbed her by the

arm, pulling her to him. Her cotton bathrobe was an unwelcome barrier between them.

"Let go of me." Sydney pulled away, the only result being her robe loosened, falling off her shoulders and revealing the satin spaghetti straps of her rose tank top.

Marcus felt a fire ignite at the sight of her soft, shining skin. "You . . . you and Bree. You and Keith. Tell me."

"Let me go." She felt naked as his eyes raked over her.

"You're trying to change things here," he said, his other hand trailing her shoulder, touching the strap. God, how he wanted her. "You've come in sheep's clothing, but you're really a wolf, out for blood."

Sydney felt her breath race. She lifted her chin. "Not with this family. The blood here is too cold. Besides, you're all too busy sticking your fangs into each other."

His eyes lit up in anger as he swung her around, bringing her body to his. His arms engulfed her, his face only inches from hers. "You're wrong about one point. My blood is warm, and right now it's steaming hot, Ms. Tanner. So it's my turn. You've turned your charms on Bree, Aunt May, and Keith. Even my father seems taken by you. A different brand of charm for each person. Convince me."

Sydney twisted and turned, but there was no fighting. His mouth came down hard, encompassing hers. The kiss was demanding, and it made Sydney light up like a forest fire. Her resistance disappeared as she was drugged with passion. Her knees went weak as his lips forced hers open and his tongue invaded her mouth. Sydney moaned, her stomach swirling. She let him kiss her, let him trail her arms with sturdy hands.

Marcus was consumed with thirst, thirst for Sydney. His mind had been a mess since he'd met this woman and his body had wanted only this. She was so soft, her skin, her lips, everything. He heard her moan as his tongue explored her mouth. She tasted like a finer wine than he'd ever had, intoxicating him more than any wine ever could. He wanted more. His hands trailed her arms, his desire threatening to take control. He took her hands in his, guiding her fingers to his neck.

"Touch me," he whispered, almost breathless in her ear. "Touch me, Sydney."

Sydney's eyes rolled back in her head as his lips touched the soft edges of her ear. She felt her body go limp, and did as he said. Her hands wrapped around his neck and head, pulling him closer. Her body began to ache, her heart fluttering wildly.

His lips sent volcano-hot kisses down her neck, over her shoulders. He thought he'd go insane from the supple texture of her golden-brown skin. His hands grabbed at her waist, forcing the robe open. He slipped in his hand, caressing the satin, wanting the skin beneath it. He wanted every bit of her. He needed her to want every bit of him.

"Sydney," he called out in a groan.

Sydney heard the sound of desire in his voice. Its tone warned her of his last reserve. Her instincts kicked in, contradicting her desire. Her eyes opened wide, leaving heaven and returning to cabinets, drawers, a refrigerator, and a toaster. Her mind used its last bit of sense to send her a warning.

"No." The words barely came out as she pushed and twisted. Catching him in a vulnerable state, her pushing caused an imbalance and Marcus fell back against the wall.

Sydney didn't look at him as she turned and ran out. She heard him call her name, but kept going. She was already in tears halfway up the steps. She cried as she locked her bedroom door and slid under the covers. She didn't stop crying until she fell asleep.

SEVEN

The knock at the bathroom door was gentle.

"Everyone is gone," Gabrielle whispered through. "They've gone to church. Can I come in now?"

Sydney unlocked the door to her bedroom and promptly returned to her bed. Pulling the covers to her chin, she sat up against the headboard. She knew she was being a baby, but she felt like it.

Gabrielle entered cautiously and closed the door behind her. Silently she sat on the edge of the bed, waiting.

"So," she said, after waiting a while. "What happened with you and Marcus last night?"

"How do you know it was Marcus?" Sydney ran her fingers through her unruly hair. Her cheeks hurt from having tears wiped off them all night.

"Well, first of all, I came to get you for breakfast and you wouldn't even open the door." She bit at the nail of her left index finger. "You told me you didn't want to talk to anyone."

"I'm sorry for being such a baby." Sydney knew she was overacting, but last night with Marcus . . . She couldn't even think about it.

"Then," Gabrielle continued, "right before breakfast, Marcus pulled me aside, asking all types of questions about you."

"What questions?" Sydney was surprised by her own eagerness as she quickly leaned forward.

"He wanted to know how you were, if you were coming to breakfast, coming to church. If you'd said anything to me."

Sydney calmed, feeling a certain sense of satisfaction. So he hadn't been too drunk to remember. At least he felt some guilt.

"I asked him what was up," Gabrielle said. "He was actually flustered—if you can say a guy was flustered. Whatever the case, Marcus never gets flustered. In public or private."

Sydney swallowed hard, tugging at the edges of her sheets. "What did he tell you happened?"

"He wouldn't say," she answered. "Well, more like he couldn't. Mother came around the corner, ranting and raving. Huge drama. She was ticked at Marcus beyond words. Before she dragged him away over some nonsense, all he could say to me was *'Tell her I'm sorry.'*"

Sydney's face softened as she imagined those words coming from Marcus. A whole night of crying and whispering to herself how much she hated him was swept away in a second with the idea that he felt some compassion for her. Sydney was certain she was going crazy.

Sydney's appetite suddenly returned. "What was for breakfast?"

"Don't even try to change the subject." Gabrielle slid closer on the bed. "Let's have it."

"You can't tell anyone," Sydney said.

Gabrielle motioned zipping her lips.

"That includes people I don't know," Sydney added.

Gabrielle pouted for a second. "Okay. You have my word. You keep my secret, I'll keep yours."

Sydney repeated last night's passionate embrace, still floored by its seduction. She knew the words out of her mouth made it seem one-sided, even though her body reminded her of her own willing participation.

"That doesn't sound like the Marcus I know," Gabrielle said after a moment's pause. "He's not a drinker first of all."

"I guess he wasn't that drunk." Sydney shrugged, her eyes looking down at her hands.

"He's not usually that abrasive and—"

"Well"—Sydney put up a hand—"he didn't hurt me or anything like that."

Gabrielle looked at Sydney, tilting her head. "You sure are making excuses for him."

Sydney tossed her head carelessly to the side, jumping up from her bed. "I might have exaggerated. I mean, he's sorry. He said so."

"So what's next?"

Sydney enclosed herself in her bathrobe, remembering how it had fallen open at Marcus's touch last night. She had to find a way to block the event from her head.

"Nothing," she said. "It was just a one-time event, an alcohol-induced mistake. I know you love your brother, Gabrielle, but I have no interest in him."

"You're sending mixed signals, girlie."

Sydney ignored her. She'd resolved to be more careful because of last night. She was staying as far away from Marcus Hart as possible.

"Besides," Sydney said as they headed for the kitchen together. "He's on the rebound. That's the last thing I need."

"I wouldn't say he was on the rebound," Gabrielle said. "He never talked about Lindsay. Mother and Daddy loved her more than Marcus did."

Sydney felt guilty, knowing she was interested in hearing more about something that was none of her business. "I'm sure they were. She's his type and has all the breeding to fit right in. Victoria was probably aching to make her a daughter-in-law."

"That's what the scene was about this morning." Gabrielle hugged McKenzie as he rushed to her just as they entered the kitchen.

"Marcus told her?" Sydney grabbed a plate and filled it with leftovers from breakfast still left on the kitchen island. No matter where you came from, breakfast on Sunday in a black household was a king's feast. Even growing up, although not as frequent as every Sunday, her own mother made grits, eggs, baked biscuits from a can, occasionally adding bacon or sausage. Sometime's she'd fry chicken or pork chops, stream rice, or heat already made french toast or waffles in the microwave.

"Lindsay told her." Gabrielle eyed the food, rubbing her belly. "Called her early this morning. Mother was furious. She went on and on, but Marcus stood his ground. He didn't want to discuss his relationship with Lindsay. Told Mother it was none of her business. That just set her off until he threw Celeste in her face. She shut up right away. Breakfast was over real quick."

Sydney asked, "Who is Celeste? I've heard her name mentioned before."

"Sounds like somebody is telling Hart family gossip." Laura entered the room in a casual T-shirt and jeans. She looked at Sydney's plate. "Someone is pretty hungry."

"Starving." Sydney smiled.

"Everyone from Baltimore to D.C. knows Hart family gossip," Gabrielle said. "Why keep Sydney in the dark?"

"Your father hates it, is why." Laura started clearing the table. "How would he feel if he found out his own daughter was fueling the fire."

Gabrielle shrugged carelessly. "I'd be surprised if he felt anything."

Laura slammed the glass cup in her hand on the table,

startling both girls. "Don't you talk about your father like that. He cares. He cares deeply. You have to understand that."

"Hey, hey." Sydney put up her hands. "Don't argue over my curiosity. I don't need to know."

"It's nothing you couldn't read at a library anyway." Gabrielle frowned. "*Baltimore* magazine archives has our whole family, breakups and makeups on paper."

"Maybe I'll try that for my project," Sydney said. "I don't seem to be getting any help from you."

Gabrielle's eyes lit up. "I forgot. Let's do it now. Laura, can you give me the keys to the photo album drawer?"

"Why?" Laura asked.

"Our project," Gabrielle said. "I need the old pictures Mother keeps all locked up."

Laura turned to Sydney. "I thought you'd given that up. Mr. Hart said he talked to you about it."

"We talked," Sydney said, "but he didn't ask me to stop. He's not too happy with it, he made that clear. But he never asked me not to do it."

"Saying he's not happy with it is his polite way of telling you to stop." Laura's hands were on her hips.

"Laura," Gabrielle said. "This project is the whole reason Sydney's here. Besides, you know Daddy doesn't care either way. Keys please."

After an uncertain hesitation, Laura retrieved the key and handed it over. After Sydney ran upstairs to grab a tape recorder, pen, and paper, the two women took over the sitting room. Gabrielle covered the floor with pictures and family albums framed in leather with gold trim.

"So we start with Jordan," Gabrielle said as she separated straying pictures. "Kelly's son. He's the newest Hart or Hart-Jorman."

Sydney smiled at the picture of the precious four-year-old. His café-au-lait skin, innocent eyes, and plump cheeks begged for a hug and kiss. When she finally had a child, Sydney vowed to give it all the love in the world. She'd spoil it rotten. Her child would never ever feel unloved or unwanted.

"Daddy and Mother are eager for a Hart boy to carry on the name. Daddy tries to hide it, acts like he doesn't care, but his name, this family's name, means everything. Mother, on the other hand, is freaking out loud."

Sydney laughed, trying to ignore that her thoughts constantly turned to Marcus and last night. She still felt his lips crushing hers and still remembered how much she liked it—still felt his hand as hot as the sun against her skin. She felt the pit of her belly pull at her at just the memory.

"Who is Celeste?" Sydney asked, the words coming without thought.

Gabrielle sighed, keeping her eyes on the pictures as she flipped page after page. "Celeste Johnson. She was pretty cool. It's sad how . . ."

"Did Marcus love her?" Sydney felt she needed to know this, if nothing else. Why, she refused to even guess.

Gabrielle looked at her, her young face softening. "I think he did. He talked about her when she wasn't around. He never does that with a woman."

Sydney crossed her legs, putting the album in her hand on the floor. "Tell me everything."

Gabrielle smiled as if she understood a secret.

"It was five years ago. She was a teacher in the public school system. Celeste was pretty, smart, and nice. Perfect, except she was also poor as all get-out. So were her parents, who by the way, were never married. She had no connections and worse, she had the nerve to get her degree at a state college."

Sydney saw herself already. She would never have a

chance in this family. Not that she would consider wanting one.

"I don't remember how Marcus met her. Some community event for the public schools. As you could guess, he got hell for it. Lord and Lady Hart weren't having it. They gave Marcus the worst time. They were hard on Celeste, too."

Sydney's anger was building. How cruel! "So he gave in. He broke it off."

Gabrielle laughed a sad laugh. "No. Marcus is a fighter. He got engaged to her. It lasted a couple of months, before Celeste broke it off. Up and moved to Phoenix, overnight almost."

"Couldn't take the pressure." Sydney recognized the sympathy she felt for Marcus. It was like last night, right before . . .

"That's what she said," Gabrielle answered. "I think there was more to it than that. Things were never the same between him and my parents. Between anybody."

There was a long silence before Gabrielle returned to the pictures and Sydney clicked on the tape recorder. They worked backward from Jordan to the Hart children, to Victoria and Anthony. Sydney decided to follow Victoria's family, the Halats. She realized the Harts were her main subject, but was more interested in what Victoria had to hide.

"You're trailing both sides?" Gabrielle asked.

Sydney nodded. "I'm planning on going as far back as I can for both families. I need that five hundred."

Victoria was one of three girls. Her sisters were Camille and Danielle. Camille, now forty-two, was a former model, now a designer in Paris working for a famous company. She was single with no children. The middle child, Danielle, had just turned fifty. She still lived in Denver, Colorado, where the family moved from the Baltimore area when the girls were young. Danielle was a dentist's wife and mother of twin fifteen-year-old boys.

"We see them every couple of years," Gabrielle said as she passed Sydney a picture of the boys. "Kevin and Jonathan. That picture was taken two years ago when they last visited. Aunt Danielle used to send pictures every year. Not anymore."

"What happened?" Sydney asked, already having an idea.

"Take a guess." Gabrielle shuffled pictures. "Aunt Dani and Mother always bumped heads. Dani was cool, and I don't need to tell you that Mother isn't into cool. This last visit . . ."

"These are those pictures?" Sydney took the pack of photos offered. Danielle looked very much like Victoria in the face, but her persona was completely different. She was smiling in almost every picture. She exuded much more warmth than Victoria ever could.

"They were supposed to be here a week," Gabrielle said, nodding. "Mother and Aunt Dani were whispering and scowling for the first few days. Then Thursday night, instead of coming down for dinner, out of the blue, Aunt Dani, Uncle Jim, and the boys left."

"A big blowup?" Sydney was caught up in the intrigue. The Hart family was a nighttime serial.

"Mother never made that clear. That morning, we were in Druid Heights. You know the hood. We'd been shopping. Of course Mama wasn't around. The area is in the urban renewal phase, if you catch my drift. She'll attend a charity for the rebuilding, but she wouldn't be caught dead in the neighborhoods."

Gabrielle pointed to a set of photos. "Those are from that day."

Sydney focused on the only picture of Danielle in which she wasn't smiling. She stood on the street corner, in front of a row of specialty stores. She didn't appear to Sydney to be sad or angry, just serious.

"That was that." Gabrielle shrugged. "You want all of these?"

"No." Sydney picked out her choices. "Just some. I want these faces to remind me when I'm putting all this together."

They moved on to Victoria's parents, Andrew and Primrose Halat. Andrew, an internal medicine doctor, packed up his family and left their hometown of Baltimore for the far west of Denver. His calling was for a black community in need of a doctor. Primrose was a nurse who worked alongside her husband until his business became prosperous enough for her to occupy her time with social events. The Halats moved to Denver, Colorado, but sent their children to school back East. Victoria was sent to Johns Hopkins, where she met Anthony and returned to her hometown. Primrose passed away from breast cancer five years ago. Andrew died in a car accident while vacationing in Greece a year later.

"This is easier than I expected," Sydney said. "I have names, birthplaces, occupations. I'm going to need exact dates and documentation."

"You jinxed yourself," Gabrielle said. "This is where it stops. This is where I was stumped when I tried. Mother isn't going to help. Trust me."

"What about your aunts?"

"I can't reach Aunt Camille, and Aunt Dani . . . well, since her falling out with Mother, she'll talk to me, but not about the family."

"What outside help did you get?" Sydney found this at least unusual, borderline mysterious. "Records? Library research?"

Gabrielle shrugged. "I gave up. Tired of the hassle Mother and Daddy were giving me. I ended up doing research on a girlfriend of mine. Got all the way back to 1920."

"Okay," Sydney said. "I'll get back to that. Let's move on to the Harts."

"What about the Harts?"

May rode in on her motorized chair, dressed in her Sunday best, white gloves and hat even in hot June. She had a warm, generous smile on her face as she stopped just short of the girls.

"What's with all these pictures?" she asked, leaning over. "Looks like a big mess to me."

"It's Sydney's project," Gabrielle said. "How was church?"

The conversation faded into Sydney's background, as every bit of her attention was directed at the door. Keith walked by with an uninterested wave. Then nothing. She sighed, not believing her own feelings.

"Sydney."

She snapped back to attention, but was unable to even force a smile for May. The old woman, whom she'd grown close to over the days, looked tenderly, knowingly.

"Marcus didn't come back home," she said. "He went straight for Georgetown from church."

Sydney blinked, her eyes turning to the pictures at her feet. "I was . . . I . . ."

"I know, dear." May touched her shoulder, patting it gently. "He was a mess at breakfast and distracted to the point of embarrassment during services today. Does that help?"

Sydney looked up with a grateful smile. It did help. It touched her even though she didn't want it to. She couldn't even entertain thoughts of this. She had to wipe it from her mind now! *Think of anything else, please.*

"Remember, May," she said. "You promised to sit with me for this project."

"Yes, but I got the impression from Anthony that you'd changed your mind about this."

Sydney shook her head. "I don't get it. I never said I wouldn't. I mean, I don't want to upset everyone, but . . ."

"You're not," Gabrielle said. "Ignore them. They're so secretive. They'd be pissed if—"

"Bree!" May admonished with a scolding finger.

"Sorry," Gabrielle acquiesced. "They'd be upset if you asked them anything, private or not. They like to brag, but they don't like to be questioned."

"I'll agree with that," May said. "The family is secretive. The Harts have always been. I think it adds to this mystique the family seems to enjoy. Well, some of us. I couldn't care less."

"You'll let go of some of the mystique to help me, won't you?" Sydney asked.

"Of course, young lady." May sat back and smiled, the wrinkles around her mouth stretching. "I have some stories about the Harts."

"What is going on in here?"

Victoria stormed in, looking at the clutter on the ground. She stood in an angry stance, her arms on peach Sunday-best thick satin covering her hips. Even angry, she was a striking woman.

"They're working on Sydney's little project," May said. She leaned closer to Sydney and winked. "We'll talk later."

Sydney winked back, and as May turned her chair and headed out of the room, she started gathering the pictures together.

"Don't start, Mother." Gabrielle helped with the cleanup. "We're working on the genealogy project and we're going to put everything back. All perfect, like you had it."

Victoria shared her vehement stare between the girls. "I thought you two had given this up?"

Sydney kept silent, avoiding eye contact. She needed the money for this project. She never expected Victoria to understand this. To understand her desperate financial situation. To understand her goal and how it meant more than anything.

Victoria sighed, seeming to realize she wasn't getting an answer. "And you, young lady. You said you couldn't come to church because you weren't feeling well. Why aren't you in bed?"

"That was hours ago." Gabrielle exaggerated the annoyance in her tone. "I'm fine now. Please."

"Don't please me, Bree. As long as you live here as a member of this family, you'll be at Saint Katherine's on Sundays."

Gabrielle stood up, her face tightening. "Why? So I can be seen? I mean, that's why you go, isn't it? You're not searching for any kind of spiritual enlightenment. Anyone who is anybody goes to Saint Katherine's. The church for the rich and powerful."

"Shut up," Victoria said. "Stop being such a brat!"

"I'm outta here!" Gabrielle brushed past her mother and out of the room.

Sydney continued cleaning, praying that Victoria would leave. She'd never been lucky in her life, and wasn't hopeful she would start now.

"You're my guest, Sydney." Victoria spoke slowly, to give the girl time to turn and face her. "I've tried to be a polite host to you."

Sydney wanted to laugh at that, but she sat frozen. *Just get through this. Nothing lasts forever. You've had worse tongue-lashings.*

"On the other hand," Victoria continued. "You have done nothing but disobey my mild requests, influence my daughter to have no regard for me, and attempt to seduce my sons."

Sydney jumped up, her anger hitting a boiling point. "You're wrong, Mrs. Hart. I never . . . I had no intention—"

"Don't you tell me about intentions." Victoria stepped closer, pointing a cold finger. "I see you. I'm watching you. I won't kick you out. It's too late for that. I'm not going to be the bad guy here."

"Listen, Mrs. Hart." All manners aside now, Sydney wouldn't stand for this. "I'm sorry for any misunderstanding, but I'm not trying to disobey you. I'm not influencing Gabrielle in any way. She has her own mind. If you want to know what's on it, sit down and talk to her without judging her ahead of time."

Victoria looked aghast. "You little piece of nothing from nowhere. How dare you even attempt to tell me how to deal with my child?"

Sydney bit her lower lip as Victoria's face took on Linda Williams's features. Those were Linda's words. *Little piece of nothing.*

"You are no better than me, Victoria." She blinked, trying to fight the image of her mother. "All your money, your nice home, your clothes, your cars, and your friends don't make you better than me."

Victoria laughed for only a second, her eyes squinting. "That's what this is all about. That's what you're all about. You want my money, my home, to have clothes like mine, cars like mine. All of it, and you think you're going to get it by hoodwinking one of my sons. Either one, you don't care."

"I have no interest in either of your sons." Sydney stepped up to only inches from Victoria, and she could see this startled her a bit. Victoria Hart wasn't used to being stepped up to—not at all, and not in her home.

Victoria swallowed, stepping back. She blinked and said, "I know you were behind Marcus's break up with Lindsay."

"I had nothing to do with that." Sydney only hoped she was right. "Besides, breaking up Marcus's relationships is your job, from what I hear."

She took Victoria's look of amazement as her cue to leave. Before she could get out of earshot, she heard the woman call to her.

"Stay out of my family's business, and stay away from my sons."

Before reaching her room, Sydney had already made the decision to get out of this house and as far away from the Hart clan as she could.

EIGHT

Keith glanced impatiently at his watch.

"We don't have time for this," he said, stuffing his mouth with a sushi roll. "We work at a law firm. There's no such thing as lunch hour. Hurry up."

Sydney and Gabrielle sped up the pace of their munching as the three of them sat in Keith's office. Gabrielle worked her persuasive wonders in getting lunch together. It was a slow Monday, everyone was in that getting-ready-to-work-but-not-quite-there-yet mood.

Sydney was preoccupied with thoughts of Marcus and her disastrous last encounter with Victoria. She had planned to check out a couple of summer sublets she'd circled from the Sunday paper, but didn't want to tell Gabrielle yet. She knew the girl would try to talk her out of it.

Gabrielle dipped her roll in Sydney's sauce and turned to her brother. "What's with you anyway? You've had a nasty attitude all day. You mad at me for something?"

Keith frowned at her. "Whenever you upset Mother, who has to hear about it? Dad? He's never there."

"Can you blame me?" Gabrielle pleaded. "You know how she is."

"She loves her children, Bree. That's what I know. We're all she has. Stop giving her a hard time."

Gabrielle slapped her plastic fork down on the table. "How am I doing that?"

"What's with the secretive behavior," he asked. "What are you up to?"

Gabrielle let out a sarcasm-laced laugh. "Mother is one to talk about being secretive. She's recruiting you for a spy now? You must love that."

Sydney wondered if this family ever got together without fighting.

"What does that mean?" Keith wiped his mouth, throwing the napkin into the shiny black plastic container that had held his food.

"Mother selected you," Gabrielle answered. "You've always wanted to be her favorite son."

"Okay," Sydney interjected, sending Gabrielle a disapproving glance. "Let's not fight. Isn't it bad enough that it's Monday?"

Keith cracked a smile. "Is that an attempt at humor? I'm surprised. You haven't seemed in a great mood today either."

Sydney shrugged. "Again, it's Monday."

"Monday sucks." Gabrielle nodded, grabbing one of Sydney's rolls. "You eat too slow."

"I'm on a diet," Sydney said, hating the word that had emanated from her lips since she was ten.

"For Marcus?" Gabrielle asked, her eyebrows lifting repeatedly.

"What's this about?" Keith turned back from throwing his food in the wastebasket behind his desk.

"Didn't you wonder why Marcus was acting like a lost puppy at breakfast yesterday?"

Keith nodded. "At church, too. I thought it was because of Lindsay."

"It was!" Sydney sat up straight. "And don't start with that, Gabrielle. There is nothing going on between us."

Keith looked surprised, his mouth a little open.

"Nothing," she repeated to him.

He blinked, slowly smiling. Well, don't diet. You look great. Women think being skinny is what men want. Trust me, men want some meat on the bones."

Fat. Fat. Fat. Sydney shook the word told to her her entire life from her mind. An image of Lindsay, her thin figure, flashed before her eyes. Was this for Marcus?

"Okay." Keith checked his watch again. "Lunch is over."

"We've been here fifteen minutes," Gabrielle whined.

"We have the lawsuit meeting in D.C. this afternoon." He turned to Sydney. "You'll come?"

Sydney nodded. "You want me to follow you?"

"Just ride with me," he said. "We'll come back here."

"We?" Gabrielle asked. "I didn't know the meeting was in D.C. Why wouldn't it be in Baltimore?"

"The partners are in D.C. today. So are some of the community leaders for that community outreach conference. Most of all, the king himself. Let's go."

"Hey, Sydney." Gabrielle nudged her as they stood. "You'll get to see Marcus."

"Shut up." Sydney grabbed her plate and Gabrielle's, trying to hide her emotions, which were heightened at the prospect of seeing him.

She tossed the remainders of lunch in the wastebasket, trying to decipher her own feelings. Dread? Anticipation? Fear? Excitement?

"Quit looking at him."

Sydney quickly averted her twelve-year-old eyes from the boy across the aisle in the grocery store.

Linda Williams rolled her eyes. "Pay attention to what I'm getting, 'cause you're gonna be doing the grocery shopping from now on. Make use of yourself."

Sydney did as she was told, even though she was distracted by Shawn Hughes, a boy from her class. He was down the aisle, shopping with his mother. He'd peeked at her a couple of times in class. She thought he was cute.

"Don't know why you want to make such a fool of yourself," Linda continued. "He's a cute little boy. What would he want you for?"

"Felicity Smith said he told Steven Collins that he liked me." Sydney stole a glance. Yeah, he was looking.

"With all that wagon you draggin behind you, I bet he does like you." Linda pulled at her. "But not for you. For only one thing. Look at his mama. She's a high-class bougie wannabe. She'd never let her son get hooked up with someone like you. You'd be entertainment. That's all."

Sydney jerked her arm away and scowled. Someone would love her one day.

Sydney was jolted from her memories by the ringing phone.

Keith cursed out loud, his hands full of files and folders. "That's probably Richard. Can you get that? Ana's at lunch. Just tell him we're on our way."

"Keith Hart's office."

"Hello, Ana. It's Marcus."

Sydney felt her body tense. "Marcus?"

Marcus paused. "Who is this?" There was a silence for only a moment. He took the phone off the speaker and held it to his face. Was he imagining her voice now? "Sydney?"

"Yes?" She answered in almost a whisper. In a tenth of a second, she relived their last encounter. *Stop it!*

"How are you?" Since Saturday night, he'd been thinking of what he'd say, do, when he saw her again.

"I'm . . . fine." Sydney looked up. She was alone in the office.

Marcus felt his collar squeezing his neck. His throat was dry. "Did Bree tell you I . . ."

"Yes." Sydney's voice wavered. She felt her composure threatened. She couldn't believe this was all from a mere phone call.

"I mean it," he said, wanting nothing more than to see her. It was crazy. This was more trouble than he needed in his life right now. "I was drinking. Not that it's an excuse. I didn't mean—"

"Don't." Sydney took a deep breath. She had to be stronger than this. "It's not important. I've already forgotten about it."

Marcus felt a tinge of pain hit him. She'd forgotten? Couldn't have! He was angry at himself for caring. He didn't need this. Fine, if she could forget, so could he.

"Is Keith there?" he asked, putting up his best front. "I need to speak with him."

Sydney felt a chill from his tone. She'd thought he'd be pleased, since he seemed so sorry it happened. Maybe he didn't care as much as she thought he did. As much as she did.

"He's on his way to your meeting."

"Be a good sport and tell him I can't make it. Political crisis on the Hill."

"Fine," she said. Good sport? "I'll tell him. Good-bye."

Marcus heard the click as she hung up. He stayed a little longer, slowly returning the receiver.

He was conflicted and had no time for it. His mental and physical preoccupation with Sydney Tanner had already slowed him up this morning. Right now he knew he needed to focus on his career, his community. Not a woman. Especially not this incredibly difficult woman who was doing everything she could to keep from caring about him.

He had to figure out a way to forget the fire and desire

he felt when he held her and kissed her. He had to stop seeing her voluptuous figure, her teasing lips, or her promising eyes every time he closed his own. He could do it. He hadn't met a woman yet that could control his every thought and action.

"This is ridiculous!"

Sydney noticed how angry the man who had just stepped into the Marriott conference room was. He'd entered the room, had been met by a woman who spoke to him for only a minute before he'd started, his voice raised.

He was tall, attractive, in his mid-thirties and almost identical to retired football player Marcus Allen. He locked eyes with Sydney for only a moment as he headed straight for Keith, sitting next to her at the conference table.

Keith quickly stood up. "Long, don't start with me. I'm not his keeper. Besides, he's on your side. This is your problem."

"What has gotten into your brother?" The man massaged his temples right between his eyes. He looked beyond stressed.

Sydney cleared her throat. "Marcus . . . Marcus had a political crisis. That's what he said."

He looked her up and down quickly. "That's the message he left with my office, too, but this is a political crisis. His community is being threatened, harassed."

"That's not true and you know it," Keith said, putting a hand on Sydney's shoulder. "Don't yell at the messenger. Your beef is with Marcus. If he really had faith in your cause, he'd be here."

David shook his head, a look of contempt on his face. "You must be loving this, Keith. But it is somewhat of a hollow victory. I mean, you can shine only when Marcus isn't around. It's always been like that, hasn't it?"

Keith's eyes narrowed, his lips pressing together. He said nothing, simply returning to his seat.

Everyone sat down and the meeting started. Gabrielle, who'd begged furiously to come along, showed no interest at any point in the meeting. Sydney knew she was up to something, but didn't really have the energy to concern herself with it.

The meeting was an attempt to identify all the major players in the lawsuit, and an attempt by the Preston Corporation to appeal to the community leaders to get their people to drop the lawsuit. Sydney didn't know too much about the civil litigation process, but knew the meeting was a waste of everyone's time. This was all about everyone getting to eye the other side down and make their own personal assessments of what they'd discuss in their little groups later.

The angry man from before was David Long, a Baltimore community activist and lawyer. He, his assistant, and neighborhood spokeswoman were here on behalf of the plaintiffs. Sydney was appalled by what David was suggesting.

"These accusations are preposterous." This from Jesse Michaels, lead counsel for the Preston Corporation.

"So you're saying my clients, the people of Fairview Hills, are lying?" David asked, his face straining to stay professional.

"No one is calling anyone a liar," Keith suggested. "Our client has denied each and every one of these accusations. Some were misunderstandings. Some were simply not us and there's no way to prove otherwise."

"You'll see when we start this case." David shook his head in disgust.

"It will be dismissed by the judge when it comes to

court in two weeks," Jesse said. He held his expensive pen at the tip under his nose. "No evidence."

"We have testimony," David said. "We have believable plaintiffs who will testify that you sent agents—"

"Agents?" Jesse laughed.

Sydney didn't like his laugh. It was pompous, condescending.

"Agents," David repeated, speaking louder now. "To use volatile, threatening language to encourage them to sell their homes."

"What some people view as volatile, threatening," Richard McDaniel said, "others view as persuasive sell."

"Threatening to expose infidelities," David said.

Jesse slammed his hand on the table. He leaned over impatiently. "Preston Corporation did no such thing."

"Conducting criminal background checks and threatening to tell police about relatives that might or might not be—"

"Mr. Long!" This from Michael Wagner. "This is too much. My client isn't the mob."

"No," David offered. "The mob is more professional with their threats, but you've come close."

This started a melee of accusations back and forth. Sydney sat stunned, trying to keep up and take notes for Keith. David ended the battle by storming out, his group following right behind. As the rest sat in silence, Jesse Michaels leaned back in his chair at the end of the table and laughed, just like he had before. Everyone turned to him in amazement.

"No," he said, smoothing out his tie. "This is good. Look at what just happened."

"Our negotiations went bust," Keith said. "How is this good?"

"Negotiations?" Sydney saw no sign of this. She turned to Gabrielle, who had eyes only for her watch.

Jesse pointed to the door. "That Long, he's a hothead. We can completely discredit him."

"Why would we need to do that?" Sydney asked, immediately regretting doing so as she garnered reproachful stares.

"What are they doing here?" Jesse asked, his eyes shifting from Gabrielle to Sydney. "Shouldn't they be interviewing residents?"

Keith pulled at Sydney's chair. "They were both leaving."

Sydney hesitated, insulted by the whole scene, but Gabrielle jumped up, grabbing her purse. No protest?

Richard cleared his throat. "Jesse, we were going to hold off on the interviewing until later this week. If we could get our way today, it would be an unnecessary cost."

Jesse rolled his eyes. "Now you didn't believe for even a second they would back down so soon. I've told you it would take . . ."

He paused, looking at Sydney, who was still in her seat. His eyes rolled to Keith.

"Sydney," Keith said, "you and Gabrielle wait outside. We need to talk confidentially now."

Gabrielle was already out the door as Sydney stood up. She was altogether uncomfortable with these people she worked for now, but as she stepped outside the room she decided there was no room for judgments now. She needed this job.

"Hold these." Gabrielle shoved her stack of folders at Sydney as soon as they were in the hallway. She reached into her purse and pulled out a mirror.

"I can't believe you have nothing to say about this," Sydney said, watching Gabrielle apply her lipstick. "About what went on in there. You were so insistent on coming."

Gabrielle wondered how this girl's mind worked. "Not

because of this, silly. I've got to go. Tell Keith I'll take the train home."

"Wait a second."

Gabrielle ran a comb through her short tresses. "I'm meeting Gary. He's in a hoops tournament on the University of D.C. campus."

"What am I supposed to say?" This agreement was turning out to be much more than Sydney had bargained for. "I have a lot on my plate, Gabrielle. I don't want to deal with your family tonight."

"Keith won't be thinking of me," she said with a devilish smile. "Not after that scene. You'll be lucky if he remembers you're out here."

With that, she turned and walked away, with a sashay in her hips that spoke of her youthful anticipation.

Sydney thought to go after her, but decided against it. Instead, she took a seat along the wall and pulled the classifieds out of her bag. What could she afford? She knew nothing of the neighborhoods in Baltimore. Which were safe for a woman living on her own, but cheap enough that she wouldn't have to spend what she needed to save over the summer for her tuition. She searched and searched, but could see nothing. It was hopeless. She knew she had to stay right where she was, no matter how painful. She needed the free room and board the Harts were offering. She couldn't afford anything else.

"I have to apologize."

Sydney's eyes shot up, seeing David Long with a remorseful frown on his face.

"You don't have to." Sydney slid down the bench, so he could sit next to her.

"That was unprofessional." He sighed. "It was stupid for me to think something could be done today."

"I was with you there," she said. "I realized that going

into it. We were all a little stupid for thinking something could be resolved today."

"What was it?" he asked, his eyes turning regretful. "What was so important that Marcus couldn't make it?"

"There is so much game playing and face time in politics, I assume." She turned to him. "I'm sorry for you that he wasn't here."

David blinked, leaning back. "You can't be a lawyer. You seem too nice."

Sydney laughed. "Aren't you a lawyer?"

"Exactly."

Sydney introduced herself with bare-bones details of her relationship with the Harts and the law firm.

"You just joined up?" he asked. "No one warned you about the Harts? No one told you what you'd be getting into?"

"I'm doing all right," she lied. "I do my best to mind my own business."

David leaned against the wall, shaking his head. "Marcus used to be different. Man, we've been buddies, best buddies since we were ten. His dad put him under an ungodly amount of pressure, but he handled it. He grew up before he should've had to. We knew his father was planning his life for him, but he was going to make his own purpose with those plans."

"What do you mean?" Sydney found herself drawn to David's words. She knew nothing of Marcus Hart, except that he was an unwelcome intrusion in her life.

"His commitment to our people." David's hands closed in hopeful fists, not anger. "Anyone in need. We both come from well-off families. Our parents had to make more of us than the average kid. They had more to prove. They had to prove it wasn't just a stroke of luck or white charity. They proved it through the kids' doing, not just as well, better even. I had to be a lawyer, Marcus a politician. We accepted that, but promised to use those positions to help those in need: our brothers and sisters who didn't have a choice of becoming a lawyer or politician—too busy just trying to survive."

"You don't think Marcus is committed to your . . . your promise anymore?"

David shook his head, his eyes lowering to the floor. "I'll never question his heart. It's a good heart. It's just that he needed to be here today."

"Don't you think he would've if he could?" Sydney realized she was making an attempt to defend a man she wanted herself to believe she couldn't stand.

David nodded. "He's been very preoccupied with something serious lately. If I know him as well as I think I do after almost twenty-five years, it's a woman."

Sydney swallowed. Must be Lindsay—had to be. If it was a woman at all.

"It's hurting his work," David continued. "When his job suffers, it's stuff like this meeting that gets pushed aside. Only now this is more important than ever. Preston's tactics . . ."

David stopped. Sydney noticed a flicker of uncertainty in his eyes.

"You're right," she said. "We shouldn't talk about this. We're supposed to be enemies."

"No." David said. "My life has been dealing with people, tagging them quick so I can cut to the chase. You're not my enemy. You're a lot softer than you want people to think you are."

She smiled, unsure of what she felt. No, she was tired. Tired of caring, tired of remembering, tired of wondering and waiting.

Keith interrupted the quiet moment, with an excessive clearing of his throat. David took the high road, quickly excusing himself before anything could get ugly.

"What did you tell him?" Keith asked with urgency. "You can't tell him—"

"I'm not stupid, Keith." Sydney placed a reassuring hand on his arm. She found him unnecessarily wound up and anxious. "I wouldn't do that."

"I know," he said after a while, calming down. "Where's Bree?"

"Ran off to meet some friends," she answered, trying to remind herself this was for young love. "She's taking the train home. She had ulterior motives in coming."

"I didn't doubt that for a second." Keith took the folders Sydney handed over. "I just don't know what to do about her. Mother's gonna have a fit when I come home without her."

Sydney could see how much Victoria's approval meant to Keith. She felt sorry for him, because he didn't see that Victoria would never, could never, be pleased.

"Look," he said, nodding at Richard who was leaning out the conference room door, trying to get his attention. "We've got to look into something in the city. It's a hush-hush, so you can't come."

"You're looking into Long's past, aren't you?" Sydney asked. "Come on, Keith."

Keith put up a hand to stop her. "It's nothing for you to get involved in."

Sydney frowned. "You've got that right. I don't want any part of it. I'll just jump the train and catch a cab home—keeping all the receipts of course."

"I hate to be a burden," Keith said, his brows centering in frustration. "Can you wait for me? You could just walk around a bit, visit a friend or something. We can meet up later. I just . . . I don't want to come home to Mother empty-handed."

Sydney couldn't hold back her laugh. "You just want someone besides yourself to explain Gabrielle's absence.

You can't possibly believe Victoria would be upset not to see me."

Keith smiled, winking at her. "If it makes a difference, I'm happy you're here."

"It does, and thanks." She stood up, stretching. "Where do you want to meet?"

"We're going to end up near the D.C. Mall, so why don't we meet at the Lincoln Memorial?" He glanced at his watch. "How does five on the dot sound?"

"Sounds like we'll be just in time to hit rush-hour traffic heading home."

"All the more reason I'll need the company. Besides, Bree'll probably get home before us."

"See you at five."

Sydney knew right away where she needed to go, and fortunately for her, Professor Maggie Shue was in her office with a few minutes to spare before teaching a summer history course.

"A slow but good start," she said after Sydney detailed the progress of her genealogy project.

"I've been a little preoccupied with other things," Sydney explained. "I will complete this. I need that five hundred dollars, and I need this assistantship."

Maggie seemed pleased. "You picked an interesting family. You'll probably have it easy for the next few generations. Easier than most."

"I'm going to visit the genealogy center at the Library of Congress." Sydney pushed the sheet of paper with her action plan across the desk to Maggie. "Also, the Harts have been written about a lot. So, like you said, I'll go through the general magazine and newspaper archives at the Baltimore public library, then the genealogy web sites on the Internet."

"I find it interesting that you want to go off on this Halat family tangent," Maggie said. "The Harts would've been good enough."

Sydney nodded. "I know, but I think there's something special about the Halats that'll make this a stand-out project."

"Okay, but don't get distracted. More is not always better. Even though you're in search of information, don't let it be like the Internet where you get lost in a melee of information and lose sight of why you got on in the first place. Focus."

Sydney enjoyed Maggie's direction, firm, but caring. She wished she'd known someone like her when she was younger.

Maggie reached over the table and handed her a card. "This is the number of Amira Hawn. She runs the D.C. chapter of the National Genealogy Society. They're also on the Net."

"I know." Sydney had seen at least one computer, and possibly a laptop, in the Hart home. She'd have to use one of those. She wasn't getting a second at work to make headway. "Thanks for the number. She can give me direction, but she'll probably guide me to my next step, finding out if Maryland has a local chapter."

"They do," Maggie said. "Maryland has a lot of history. There are probably several chapters throughout the state. The web site will tell you. Now what else?"

"A trip to the Latter-Day Saints Family History Center in Baltimore. They're supposed to be a source for anyone, not just Mormons."

"Right," Maggie answered. "What else?"

"Most importantly . . . ," she added.

"Interview, interview, interview."

"This Aunt May"—Maggie pointed to her mark on the

early, first draft of the tree—"she's going to be a wealth of information. Priceless."

Sydney agreed. She knew she'd been very lazy with this project, caught up with the job, thinking about Marcus and how much she couldn't stand him. It was time to get serious.

Sydney and Maggie exchanged pleasantries before Maggie headed off. Sydney realized she still had an hour, so she headed to her favorite coffee shop near the D.C. Mall, the area made up of political offices and famous monuments. She needed to put together a plan, and figure out how she was going to avoid Marcus for the rest of the summer.

Sipping on a cup of hot chocolate, she stared out the window, seeing nothing, thinking of Victoria's warnings—or threats—depending on how one perceived them. It was out of her hands. This project was all she had to reach her MBA, and she couldn't wait any longer. It was starting to look bad, and she wasn't proud of her *ends justifies the means* decision, but this *had* to happen. She *had* to do it now. Coming this far would only be a failure, and that was unacceptable.

"You'll fail, you know." Linda Williams tossed a dirty plate into the sink where her seventeen-year-old daughter was washing dishes. "Why even set yourself up?"

Sydney ignored her mother. Nothing could hurt her feelings today. She'd gotten her acceptance letter from Chicago State University today. She was getting out of this hell on earth.

"How much it cost?" Linda asked.

"I can afford it," she said. "I'll apply for financial aid. I'll get scholarships. I'll work."

"You're not living here," David Williams spat out from his drunken stupor. He was leaning against the wall just

to keep from falling to the floor. "Once you turn eighteen, you're out of here. I'm tired of paying for a kid that ain't mine and don't mind me neither."

Linda laughed. "Shut up, you drunk fool. She'll last half a year."

"No, I won't." Sydney didn't care that she was only encouraging more wrath by responding, disagreeing. "I'm going to finish. I'll get my degree and go to business school."

Linda laughed louder now. David joined her.

"After that," she continued, "I'll get a big job, be very important, and make a ton of money."

"You'll kill yourself." Linda turned, still talking as she walked away. "You'll kill yourself trying to be something you're not."

"It won't happen, Syd." David stood up straight for one second before hitting the floor.

That was where he slept that night.

NINE

"Sydney? Sydney?"

Sydney snapped from her flashback, blinking rapidly. Looking up, she recognized her greeter and smiled as he sat down across from her. Her mind raced with questions, analysis. She'd anticipated more emotion on her part, but it wasn't there. She'd expected anger, hurt, attraction. None of those.

"You're always blanking out like that," he said. "Where do you go? What's the point, right? You'd never tell me when we were together. I'm not expecting it now."

"You don't want to know," Sydney said.

Darrin Matthews looked his usual charming self. He was almost a twin to Blair Underwood, the actor. Very attractive, but in a sweet, small-featured, dependable way. He always dressed preppie, today decked out in a purple polo shirt, khaki shorts, white foldover socks, and dark brown loafers.

"How are you, Sydney?" He placed his books on the table. They were thick, premed books.

"Fine," she answered. He had such a nice smile. "You?"

He pointed to his books. "You know"—he blinked—"I miss you."

Sydney smiled nervously. Not only did she realize she

had somehow gotten over him without trying, but an image of Marcus flashed in her mind, and its presence at that moment made her want to scream.

"It's okay," Darrin said. "You don't have to respond. I know I'm the one who ended it."

"It was the right thing to do," Sydney said. She blinked away a vision of her and Marcus dancing together. No. Never.

"Look at this mess." He looked at the papers spread out on the table. "I didn't know you were taking summer classes."

"It's just a project." She had to admit, a small part of her missed him still. Not so much him as someone familiar. Sydney couldn't believe she was hinting at a desire for stability.

She knew it was high time for a serious, lasting relationship. She had that consistency with Darrin over the past year. She missed that. She knew there was no chance of anything like that with Marcus, so why was he on her mind every second?

"There you go again," Darrin said, his teeth white and shining. "Look. if you want to be alone . . ."

"I'm sorry." She didn't want him to go. Sydney knew it was over, but she was feeling a little lonely right now. "Have a cup with me."

He paused, seeming uncertain. "I guess I can."

He ordered a cappuccino from the waiter who approached them and settled in. He asked for an update on her life and she gave it. Sydney was reminded of how good a listener Darrin was.

"Can you handle such a full plate?" he asked.

"Par for the course for me." Sydney shrugged, leaning back. She'd left out the nonsense with Victoria and especially Marcus, hoping that for at least a few minutes, she could forget it herself. "I'll do fine."

He shook his head in admiration. "That's one of the things I love about you, Sydney. Never one to complain."

"Takes up too much energy."

There was an awkward silence as Sydney felt the mood dampen. Darrin looked unhappy.

"All I wanted was"—he turned away, swallowing hard—"I think I made a big mistake."

Sydney waited until he turned back. "No, Darrin. You were right. I can't do more now and you need much more. You deserve more."

"You say that like I could get better than you. I don't agree with that."

Sydney smiled, feeling warm appreciation. "Not better. Just right. Look, Darrin, I'm not gonna play that *it's not you, it's me* routine. You saw it ending and that's why we did just that. It was time."

Darrin shook his head. "Nothing. Not all the reasoning and good sense in the world makes up for—"

"We'll get nowhere dwelling on this." Sydney understood his frustration. She could never fully explain her feelings, her motives. No one would understand. "We agreed to be friends. Let's see if this works."

He nodded, his shoulders releasing tension. "Let's try."

Marcus impatiently glanced at his watch: five-fifteen. Where was she? An hour ago, David had given him a tongue-lashing to match anything Victoria Hart could put out. The guilt from not showing up made him a sitting duck to the next favor asked of him. He'd give a kidney to a stranger to feel better about himself at that moment.

But it wasn't a stranger who called, it was Keith. After enduring his little brother's gloating, came the favor. A legal emergency was what Keith called it, but Marcus suspected he used these precise words to further annoy him.

HEALTH, FITNESS AND BEAUTY FOR AFRICAN-AMERICAN WOMEN

heart & soul

1 year (6 issues) $16.97 plus receive a FREE HEART & SOUL
Healthy Living Journal with your paid subscription.

YES! I want to invest in myself and subscribe to HEART & SOUL, the health, fitness and beauty magazine for savvy African-American women. I'll get a year's worth of helpful information that will inspire me to discover new ways of improving my body...my spirit...and my mind. Plus, I'll get a FREE HEART & SOUL *Healthy Living Journal* to keep a daily record of my wonderful progress.

Name _____ (First) _____ (Last) _____

Address _____ Apt # _____

City _____ State _____ Zip _____ | MABM4 |

□ Payment enclosed   □ Bill me
Rush my HEART & SOUL
Healthy Living Journal

Please allow 6-8 weeks for receipt of first issue. In Canada: CDN $19.97 (includes GST). Payment in U.S. currency must accompany all Canadian orders. Basic subscription rate: 6 issues $16.97.

BUSINESS REPLY MAIL

FIRST-CLASS MAIL   PERMIT NO. 272   RED OAK, IA

POSTAGE WILL BE PAID BY ADDRESSEE

heart&soul

P O BOX 7423
RED OAK IA 51591-2423

In the end, he wasn't going to be able to meet Sydney at five, so Marcus had to be there. He had to hold onto her until Keith arrived. Keith wasn't going back home empty-handed.

So Marcus found himself racked with guilt, angry at himself, annoyed with Keith, anxious about Sydney, whom he had no idea how to act toward since their last encounter, and altogether ticked off that Bree had disappeared again. Now here was Sydney, topping the day off by being late. He had a late business meeting he couldn't miss, so he needed to eat quickly and get ready. His impatience grew with every second past five.

As he saw the beat-up TransAm stop in front of the walkway to the monument, Marcus felt a spur of excitement at the sight of her, but his anger fought to stay in control. It succeeded as he watched her walk around to the driver's side of the car, lean over and converse with casual flirtation with the young man in the driver's seat.

"Look at this." He threw his arms hopelessly into the air. "She knows she's late and she still stops to flirt with this joker."

He sighed out loud even though he knew no one could hear him. "Even as this boy drives away, she stands and watches. Does she think the world revolves around her schedule?"

His impatience turned to uncertainty as she turned and started walking toward the monument. She walked with a protective confidence, her curvy hips moving left to right. Marcus wondered how she would react when she saw him. He still tasted her sweet lips, and wanted more even though he knew it was the last thing he needed right now. Would she be civil, having accepted his sophomoric apology through Gabrielle? Or would she return to her cold, unpenetrable self? He hated that he cared so much. He hated that this woman made him feel like a kid.

As soon as Sydney saw him, discontent set in. She knew immediately it wasn't Keith. This man was taller, broader. It took only a second to realize it was Marcus and Sydney didn't know what to do.

Why? she asked herself. She wasn't prepared to face him now. She was doing everything she could to forget their last encounter, now here he was again. Looking good at that. Please God, she prayed to herself, let Keith be there somewhere. Hiding behind a bush. Anywhere.

No such luck.

"Keith isn't going to make it," he said coldly. He could see from the look on her face as she approached that she wasn't happy to see him and that bit at him.

"What's wrong?" Sydney reacted to his coolness, keeping a good distance. Lines formed on his brow. Apparently he wasn't any happier to see her than she was him.

"Legal emergency," he said. He couldn't fight those eyes. They dared him to look away, promising rapture swirled in her black irises.

"He sent you to tell me?" Sydney found that an odd order. Keith wasn't the dominant brother, and Marcus wouldn't offer to see her. "Well, thank you. I'll just jump the train now."

Her quick dismissal made him even angrier. He was not sure why. "I'm not his errand boy. He didn't send me. I'm doing him a favor."

Sydney placed her hands on her hips. "So nice of you, big brother. I'm sure he appreciates it."

"It's a good thing he wasn't here," Marcus called after her as she turned to walk away. He didn't want her to go, and not because of Keith.

Sydney turned around. He was striking when he was angry. Man, she'd give him that. "Why? Because I was a little late?"

"Because you drove up with that boy," he said, pointing

to the street as he caught up with her. "Flirting, hanging off his car. You practically had your whole chest in his face."

Sydney's eyes bulged as she grabbed her purse straps so tight it hurt. "You . . . you—I did not!"

"If Keith had seen that . . ." He found a little guilty pleasure in getting her riled up. He loved her fire. It did something to him.

"He wouldn't have cared less," she said. "Neither should you."

He was stumped for a second. Only a second. "Don't flatter yourself, Sydney. I don't. I just don't care for baby-sitting grown women."

"Then don't." She eyed him with icey contempt before resuming her walk. Oh, how she hated him. One night he's kissing her, the next he treats her like a child. She had no time for these games.

He called after her, following a few feet behind. She ignored him, picking up the pace. He called again, sounding more frustrated. She smiled and kept walking. Then she felt his hand grab her arm and she jumped. Memories of him grabbing her, kissing her, flashed in her mind and she jerked away.

Marcus was shocked with the urgency of her jerk. "Sydney . . . I don't want you to be afraid of me. I—"

"Then don't grab me!" She was louder than even she expected.

"I've apologized." He stammered through his words. Her eyes were full of anger, her lips pressed so tight together. "I'm sorry about the other night. I was drinking. I mean, that's no excuse. Really, I—"

"You already said that. It doesn't matter. Just let it go." She turned away. She wanted to cry. Why? Maybe she was tired of all the obstacles. Marcus Hart was an obstacle.

"You have to stay with me," he said gently.

She looked into his eyes, speechless. What was he saying? Oh, God, she thought. Was he asking her to . . .

"You have to come with me!" Marcus couldn't comprehend her expression. She was as confusing a woman as he'd ever met. "Keith is begging you to."

Sydney blinked, thinking herself an idiot for even suggesting . . . She couldn't even repeat it to herself.

"Keith doesn't want to go home empty-handed," he said. "You have to wait for him."

"Here?" she asked. "How long?"

"Another hour or so," he said. "But not here. They'll be near Georgetown, so you can come home with me."

Bells went off. "No. I'll catch a train. I'm not going home with you."

He fought to control his anger at her obvious rejection of his company, even though she had every right not to want to be near him. He'd practically attacked her the other night. Still he hadn't been so drunk that he couldn't remember her responding in kind at some point before pushing away. Hadn't she?

"Look, woman," he said sternly. "You have nothing to fear from me. I'm not too excited about playing host to you, but you haven't left my brother and me any choice.

Sydney gasped. "How did this become my fault?"

"If you hadn't let Bree run off—"

Sydney threw her hands in the air. "Here we go again. You with Bree. She is not a child!"

"Where is she?" he asked. "I demand to know."

She looked him up and down with a laugh. "Now you know better than that."

"I'll find out," he said, feeling a spark in response to her sassy tone and posture. She was a shapely, sexy fighter, stubborn and unyielding. He wished he could be an exception to all her rules.

"I'm sure you will find out," she said. "You'll use your

money to track her, follow her. Spying on your own sister. That sounds like something a politician, a Hart, would do."

Marcus's eyes squinted, his teeth gritted. "You watch your mouth, woman."

Sydney knew she should've been insulted by his comments, but she was excited as his nostrils flared and he stepped even closer to her. At that moment, she felt such a strong sense of desire, it almost slapped her in the face.

"Let's go."

With that order, he took her by the arm and guided her to his waiting sedan with driver. Her skin felt soft under his hands and it distracted him from the annoyance of her purposeful resistance to his direction. She forced him to stop a few times and look back with a tug before walking along. She knew she was being difficult with a smug smile on her face and it infuriated him, even though he knew he wouldn't rather have it any other way.

Sydney sat alone, like a punished child, on the sofa of Marcus's Georgetown brownstone. It was a charming place, with a little more styling than Sydney expected of Marcus, with hardwood floors covered by wool rugs in shades like charcoal, brown, and green, and maple wood cabinets, bookcase, and natural furniture in various shades of black and green. Everywhere, one could see paintings of rivers, sunsets, and prairies. It was warm, but still masculine.

Sydney wondered if Celeste Johnson had ever lived here.

Marcus hadn't spoken a word in the car, and as soon as they'd gotten inside he'd only given her orders. He'd ordered her to follow him to the big black-and-white marble designer kitchen.

As he threw frozen pizza into the oven, he informed her he was taking a shower upstairs to get ready for a business meeting later that night, and she was to take the pizza out in fifteen minutes. Until then she was to sit on the sofa in the living room.

"Do nothing else," he said with a warning stare. "Touch nothing."

Sydney smiled wryly. "It's the weirdest thing, but all of a sudden, you bear a striking resemblance to your mama."

He sent her a searing glance, with no response as he left for upstairs.

It was too much. Ten minutes had gone by. Sydney ached to do as she was told for the only reason being that Marcus would leave her alone. She couldn't help it. She walked along the bookcase, running the tips of her fingers over the books and miniature statues. She glossed over the photos of political figures and others she didn't recognize.

Over and over again, she noticed Marcus's magnetism, his attraction. His smile was magical, his figure so worth consideration. His charisma leaped off every photo as if he'd been destined to stand out.

Sydney made her way back to the sofa and reached under the coffee table, opening the little cabinet's door. She pulled out one of several miniature photo albums and opened it up.

One picture stood out right away. She was beautiful. Sydney noticed that in an instant. She was shapely and young with a naturally regal face. Her hair was in a ponytail, giving her a sporty look to contrast her features. She seemed so content with Marcus's arms around her. He appeared happy, too, looking down at her. In the near distance, sitting at what Sydney recognized as the Harts' main dining-room table, was a very unhappy Victoria. She was eyeing the couple with contempt and disapproval.

Sydney knew the girl in the photo had never had a fighting chance.

"You'll never be good enough for them," David Williams said as soon as he entered Sydney's room.

"You said you would knock," Sydney yelled. She was sixteen now. She hated his barging into her room whenever, unannounced.

"I lied." He laughed teasingly. "I'm paying the rent here. I own every square foot of this hellhole. I don't have to knock. Besides, you ain't got nothing I ain't already seen looking ten times better anyway."

Sydney sneered. Hate didn't even describe how she felt about him.

"Anyway," he continued standing at the foot of the mattress. "I'm here to give you some advice."

"What you gonna do, David? Sing me a 'Schoolhouse Rock' song you learned watching cartoons this morning? Spare me. I know conjunctions and how a law becomes a bill."

"I'll haul off and slap your little smart mouth, girl!" He frowned, seeming confused as always whenever she made a snappy comment. "This is your problem. Thinking you're someone you're not. You're not someone to spar with a grown man like me. Just like you're not someone a rich boy would be interested in. If you'd listen to me, he never would've hurt your feelings 'cause you never would've tried to ask the boy out."

Shut up, her head screamed. Go away! Brad Watson had laughed in her face when she asked him out. She saw him only once a week when she traveled downtown for her college test preparation class. He was so cute, and she'd sworn he'd been looking at her.

"You're cute and all, Sydney," Brad had told her, *"but my parents would kill me if I dated someone from . . . the projects. Nothing personal."*

Sydney was broken from her trance as she heard her name being called in between swear words. It was Marcus. From the smoke-filled kitchen, he came storming into the living room.

"What in the hell is the matter with you?" he yelled.

Sydney was speechless as she stared at his chiseled body, covered only slightly by a fire-engine-red towel around his waist. His chest was smooth, showing shiny, sleek skin that raised at his pecs and indented in a six-pack down his stomach. The towel hid unmentionables, stopping just above his knees. Sydney had seen his thighs before. Outside the balcony of her bedroom. The first time she'd seen him. He'd made her knees weak then and she was sure they'd buckle under her again now.

"You trying to burn down my house?" He'd been too excited to even realize he was almost naked. He'd been drying himself off in his bedroom, his door open, when he smelled smoke.

"I . . ." She turned away, but turned back. He was walking toward her! *Stop!* she heard herself yell, but the words never come out. *Stop it! He's Brad Watson all over again.*

"I smelled this from upstairs!" He stared her down.

She swallowed, thinking of anything to say. *Speak! Speak, you idiot.* "You're smoke alarm doesn't work."

Marcus blinked once, twice. He leaned back. "Okay. Is that all you have to say?"

Sydney shrugged, her eyes as wide as saucers. Her fingers, all ten, gripped the photo album tightly as if they didn't they would surely have to reach out and grab him.

"Well, yeah. I mean, yeah. You need batteries. That's . . . dangerous."

Marcus coughed, the smoke sending a haze through the apartment. He looked her over, noticing her knuckles were losing color as she gripped the photo album. He snatched it from her, surprised that she resisted at first.

"What are you doing with this?" he asked. "I told you not to touch anything."

"I didn't." Sydney didn't even hear her own words. She thought she wanted him to put some clothes on, but she heard a voice inside say *Lose the towel.* Then she'd lose control.

Marcus looked at her closely, then the album. He held it up to her. "You didn't? Then what's this, and what's the matter with you? You're acting weird."

Sydney let out a childish laugh. She was, deep inside, begging herself to come to her senses. It wasn't working yet. She'd keep trying.

Marcus looked at the photo open on the first page. Celeste. Memories, good and bad flashed back to him. Mostly one memory, and it was bad. "Why did you take this? Why this one?"

"It . . . was the first . . . one I grabbed." Sydney coughed through the smoke, as it clouded her eyes. "That's Celeste, isn't it?" Sydney joined him on the sofa as he returned the album to its home.

He looked at her startled. "How do you know?"

"Gabrielle told me," she answered. "I didn't ask. It just came up. Don't be mad at her. She didn't say much."

"I'm not mad." Surprisingly he wasn't, even though he expected to be. "She told you Celeste was my fiancée"

Sydney nodded. She could see, as the smoke began to clear, this wasn't easy for him. "You don't have to say anything."

Good, Marcus thought. She was acting normal again.

He relaxed, smiling at her. She was beautiful. She made him want to talk, tell her everything.

"I thought I loved her," he said softly. "I might have at one point, but it became something else entirely. She was nice and caring. A teacher. Funny, pretty. From the start, Dad, and especially Mother, weren't having it. She didn't come from . . . well, I hate to say it. To use their words."

"You don't have to," Sydney said, feeling anger seep through her. "She wasn't good enough for your parents— not good enough to be a Hart."

He looked deep into Sydney's eyes. She did understand. Still he couldn't tell her everything, could he? "You've had to deal with this before."

She nodded, closing her eyes for only a moment. "Go on."

"I stayed with Celeste far longer than I should have. I just got so sick and tired of them and their elitist nagging. It was over long before it ended. I knew I didn't love her, but I asked her to marry me. I used her to hurt them."

Sydney was surprised, expecting to hate him for such an awful thing, but his emotions were too familiar. "How did it end?"

Marcus couldn't tell her that. It made him sick to even think about it. "Celeste ended it. It got to be too much for her. She broke it off and left town. That year I lost my first bid for the House seat. It was a bad year. Nothing has been the same since. Not that it was so great before that."

"I'm sorry, Marcus." Sydney placed a tender hand on his bare shoulder. In a moment of sincere confession, she'd forgotten how attracted she was to him, but it came hurtling back in a second's time.

Her touch was so soothing, so warm, so right. As desire swept over him, Marcus heard one last voice of caution.

You don't need to fall for anyone now, it said. Not now. He ignored it as everything in his world became a blur except for her welcoming, caring eyes and her full, seductive lips.

When he kissed her, Sydney's mind went to oblivion. Her stomach exploded in a lava flow of heat that spread throughout her body in less than a second. She realized that she'd been waiting for his kiss all along. His lips were demanding, but not harsh like before. Now they were needing, caring, full of emotion and tasting of painful regret.

She returned his kiss, wrapping her arms around his neck. Marcus wasn't thinking anymore, only wanting as he pulled her to him. His tongue entered her mouth, slowly tasting her warmth and seducing her. His hands caressed her waist, moving passionately up and down her sides. Anticipation would make him go tantalizingly insane.

Sydney felt waves of passion sweep through her as his hands explored her body. Her thin cotton dress shirt was too much clothes at this moment. She could feel his muscled chest against hers and she kissed him deeper. Her hands moved from his neck, down his back. She heard him moan and she kissed him harder.

Marcus wanted this woman more than he had ever wanted any woman, he knew that one thing to be true. He scooped her lower back with one hand and supported her head with the other as he lowered her flat on the sofa. He rested himself between her legs, all the while caressing her mouth with kisses.

Sydney whispered his name as his mouth moved to her chin, then her neck. His hands moved everywhere, only making her want them in each spot again. His body moved against hers, making her skirt rise. She felt his towel fall between her thighs. Oh, no, she thought, knowing where this would take them—afraid of how much she wanted it.

Marcus reached to remove his towel completely, but just as he touched the edges of the material, a screeching sound reverberated through the house. They both jumped sky high as the noise was deafening and nonstop. They stared at each other. Sydney looked down. The towel was on the floor, it was obvious to both how affected Marcus was by their encounter.

Their eyes met again. He was speechless. Sydney blinked.

"Your smoke alarm does work," she said, as she covered her ears.

Marcus smiled as he reapplied the towel. "Yes, it does. It just needed some real fire."

Sydney blushed and looked down. She saw her shirt was out of her skirt and several buttons were loose. As Marcus ran to the kitchen, she pulled herself together.

The doorbell rang, making her jump again. Her mind hadn't fully returned to her yet. She didn't know what to do as, within a second, the phone rang. The noise was too much. She hurried to the door, checking herself in the hallway mirror.

The smoke alarm stopped just as Sydney opened the door. The phone stopped only a second after.

Keith Hart stood in the doorway with a smile as wide as ever. He looked Sydney over. "What's wrong with you?"

"What do you mean?" Sydney smoothed her tousled hair.

"You look dazed," he said, walking past her. "You look . . . What's with that smell? Who burned something?"

Sydney followed behind. "The pizza burned. The alarm doesn't work."

He turned around, looking confused. "I could've sworn I heard it from outside just now."

"Yeah, now." Sydney fanned herself as Keith looked at her in confusion. She needed a few more seconds to cool down. She couldn't even begin to deal with what had just happened.

"Where is he?" Keith looked around.

"The phone." Sydney prayed he'd heard the doorbell and wouldn't come out here in his towel. All she needed was for this to get back to Victoria somehow.

"Fine," Keith said, turning and heading for the door. "Thanks for waiting. Let's go."

"Wait." Sydney didn't want to go. No, she thought, maybe she did want to go. Just because it felt good, didn't mean it was good. She wasn't sure. She hated this. "What about Marcus?"

Keith shrugged. "He knows I'm coming for you. He won't care. When we talked on the phone earlier, he said he had plans for tonight anyway."

Sydney reached for her purse. "Still I should say bye. Thanks. Something."

Just then Marcus came storming into the foyer still only in his towel. Sydney felt herself shrink. She was horrified. She couldn't even look at Keith.

"What the—" Keith's eyes widened.

"You little bastard!" Marcus stepped just inches from Keith. "How dare you?"

Sydney was taken aback, not knowing where this vehement anger was coming from. She looked at Keith and saw he was braced, a little intimidated, but not at all surprised.

"Sydney and I were just leaving," Keith said. "Carry on getting ready for your meeting."

As he turned, Marcus grabbed his arm. Keith jerked back and pushed his older brother. Marcus moved only an inch or two back. He slammed Keith against the wall, cocking his hand in a fist, pulling back. Keith braced.

"Stop it!" Sydney leaped forward, positioning herself between the two. "Marcus, please."

"Get in the car, Sydney." Keith's eyes never left his brother's. "This is between me and Marcus."

"You didn't think I'd find out?" Marcus asked. "You didn't think he'd find out?"

"Didn't care," Keith answered. "It's part of the game. Come to play or don't come at all."

"You leave him alone!" Marcus grabbed Keith's collar, pulling him close, but Keith pushed away.

"What is going on?" Sydney asked.

"Big bro is upset with us," Keith said, his voice laced with cynicism, unable to hide a slight quiver of fear. "He doesn't like us snooping in his buddy's biz."

"Did you know about this?" Marcus turned to Sydney. "Did you know about them investigating David Long?"

Sydney turned away. "I . . . I . . . I don't approve of—"

"Get out," he said, waving his hand at them. He wanted to throw something, anything, he was so angry. "Both of you. Get out of my house."

Sydney was stunned, the pain of his words catching in her throat. Before she could say a word, Keith gently took her arm and began leading her to the door. She watched speechless as Marcus turned his back to them both.

"Let's go, Sydney." Keith opened the door. "He can't take it. He's a politician. He knows how to play dirty."

Sydney felt her stomach turn as the car headed out of Georgetown. What had just happened?

"Why?" she asked. "What? How so soon?"

Keith kept his eyes on the road as his BMW traveled the brick side streets. "We hire only the best. In less than three hours, we found out that David Long had an affair three years ago. He cheated on his wife. A law clerk he hired, all of twenty-one years old. Our guy found out she stills lives in Adams Morgan, so we paid her a little visit—just to verify of course. She must have called David, who probably went whining to Marcus."

"Oh, Keith." Sydney felt dirty just for knowing this. "This can't be our business. This can't have anything to do with us."

"It's war, Sydney. You're an adult. You're not a kid, you know this."

Sydney shook her head. "No. If Preston didn't do these things, it doesn't matter what David Long did three years ago."

Keith smiled, but only for a moment. Then he became more serious than Sydney had ever seen him. "It's never that simple, Sydney."

Nothing ever was. She knew that now more than ever. If uninterrupted, she and Marcus would have made love, she knew that. Nothing, nothing could have stopped them. Then only seconds later, he'd given her the most contemptuous look and thrown her from his home.

Stupid, she thought to herself. *You are so stupid.* She should have never set foot in that apartment. Never. She should have never touched him. There was no chance of anything happening between them, not with him being a Hart and her being the second coming of Celeste. No, Sydney wouldn't be driven to insanity the way she was certain Victoria had driven Celeste. She wouldn't do that to herself. Life was already too hard.

"Just survive the summer," Sydney said to herself later as she soaked in a warm bath back at the house. To top off the day, the tub faucet had fallen right off when she turned it, but the water still came, so she didn't care.

"Just survive the summer," she repeated. "Do this project, get back to school. Only three months, babe. You can do it. No distractions. No Hart men. Just work. Nothing else."

Marcus still smelled the burnt pizza the second he returned home from his meeting. He couldn't even remember what the meeting was about. He felt so many emotions—anger, sorrow, confusion, and frustration. He wasn't going to let Keith's firm get away with what they were doing to David. He and his wife had resolved that issue and that's where it was left. They had children to protect.

Marcus knew Keith hated him. This lawsuit was going to be it for them. Marcus couldn't see a way of avoiding this. He wanted to, so badly, but his distractions threatened to overwhelm him.

Sydney Tanner.

Marcus sat at his kitchen table, running his fingers through the decorative jar of colored egg noodles there for display only. He wanted her, ached for her. At the same time, he was furious with her for knowing about David, being a part of Keith's plans and not saying a word to him.

He'd known this woman was going to stir things up, but he'd had no idea how much until now. What was he going to do with her? This wasn't a good thing, even though it felt better than heaven.

TEN

Sydney had known Gabrielle had a plan all along. Wednesday came, and the interviews were to begin. Sydney was partnered with Kira, and together they'd charm the pants off the citizens of Fairview Hills, making the lawsuit a lost cause. It hadn't been said in exact words, but Sydney understood that those she couldn't win over she was supposed to at least ask the right questions to confuse them enough.

Gabrielle begged and pleaded to come along, even though she knew she wasn't supposed to. In a display Sydney had to admit was impressive, Gabrielle convinced Kira that her life would be in danger if she stepped foot in Fairview Hills. Sydney didn't bother to protest. There was no controlling the girl.

"I'd say I was excited about having your company, but I have a feeling I won't have it long." Sydney drove cautiously down the streets of Fairview Hills.

"I can hang with you until noon." Gabrielle didn't miss a beat. "He's got to be at his second job at the zoo by two, so you gotta pick me up there, okay?"

Sydney felt like the girl's chauffeur. Whenever they went out, two cars would bring suspicion, so Sydney was left dropping her off and picking her up.

"So you want to protect Kira," she said, "but I can be all by myself in a crime-ridden neighborhood."

"That was show." She waved her hand. "Fairview Hills is harmless. At least during the day. You know where the zoo is, right? Right out of Fairview Hills in Druid Hill Park."

Sydney nodded. "We passed it coming in. Right off the Jones Falls Expressway."

"You're a quick learner," Gabrielle said. "Exit Seven."

Sydney wasn't too excited about being alone despite Gabrielle's reassurance. Fairview Hills reminded her too much of her home, where days and nights, especially nights, were filled with loud music, bumping cars, and gunfire. More patches of dirt than grass, bars on the windows, graffiti, litter in the streets. You never saw the decent people, even though you knew so many of them were still there, couldn't afford to live anywhere else. They stayed inside avoiding the others. Others—like the group of men a block away from where Sydney parked— grown men in their twenties and thirties playing hoops with a stringless basket in the middle of a weekday, music blaring obscene lyrics.

"It's 2018 Glaser Avenue," Gabrielle said as she read the first folder. "Right here. You ready?"

Sydney swallowed. As much as she'd ever be. For the life of her, she wouldn't understand why this was happening. Why wouldn't anyone want to leave here? They were being paid to leave a place no one but criminals wanted to come to. And they were probably being offered much more than it was worth.

"Yeah, they threatened us."

BeBe Foss leaned against the wall of her doorway. She

held the torn screen door open with her foot as Sydney and Gabrielle stood on her porch.

"Preston Corporation?" Sydney asked, her notepad out. "Can you explain a little more?"

She eyed the girls, appearing hesitant. "They called here and talked to Lenny—you know, my husband of forty-two years. Well, they told Lenny he shouldn't be surprised if he woke up one day and found his fruit cart gone."

Sydney nodded for her to continue.

"Lenny has a fruit cart. Pushes it along, sells all kinds of fruit. Mangoes, cherries, strawberries."

"You were saying . . .

"Watermelon. Cantaloupe."

"Preston called and threatened to take his cart if . . ."

"We live on social security," BeBe said, smoothing out her housedress. "That little cart, spring through summer, helps us a lot."

"If, Mrs. Foss." Sydney wrote on.

"No if. They called three times, said the same thing each time. 'Don't be surprised, old man, if you wake up one morning and find your cart gone.' "

Sydney wasn't clear on this. "Who exactly was it that called you?"

"Preston Corporation," she answered. "That's who we talkin' about, ain't it?"

"How do you know?" Sydney asked as she nodded. "How did they identify themselves?"

"They didn't."

"Then how do you know it was the Preston Corporation?" Gabrielle interjected.

"Who else would it be?"

Sydney looked at Gabrielle, her glare advising silence. "Maybe someone who wants to play a trick on your husband. Play with him. Someone in the neighborhood."

Mrs. Foss looked stunned as she held her hand to her ample bosom. "No one. No. My husband is loved here. The kids love Mr. Foss. No. It's the Preston Corporation that calls here. They're trying to make us sell and move out."

"Maybe you're assuming this because of the lawsuit." Sydney could see she was aggravating the woman, but she had to ask these questions. "If it was Preston, don't you think they would add something like 'If you don't sell your home, your cart will be destroyed.' Something like that?"

"They don't have to." BeBe folded her arms across her chest. "Three times they called. Each time, the same time of day, said the same thing with the same mean, scratchy voice. Each time it's the day after Preston came on over here and offered us money. I'm not stupid."

"It's still not proof," Sydney said, with very little conviction as she and Gabrielle headed for the next house.

Gabrielle was pouting. "What's with the attitude? I was only asking a question."

"Just chill with me today, Bree." Sydney sighed. "Besides, you won't be here long. And I'm not in the best mood. I have a feeling all these interviews are going to go just like that first one did."

Sydney almost fell back as Gabrielle attacked her with a bear hug.

"What is wrong with you?" She pushed the exuberant girl away.

"You don't even know what you just did." Her smile was ear to ear. "You called me Bree. I've been telling you since I met you that my friends call me Bree. You kept calling me Gabrielle. So we're friends then?"

Sydney shrugged. "I guess. I didn't even notice."

"I did." Gabrielle squeezed Sydney's arm until Sydney pulled away. "Buddy."

Sydney ignored her. "Can we get on with this? Next is Lester Owens."

She knocked on the door. A tall, burly man with skin the color of raisins and hair as white as snow opened the door. He was in his late fifties at least—a blue-collar working man all his life, and proud of it.

"What is it little girl?" He looked Sydney over, letting go of a quick smile before returning his face to a more comfortable frown.

Sydney introduced herself and Gabrielle. Before she could ask the first question, he started in.

"Yeah, I'm suing them," he yelled. "They cost me my marriage, 'cause I wouldn't give in."

"Can you elaborate on that?" Sydney asked.

He was reluctant, biting his lower lip. "I'm not going into detail in front of two females, but they blackmailed me. Threatened me with pictures."

"Who blackmailed you and what pictures?"

"Your client!" His eyes were filled rage. "Rachel and I been having some . . . disagreements. A few things going on. I had a little moment of weakness. Well . . . a few moments of weakness. This was about the same time Preston started sending flyers and calling us, trying to organize neighborhood meetings. I told 'em no. See, if they wanted to tear this down to build homes working-class folks can afford, then I'd consider it. But they're building luxury condos and town homes for rich white folks. Then one day, I get these pictures. I guess they been following me when they noticed I was going to be trouble."

"They?" Sydney asked.

"I got a call the day the pictures were delivered. From one of those Preston suits. Asking me to reconsider. I said, no! Damn, I had other things on my mind that day.

Then the guy, with that scratchy, shifty voice he has, says 'Didn't you get your incentive today? Your incentive to move?' I'm thinking, what? Then, he's going on about how I should say hello to my wife. That I was such a lucky guy to have her. Then hung up."

Sydney sighed. Gabrielle smacked her lips.

He continued. "They called a week later. Asking me if I'd had time to rethink my decision to sell. I said no, no, and for the last time, hell no! I mean, I had broken it off with Jessi . . . the woman. I was feeling confident I could handle the situation. Too confident. Rachel got the pictures the next week. She left me. She ain't spoken to me in two months."

He lowered his head in shameful self-pity and Sydney actually felt for him, although she assumed he deserved whatever he got. A cheat is a cheat, right?

"It ain't just me." Lester's tone was less aggressive now. "They threatened Alma Maxwell. Somehow they knew her son, out on parole, was visiting her and they threatened to tell the police."

Sydney raised a brow? "Why would anyone do that?"

"Well, his parole is . . . well, it's sort of self-initiated. But that ain't her fault! They had to been spying on her, 'cause none of us knew. She gave in. She sold, but someone anonymous called the police anyway. You won't find her on your list. She won't talk about it. It's just wrong. I mean, they can't be doing this to folks."

Sydney wanted to nod in agreement, but resisted. She looked at her watch. This day needed to end soon.

"You look like you've had one of my kind of days."

Sydney smiled appreciatively at Laura as she entered the kitchen and grabbed an apple from the basket. "It hasn't been a good one."

Laura checked on her Cornish hens in the oven before preparing the salad. "I'll have you know, Mr. Hart isn't at all happy to know Bree is walking around Fairview Hills."

"I thought he'd be happy to know she's working," Sydney said. "Really working."

Laura sat at the table across from Sydney and started peeling onions. "She's still a baby to him. He loves her very much, even though he won't show it. He worries about her. He doesn't think she understands the ugliness that's out there."

"Bree is quicker than he thinks." Sydney took a bite and leaned back. "Has Mr. Hart discussed any of his concerns with Victoria?"

Laura shook her head, concentrating on her onion. "He doesn't talk to her about much of anything. Likewise for her. I think this weird behavior with Bree and your insisting on doing this project is all they've discussed in the past month."

Sydney sighed. "With this project, do you think he really cares? Or is it just Victoria?"

Laura shrugged. "I figure it's more Mrs. Hart than anything, but she's better left unfettered."

Sydney didn't reply. There wasn't much she could say. She needed this. Her life, for lack of a better word, depended on it.

As if on cue, Victoria paraded into the kitchen, her eyes meeting with Sydney's. There was no emotion, no expression, on her face. She quickly looked away.

"Laura," she said softly. "Have you made the list for shopping yet?"

"No, ma'am," she answered. "I was—"

"Add roast beef for this Saturday night. Make it with something nice." With that, she eyed Sydney once more before turning to leave.

Sydney felt her shoulders release as she turned to Laura, who was staring at her in a peculiar way.

"What?" she asked.

"What have you been up to?" Laura gathered her chopped onions, carrying the board to the large bowl of salad.

"How could I have anything to do with roast beef for Saturday night?"

"That's Marcus's favorite dish," she answered. "He'll be here this weekend. Again."

Sydney felt the excitement stir in her. She hadn't stopped thinking about him. Even though he must hate her now, she couldn't stop fantasizing about their passionate encounter on the sofa. Her mind was stuck on what could have happened.

"Marcus hasn't been a regular at home in a long time," Laura said. "It's quite obvious why. Are you prepared for this?"

"Could anyone ever be?" Sydney asked, knowing very well she wasn't. Marcus coming home was the last thing she needed. Even if it was the only thing she wanted.

Gabrielle spread the documents and family papers over Sydney's bed.

"This is all I could find," she said. "You have to thank me. This wasn't easy."

Sydney talked her eyes. "Where were they?"

"Not in Daddy's private library like they used to be." Gabrielle made a smacking sound with her gum. "That's where I found them all locked up when I was working on this project before."

Sydney was looking the papers over. "How did you get them if they were locked up?"

Gabrielle winked. "I was desperate. No one here was

helping me. Daddy was ticked. I guess he moved them, thinking I wouldn't find out."

Sydney saw the deed to the house she was in, her eyes bulging at the price. "So where were they?"

"Still in his office," she said. "Not in his desk. Over in the old chest drawer in the corner."

Sydney set aside a stack of investment reports and CD holdings. "Did these help? They all seem to be financial."

Gabrielle looked them over. "This is weird. They aren't all here. There were some really old papers. I remember something looking foreign."

"What kind of foreign?"

Gabrielle shrugged. "Couldn't tell ya. Anyway, they looked interesting, but I needed Mother or Daddy to help me figure them out. That was my mistake."

"Anthony snatched them back, huh?"

"Right away," Gabrielle said. "I think he might have put those older papers somewhere else. These are all a bunch of receipts."

Sydney was ready to give up until she saw something that struck a chord.

"What's that?" Gabrielle asked, noticing Sydney's interest.

"Hearn Investigations," she read the full-page-size receipt. "This was stuck to a deed to a condo in Vail, Colorado, but it's got a Baltimore address dated only a year and a half ago."

"Never heard of them," Gabrielle said, scooting closer. "Knowing my parents, they probably had one of my boyfriends or my brother's girlfriends investigated."

Sydney didn't have the heart to tell her Victoria had sent someone around to Howard University to see what she was up to. She thought Gabrielle probably knew.

"Look at this," Sydney said, pointing to a line. "Under

description of service, it says source, Merricka Tesler—Owner—Family Traits."

Sydney reached for her folder at the edge of the bed. She knew what she was looking for, needing only to confirm it. When she had, she showed the picture to Gabrielle, whose eyes lit up.

"You think it means something?" Gabrielle asked.

"You said this picture of your aunt Dani was taken the last day she was here?" Sydney asked. "The day she and your mother had that big fight?"

Gabrielle nodded. "It couldn't be a coincidence."

"That your aunt would be standing outside a store called Family Traits that same day? No."

"The phone book is in the kitchen."

Sydney and Gabrielle headed downstairs. The house was quiet on a lazy Saturday morning, so they got no questions as they grabbed their purses and headed for Druid Heights.

They didn't see Marcus, but he saw them. As Sydney and Gabrielle ran out of the house, he could see the excitement in their steps all the way from his car further down the driveway. They were up to something.

Marcus hurried out of his car. He wanted to know what they were up to, but most of all, he wanted to talk to Sydney. He had to see her, touch her, kiss her. No matter how angry he was at her for what part she played in investigating David, he wanted her with a passion beyond words. Even if she had chosen to never speak to him again, he preferred that to never seeing her. He preferred anything to that.

But there was no time for that. Gabrielle was already taking off out of the driveway in a second. He had to find out what was going on. Marcus made up his mind to end this mystery with Gabrielle and find out what Sydney had to do with her behavior. He was getting an answer to his questions now.

"I'll be waiting outside for you, babe."

Sydney knew what was coming as soon as Gabrielle flipped her cellular phone closed. "Come on, Bree. Aren't you excited to find out about this?"

"Yes, I am, but I gotta take what I can. Gary is gonna meet me at the store. Just a couple of hours. Please, Sydney. I feel things closing in. It's coming out soon, no matter what I do. I want to enjoy the peace while I can."

"I could really use your help here, Bree."

"Who got you the papers, huh?" She winked playfully. "I've taken you out of this funk you've been in all week. You're excited about something now."

Sydney had to agree with her. This was the first time she had thought of anything but Marcus. As they parked across the street from the store, she vowed to get over whatever it was she felt for him. Anything else would only guarantee more problems for herself.

"Ms. Merricka Tesler?" Sydney approached the woman folding kinte cloth sweaters behind the counter.

She looked up, her middle-aged eyes large, green, and welcoming. She was petite, her complexion caramel, her hair a light brown with flecks of sandy blond made up in corn rows. She smiled with a little uncertainty. "I'm Mrs. Tesler."

Sydney introduced herself before handing her the picture. She knew she'd struck gold when an immediate look of familiarity hit the woman's face.

"You recognize this woman?" Sydney asked. "She's a . . . a relative of mine. Danielle Maple. Or it used to be Halat."

The woman smiled wider, her long, colorful earrings dangling. "In that case, nice to meet you, cousin."

Sydney blinked. "You're . . ."

"Distant," she answered, "but yes. What is your connection to the Halats?"

"The Harts," Sydney said.

Merricka raised her brow and handed the picture back to Sydney. "Oh, dear. Then I can't imagine how you heard of me. I'm sure Queen Victoria never said a word about me."

"How did Danielle hear of you?" Sydney asked. "And what did you tell her?"

"Danielle had been doing a little soul searching of her own," she answered. "She wanted to give her boys some history, some sense of self, so she hired an investigator to find her family."

"Your families never kept in touch?"

Merricka laughed. "Oh, no. The Halats don't keep in touch. At least not across class lines. Victoria has decided this side of the family doesn't exist."

"What is she trying to hide?" Sydney leaned forward. "I'll tell you the truth. I'm doing a genealogy trace and she's dead set against it."

"Of course she is. Like everyone else, she has skeletons in her family tree. But Victoria doesn't accept being like everyone else. She has to be better."

"Do you have some time to explain that?"

Merricka surveyed Sydney for a second, then glanced around her empty store. "I have some."

Sydney took notes as Merricka told the story of the Halats. They'd been separated for several generations, dating back to a racial scandal in the family's hometown of New Orleans, Louisiana.

"Her name was Sarah. She was the daughter of our great-great-great-grandfather, Louis. They were slaves on

Frank Halat's plantation. Louis's wife, Mary, was a beautiful woman. At least the slave master thought so."

"How do you know this story?" Sydney asked.

"The same way we all know much of anything about the more burdened of our culture: stories told from generation to generation. Too much respect to lie or embellish. We don't need paper to know our story."

"Go on," Sydney said, excited about what she was going to hear.

Merricka frowned, her face saddened. "Our men back then . . . our strong, courageous black men had to endure such . . . And our sisters, even worse. As I said, Mary was beautiful and the slave master took advantage of his position as so many did back then.

"Frank Halat was an all-over bad man, involved in all kinds of stuff. Well, when our Sarah was only twelve or so, Mary gave birth to her baby brother. The lightest child on that plantation. It was unexpected, because the grateful rumor was that Halat was shooting blanks. Of all the slave women on the plantation he violated, none were having light-skinned babies. All as dark as their slave fathers. At least dark enough to believe they belonged to their daddies. Halat's own wife was childless.

"All of a sudden, Halat decided he could love something. He took the baby to the house and took Sarah as well. Demanded she stay as nanny for the little boy he named Michael. He wouldn't let Mary anywhere near Sarah or her new baby, which she loved no matter who the father was. It was still hers. Drove her to distraction."

Sydney wasn't taking notes anymore, just listening, soaking in everything.

"As this went on, the mistress of the house had a fit over the turn of events. She raised mighty hell in the house, and was going to have her way eventually because she had the money from her Mississippi family. Halat had been a poor immigrant from France. Only a year after the baby was born, Halat's wife was found stabbed to death in her separate bedroom."

Sydney couldn't have seen anything more tragic or dramatic on a soap opera.

"Everyone on that plantation knew Halat had killed her—his behavior with the baby . . . And by then young Sarah was the talk of the town. He tried to pawn it off on Louis, who was then lynched by a white mob. He was a slave after all. No such thing as a trial. Suspicions died down for a while, but Halat just got worse. He was trying to bring Sarah and Michael with him to white social functions.

"As he felt the heat, he grabbed Sarah, Michael, and all that cash and left for the North. They settled in Baltimore."

"No one ever came after him?" Sydney asked.

"No. They only suspected. Then the war. Halat's money silenced the whispers about the race issue. Sarah always looked older than she was. Halat and Sarah went on to have children of their own, but none of them meant anything to Halat. He loved Michael. Spent all his efforts, his time, his money making sure that Michael was accepted into high society. They say it was because he was obsessed, and because Sarah's children were neglected. Sarah left Halat with her children, my ancestors, but wasn't smart enough to get any money. They were never legally married. Michael, from where Victoria came, was the first of the wealthy black Halats."

"What about your Louisiana relatives?" Sydney could see why Victoria didn't want people looking into her background. "The ones left behind."

"Gone as much as I know." Merricka shrugged. "Mary died shortly after Sarah and the baby left. She had no one. No husband, no other children. Lost her will to live."

Sydney sat down in a straw strewn chair next to the counter. As horrible as it all sounded, it was so incredibly interesting. "I think Danielle's interest in you came up at the Hart household and caused a big rift."

Merricka laughed, greeting a customer at the same time. "I would've loved to have seen her tell Victoria about knowing me."

"Did you ever make any attempt to reconcile with her?"

"No. I'm not proud of that, but I think we both know what the outcome would have been. Victoria knows I exist . . . that this side of her family exists. I think a couple of generations back someone might have tried, but found a dead end. It's better this way, just left alone."

Sydney thought to tell her of the private investigator receipt she'd found among the Harts' papers, but thought against it. What good would it do? So they had her investigated. Probably to gauge how much of a threat she might be. She was obviously none.

"Unless," Merricka said, "unless you decide not to leave it alone."

Sydney sighed, understanding the double meaning of her words.

"I don't know," she said. "I'll have to check for papers to document names and places. It's very scandalous, serious stuff."

"Yes, it is." Merricka's eyes lingered on Sydney for only a moment before she left to help a customer.

Sydney took down some notes and names Merricka had given her. She was going straight to the National Archives and Records Administration in D.C. to back this up with documentation. The other part wanted to slap it in Victoria's face, remembering the horrid things the woman said to her. Part of her saw such revenge as a way only to bring more of Victoria's wrath upon her, at the same time upsetting Gabrielle, Keith, and of course Marcus.

Marcus.

As she toured the store, looking over the ethnic odds and ends, Sydney and Merricka exchanged pleasantries for a while. Sydney thanked her before heading out into the hot June sun. She glanced at her watch as she stepped out of the way of passersby on the street. She had another hour before meeting Gabrielle. She intended to toss her pad and paper in the car and stroll the stores along the streets, but as she started across the street, she stopped dead in her tracks.

Marcus was leaning with his back to the passenger's side window of Gabrielle's car. His arms were folded tightly across his broad chest. He was wearing jeans and a T-shirt, clinging loosely to his muscled chest. Sydney could tell he was fuming, even though sunglasses hid his eyes.

Marcus felt a certain sense of satisfaction at Sydney's sheer surprise. As the waiting, honking cars forced her to cross the street and walk toward him, he was ready for her. All the beauty she held, the attraction he felt wasn't going to deter him.

"Where did he take her?" Marcus stood up and took Sydney's arm, pulling her up on the curb.

Sydney tried to find words as she felt a not so tiny spark from his hand on her arm. "I . . . what are you doing here?"

"Who is he?" he asked, with a hardened, ruthless voice. "Where is he, and where did he take her?"

Sydney pulled her arm away, thinking at first she'd play dumb. Only the look on Marcus's face told her not to even try. "How did you—"

"I followed you both here," he said. "I knew you were

up to something. I waited and watched as this thug drove up and Bree jumped on his motorcycle and drove off. No helmet in sight, mind you."

"Sorry," Sydney said as if that was partly her fault.

"I tried to follow him," Marcus went on, trying to ignore that he was touched by her apology. "But he lost me down an alley, my car wouldn't fit."

"You were chasing him with Bree on the bike and no helmet?"

"No. I was following. He had no idea."

Sydney opened the car door. "You'd better be glad. If he'd seen you and started flying, Bree could've been hurt."

Marcus moved to block her from getting in the car. "Nice try. Making me the bad guy. Who is that man and what is he doing with Bree?"

Sydney stubbornly pouted. "You'll have to ask her. Will you move?"

"I will not. Have you no shame?"

Sydney glared at him with burning eyes. "How dare you?"

"You've been lying all along about Bree and you know it." He was trying to keep his anger in check, remembering what had happened the last time.

Sydney felt the guilt all over, but her pride wanted to protect her from him. She hadn't seen him since he'd banished her from his home. It was so confusing for her. On the one hand, she had hoped he'd been aching to see her again. On the other, she'd wanted nothing more to happen between them. Now here he was, hating her for the lies and coverup. She couldn't blame him, but wanted to. Wanted to completely.

"I won't tell you," she said. "Because you're all trying to control her. Let her be in love, for Pete's sake. All you Harts—you're so cold, uncaring."

Marcus felt stung by her words. That's really what she thought of him and he'd given her every reason to back that up. It drove him crazy that he cared so much what she thought of him, but he did. Even as angry as he was at her now.

"Sydney," he said softly. "I know you hate me and I'm sorry for what I've done to cause that. But you're wrong if you think I want to know what Bree is up to in order to control her. Yes, Mother wants to know what she's doing, too, but we're all concerned. Believe it or not, my mother loves all her children. You've known Bree for only a short while, but I've known her all her life. She's done some crazy things as a kid, and she's still a kid—as much as she is a woman."

Sydney felt her body turn to mush as she was softened with compassion for him. Looking into his magnetic eyes, she believed every word he said, despite wanting not to.

"He's her boyfriend," she said. "His name is Gary. She's been seeing him behind everyone's back because she knows you wouldn't approve of her dating a mail clerk."

Marcus had suspected as much, but needed to hear it. Bree was a romantic. "Where did he take her?"

"I don't know," she answered, noticing his skepticism. "I don't. All I know is I'm meeting her at the entrance to the zoo in an hour. He works there nights."

Marcus wanted to say so much. He had missed Sydney terribly. This was more complicated than he'd ever imagined, and at the same time it was so very, very simple. He was falling for Sydney Tanner at the worst possible time in his life.

"You can follow me," he said, turning and heading to his car parked only two spaces away. He had to fight his feelings. This woman hated him. He'd only be setting himself up for pain.

Sydney felt like she wanted to cry for no known reason. She got into the car, feeling more depressed than she had all week. In life's cruel irony and unexpected turns, she'd come to understand that she cared for Marcus Hart. How much, she wasn't sure, but she knew it was more than physical, and that was a problem. A big problem.

As she started the car and followed Marcus's Lexus, Sydney felt defeated. She had to do something. There was no way she was going to allow herself to be pulled into this family further than she'd already been. It would be a living nightmare. She had to do something.

Marcus waited as Sydney pulled up behind him outside the park. He wanted to touch her, hold her as he could see she was sad. She really thought this was horrible, and he blamed himself for that. He wanted her to understand his intentions with Gabrielle came out of love.

Sydney took a deep breath as he walked toward her. He was so handsome, so out of her reach. How could he ever want her? she wondered. Really want her, not just as a temporary distraction, a physical diversion.

As they stood at Sydney's car, the silence was deafening and it grew tight with tension. Their eyes searched everywhere but each other's. The day was turning into a humid, hot one and sweat started to form at both of their brows only a few minutes after leaving the safety of the air-conditioned cars.

Marcus fought the desire that knocked at his door, as he watched a bead of sweat roll down Sydney's cheek, hit her chest right under her neck and trail down her thin cotton tank top, disappearing into heaven. He couldn't say he wanted her again, because he had never stopped wanting. He didn't see any way of getting out of this. He averted his gaze from her to the car. Think of anything, he told himself. Anything but her.

Sydney couldn't take it anymore. His nearness was becoming unbearable, the silence serving only to make her more aware of the tingling sensation in her stomach. It was too much. She'd already looked at her watch ten times, and couldn't think of anything else. She had to say something.

"You'll tell Victoria about this, won't you?" she asked.

Marcus nodded. "It's killing her, Sydney. She's worried, honestly. I have to tell her."

"She'll hate me more than she does now." Sydney had spent the last week resolving to stay at the Hart home. Now she couldn't see Victoria letting her stay. "If it's possible."

"I'll leave you out of it." Marcus could only hope Sydney was surviving his mother. Most people couldn't, but she seemed tough enough.

"You can't," she said. "Unless you lie, and there's been enough of that already. I'll have to leave."

"No." Marcus felt his adrenaline level pick up. "No, Sydney. Don't leave. I mean . . . where will you go? No, you can't leave."

Sydney didn't know what to make of his suddenly urgent behavior. Did he care? Could he care? Was she interpreting what she wanted to?

"It's just . . ." Marcus shook his head. "No, don't worry. Mother won't know about your part in this. I'll take care of everything."

"What about Bree?" Sydney asked, believing him. Believing his every word, and feeling a sense of comfort in doing so that scared her. "Will you take care of her?"

"I don't know." He looked into her hopeful eyes. She cared for Gabrielle, and he felt good about that. "I don't know this Gary."

"I don't really know him either," Sydney said, turning away. He was too handsome. "But Bree loves him and he seems to treat her well. I think he loves her. You know, just because he doesn't have any money doesn't mean he can't offer her anything."

"I know that. But I want the best for Bree. I'm sorry if this makes me a bad person, but that involves a guy who can take care of her in ways outside of her heart. I'm her big brother. That's what we do."

Sydney understood of course. She wished she'd had a big brother, anyone who loved her like that. "You think he might be after money?"

"Could be," Marcus said. "Or he could genuinely care for her, but I don't want her to fall for a guy with no direction or ambition."

"You can't control who someone falls for," Sydney said, understanding the irony of her words as she said them. "That's nature, chemistry."

As she spoke, Marcus knew he was completely taken. She was right and that was that. That was all there was to it, and he knew what he had to do.

He gently cupped the back of her head with his hand and lowered his face to hers. He wasn't fighting this feeling anymore.

Sydney let out a sighing breath as his mouth descended sweetly, softly onto hers. She wanted to cry because of the frantic relief that felt so good. Every muscle in her body relaxed as she stood still, letting the fire engulf her. He kissed her once, twice, then opened her mouth and explored it with his tongue. His other hand wrapped around her waist, bringing her soft, pliable body to his. Sydney felt her body melt into his as she raised her hands to his chest. The world was erased, she was in ecstasy. She could taste the sweetness of his mouth, and it made her soul weaken.

"Oh, Syd." Her name whispered from his mouth before it trailed to her warm cheek. "I want you so . . ."

Sydney felt herself freeze like ice and she pushed away. The look of horror on her face told only half of what she felt. She looked at a stunned Marcus, his face morphing with David and Linda Williams's. She couldn't breathe.

"Sydney." Marcus didn't know what had just happened. He could feel only her cold rejection and see the horrified look on her face. "What did I do?"

"Don't ever," she said, the words coming through choked. "Don't you ever, ever call me that!"

"What did I call you?" Marcus couldn't even remember. He couldn't have possibly said another woman's name. No other one was on his mind.

Sydney couldn't even repeat the hated nickname that flooded her mind with horrible memories. "Don't ever."

He stepped to her, wanting to understand, but she stepped back. What was going on? "Sydney, please. What is wrong?"

"Stay away from me." She felt sick to her stomach, completely nauseated. "Just stay away."

Marcus felt an arrow through his gut as she turned her back to him. He couldn't imagine what he'd said to cause this, but realized it was more than any one or two words out of his mouth. What had happened years ago to cause this? He knew it was something deep. That same something that held up those walls she carried around all day. He had come so close, then only a second later he felt further than ever.

Sydney fought back the tears as she thought of that name. That name that preceded insults, pain, criticisms, and coldhearted hatred. It made her sick every time someone called her Syd, but at that moment, it was worse than ever. She'd been so open, so vulnerable, so expecting of the opposite of everything that came with that name. She turned back to Marcus, who was still in amazement. He could never understand.

The roar of the engine brought the rest of the world back to both Marcus and Sydney as Gary's motorcycle pulled up to Gabrielle's car. She didn't get off, only stared at Marcus with her mouth wide open. Gary looked so scared, his hands were shaking as they gripped the handles of his bike.

"Get off, Bree!" Marcus's words didn't come through as authoritatively as he'd intended. He was still reeling from Sydney's rejection.

Gabrielle frowned, seeming to contemplate whether or not to obey. As soon as Marcus took one step toward the bike, she jumped off, eyes wide and innocent.

"Marcus, please." She shielded Gary as if she thought her brother meant him harm.

Marcus pulled Gabrielle aside and stared at the frightened young man. "Get the hell out of here."

Gary looked at Gabrielle, who nodded. He sped off as fast as lightning.

Gabrielle attempted to pull free of Marcus's grip, but he wasn't having it.

"Bree," Sydney said, as Marcus pulled her by. "I'm sorry, I didn't know. He followed us."

"A spy for Mother, no doubt." She sent a hateful stare at Marcus. "What are you going to do with me?"

"I'm taking you home." Marcus stopped, pulling his sister to him. "These lies and secrets end here."

"Sydney." Gabrielle's tone and expression pleaded with her as she was dragged along. "Come with me. I need you."

"No," Marcus said. He couldn't look at Sydney, knowing she'd make him lose his concentration. "You're not dragging Sydney into this anymore. You'll deal with this yourself. Come on."

Sydney felt for Gabrielle. She wanted to help her, but she couldn't be anywhere near Marcus right now. Her mind was racing. She felt anxious, restless. She had to get away.

Sydney took the coward's route when she finally came home that night, entering from the back of the kitchen. It was nine in the evening, late enough for dinner to be over and put away. She crept through the house, hearing idle conversation in the sitting room, possibly a television on down the hall. She headed for Gabrielle's room, but just as she set upon it, Laura opened the door and stepped out.

"Where have you been?" she whispered. She was holding an uneaten dinner in her hands.

"I had errands. Sorry I missed dinner. I need to talk to Bree."

Laura shook her head. "She's asleep. The whole uproar took all her energy. I brought her dinner, but she didn't eat a bit of it. She's cried herself to sleep now."

Sydney felt awful, although she wasn't sure how she could've helped her. "What happened when Victoria found out?"

"You can't imagine," Laura said, making a smacking sound with her mouth. "Mr. Hart couldn't even calm her down."

Sydney walked with Laura toward her bedroom. "Did Marcus . . . ?"

"He didn't mention you," Laura said with premonition. "Didn't have to. You know Mrs. Hart. She kept trying to drag your name in, but Marcus and Bree wouldn't let her."

"How did it end?" Sydney asked, grateful for their efforts. After the way she'd treated Marcus, she wasn't sure what to expect from him.

"May finally rolled in and established order." Laura laughed. "That old girl can control a room. She ended the fighting, but not the problem."

Sydney stopped at her door. "Thanks, Laura."

Laura smiled before heading for the stairs.

Sydney skipped her nightly chocolate milk, too afraid of running into Marcus, or worse, Victoria. She dressed in her nightgown and pulled her covers back. She had no expectation of getting any sleep. Just as she was about to slip in, she heard a knock at the door.

Her heart jumped, her senses coming to life. "Who is it?"

"Keith," a voice said from the other side. "You decent?"

Sydney grabbed her satin bathrobe, threw it on, and opened the door. Keith was dressed only in plaid pajama bottoms, revealing a thin, slightly hairy chest and holding a can of soda in one hand.

"Where's your bathrobe?" she asked. "What would Victoria say if—"

"She's asleep," he answered, inviting himself in. "You missed the show."

Sydney opened the door wide. "I know. On purpose. I chickened out, couldn't take it. Bree is a mess now, isn't she?"

"She'll get over it." He sat on the ottoman in the corner, between the bathroom and balcony.

"Keith, Bree is in love. Even with all your cynicism, you have to believe in that."

"A mail boy," he said, taking a swig.

Sydney sat on the bed, eyeing him discernibly. "You don't mean that."

"He's twenty-two years old, Sydney. A little old to be

wavering around this world. He never even went to college. He'd never survive my parents anyway. This is for the best."

His words sounded all too familiar to Sydney. "What is for the best?"

"They've forbidden her to see him," he answered. "Mother and Dad. She dialed Dad up and got his support. Put him on speaker and everything. Funny, the things they'll agree on."

"They can't do that," Sydney said.

"As principled as Bree is, being threatened with a cutoff of funds always brings her around."

"You stood there," she said, "letting them gang up on her."

He nodded unapologetically. "Marcus stood up for her enough. Mother needed someone in that room on her side. Not just Dad on the phone."

"Would they do it? Cut her off?" Sydney's heart sang with a bittersweet pleasure at the idea of Marcus protecting his sister. She found such pride in the things that he did, hoping that he was different than his mother, his brother. Then again, it didn't matter. She couldn't be with him. Not now.

"Don't think so." Keith took another sip, frowning at the taste. "This is warm. Besides, if we keep them apart long enough, her fancy is likely to change. We're talking about Bree, remember."

Sydney realized she didn't know Gabrielle as well as her family did. She hoped this was true. "Still, threatening her into submission is wrong. Can't you help her?"

"I have enough to deal with without getting involved in that silly girl and her nonsense." He stood up. "I'm gonna empty the rest of this in your sink."

As he left for the bathroom, Sydney leaned against the

headboard, anticipating sleep that she wasn't sure would come.

"Sydney."

Her heart was racing in less than a second as Sydney saw Marcus standing in the doorway. Still wearing his shirt from earlier, he had exchanged the jeans for a pair of thin black shorts, revealing his powerful thighs. Every time she saw him, Sydney wanted him.

"I just . . ." His eyes moved from her to the wall, the chair, then back to her. She was beautiful, and looking at her made him forget his own words, his own thoughts. "I wanted to apologize."

"For today?" she asked. "Don't. I really can't talk about it."

"I know I touched a nerve," he said. "Said something that triggered . . . Well, I only meant to . . ."

Keith, returning from the bathroom, stopped Marcus in the middle of his sentence. He saw him, half naked with a careless smile on his face, and Sydney in the bed, bathrobe on, covers down. He felt himself catch on fire as his hands closed in fists.

"Never mind," he said in a dark ominous tone before storming off.

Sydney knew what he suspected and part of her wanted to call after him and correct him, but she was too tired, too conflicted, too frustrated herself.

"What's up his craw?" Keith asked. "What did he want?"

"Nothing," she answered lazily. "I'm pretty tired, Keith."

"I'm leaving." He headed for the door. "But not before you come to the Orioles/White Sox game with me tomorrow. Preston Corporation has a box. It'll be fun."

Sydney would be grateful to get out of the house as

long as Marcus was here. "I'm looking forward to it. Close the door on your way out."

Marcus didn't get to sleep for a few hours. He paced the room he'd grown up in, trying to calm down. Could he have been wrong about Sydney and Keith? Did she prefer him? Was that why she pushed him away? Marcus wasn't able to accept that.

"Damn you, Sydney," he said to himself, sitting up in bed. "Why did you come into my life now? Things are bad enough between me and Keith."

He knew life was never simple, and he knew his feelings for Sydney were real and getting stronger every day. Most disturbing was that he also knew he wasn't about to ignore that. Not even for Keith.

ELEVEN

"They're trying again?" Sydney asked as she accepted a glass of wine from the steward working the Preston box.

She was referring to Preston Corporation's inviting David Long and the Fairview Hills community leaders to the box. As she watched a few of them enter, Sydney got a little nervous.

Keith guided her back to their seats. "We all know it's not going to work, but it makes us look good. The whole olive branch thing twice over."

"After what they . . . we did to David, why would they accept?" She noticed the ugly stares that followed fake smiles as soon as the recipients turned away.

"That's business sweetie." Keith leaned back, propping his feet on the chair in front of him. "They don't want to be here, but what do they look like if they don't come? We've got the playing card with what we know. They're not in a position to blow us off."

Sydney shook her head. "This is awful. Enough of this game-playing. Let's just get on with the lawsuit."

"This is law," Keith said, turning to the small crowd entering the room. "Ooohh. The opposition scores a point."

Sydney was struck with envy as soon as she saw them. Marcus entered the box, looking clean cut and smooth in a thin, white evening jacket over a tan polo shirt and jeans. With him was a coffee-colored woman, medium height, and in her early thirties, looking almost angelic in a white-and-peach-striped sundress. Her jet-black hair was wavy and long, her eyes were light and large. She didn't wear makeup. She didn't need to. She was beautiful.

"Excuse me, Sydney." Keith quickly stood up. "I have to discuss this new turn of events with the partners."

As Keith headed for Michael Wagner and Richard McDaniel in the far corner, Sydney struggled inside with her vulnerability and curiosity. Who was this woman with him that the firm would care so much to see them together? Her jealousy grew as Marcus wrapped an arm around her. She had no right to feel this way, knowing she had no claim to him. It was confusing, believing he wanted her one moment, then someone else the next. A woman could go crazy trying to understand a man's motives. Not her, Sydney vowed. No more.

"Be strong, Callie," Marcus whispered into her ear. He could feel her shaking as he held her. "I know you want to go over and curse out every single one of them, but staying calm is the best revenge now."

Callie smiled nervously. "I just wish David would get here."

"Your husband will be here in a few minutes." Marcus searched the room. "He never expected to run into one of his clients downstairs. He'll be finished in a second. Until then, I'm here for you and no one else."

When he saw Sydney, a ripple of excitement hit him, at the same time that sense of uncertainty. As her own eyes wandered the room, Keith came and sat beside her and Marcus felt his blood boil at the sight of them together again. He gritted his teeth as Keith leaned over and whispered into her ear and she sipped the glass of wine he'd handed her. Thinking them lovers, or something close, Marcus knew this was going to drive him crazy. He wanted, needed, to be with Sydney. The torment he'd felt last night after seeing them told him that, but what would it make him if he went after his brother's woman? What would it make him if he let this woman get out of his grasp?

"No one else?" Callie asked. "It looks like someone in particular is definitely on your mind. Who is she?"

Marcus knew he had to fight it. He had to somehow. "She's a friend of my family. Of Keith."

"Keith's a lucky man," she said, looking again to the door. "Thank God. He's here."

"David's wife?" Sydney felt herself exhale at the news. "Wow. I . . . That's good."

"No, it's not," Keith said as Richard and Michael joined them. "It's David's little way of sending us a message. Although it would be more effective if he was here, too."

"He is," Jesse said, nodding toward the door.

They all watched as David joined Marcus and Callie.

"Son of a . . ." Michael looked at Sydney and blinked. "Gun. Son of a gun. Does he think he's telling us something? So what if his wife doesn't care about the girl? The press will. The public, all potential jurors, will."

"I think the public has proven, in recent events, that they don't care about this stuff." Sydney accepted the disappointed stares of the four men.

"It's a game of poker," Richard said, as if Sydney never spoke. "He matched. Now we raise."

"It could be dangerous," Keith said, his eyes blinking nervously.

"What?" Sydney asked, feeling the tension.

"Plan C," Jesse Michaels said.

Richard put his hand forcefully on Jesse's shoulder. "Sydney, we need to talk. Us lawyers."

Sydney looked at Keith. He wouldn't make eye contact with her. She could see he wasn't comfortable with this, but wouldn't say a word. She pressed her lips together, walked away, wondering at first what in the world Plan C was, then understanding that she probably didn't want to know.

"Sydney! Over here."

Sydney turned to see Kelly Hart-Jorman standing near the mini-buffet table. She was handing a plate of tiny chicken wings to her son, Jordan.

"Haven't seen you in awhile," she said as Sydney approached. She looked tired, but happy. Like most working mothers. "So how's life in my old room? It was a safe haven in the middle of chaos for me."

"Considering it's bigger than my entire last apartment," she answered, "I'm loving it. And this must be Jordan."

The little boy smiled as Sydney knelt to face him. "How do you know my name?"

"Your mama told me about you." Sydney tugged at his Orioles jersey. He was a cutey, looked like his father. "I'm Sydney. I live at your grandparents' house."

He nodded, smiling wider now, showing a few missing teeth. "You're Uncle Marcus's girlfriend. You're Sydney."

Sydney stood up, her widely amazed eyes facing Kelly, who smiled with embarrassment.

"Sorry," she said with a giggle. "He . . . uh . . . I . . . Bree sort of keeps me updated on some things. I might have let it slip. You know kids. They blow everything out of proportion. I never said that."

"Yes, you did!" Jordan tugged at her shorts, a stubborn frown on his face. "You said Grandma's going crazy cause Uncle Marcus likes Sydney. Daddy said how did you know that. Then you said Aunt Bree told you that Marcus kissed Sydney. Then Daddy said—"

Kelly clamped her hand over his tiny mouth. "I . . . not exactly."

"I'm not his girlfriend." Sydney managed to maintain a smile for the boy's sake. "No matter what Bree told you, there's nothing going on between us. I'm not the least bit interested in Marcus."

"Who would suspect otherwise?"

Sydney jumped as Marcus appeared in their little circle, standing right beside her.

Marcus hid the sting of pain he felt at Sydney's comment. Make light of a bad situation, a wise man told him once. No matter how bad, and you'll be able to deal with it better that way. Marcus didn't feel any better.

Sydney felt herself heat up with embarrassment as Marcus leaned so close to her in order to kiss his sister on the cheek. She could feel his arm brush against hers, and smell a cool, sexy scent as well. She felt light-headed for a moment and blinked.

"Just ignore me," Kelly said to Sydney. She smiled at her brother. "Thanks for the invite. You know how Mike loves the games."

"Don't thank me," Marcus said, trying to concentrate despite the desire he felt being so close to Sydney. She wouldn't look at him, and it drove him crazy. "This was your twin's doing."

Sydney stepped to the left, not able to stand being so close to him. As she did, she caught a less than kind look from Marcus. Kelly cleared her throat, appearing nervous.

"Where's the big boy Mike anyway?" Marcus was insulted by Sydney's obvious revulsion to him as she stepped away. He felt like a fool coming over in the first place. Kelly and Jordan were an excuse—he'd wanted to be near Sydney, but that had only made matters worse.

"He's in the dugout!" Jordan said, pushing the tiny plate back to his mother. "Hot. I don't like it."

"He's stopping in the clubhouse to visit a couple of pills," Kelly said. "Can you believe it, they said no kids. Anyway, Mike loves utilizing the face power to build the business. He'll be up soon."

Marcus grabbed his nephew as the boy was jumping all over him. He kissed Jordan's cheeks over and over again. He loved the kid, although he hardly ever saw him. He knew why Kelly kept him away from Baltimore, stayed away herself. He couldn't blame her.

Sydney felt a tug at her heart, watching Marcus hug Jordan. An image of forever flashed before her and Marcus was there, kissing the son the two of them made together. Sydney smiled, her eyes closing briefly at the feeling of happiness that washed over her.

It lasted only a moment because she knew that would never happen. *Remember Celeste. Remember Gary. You'll never belong*, she told herself. *Never. Let it and him go.*

"Let me show him off to David," Marcus said, already setting off with the boy. It was harder than he'd thought, being next to Sydney. "He hasn't seen him in over a year."

Kelly waited until Marcus was out of earshot before whispering, "Does my brother have leprosy?"

"What do you mean?" Sydney reached for a carrot stick to busy her hands. Her eyes sneaked peeks at Marcus.

"The step-off was obvious," she said. "Just now. It was like he smelled like rotten eggs."

"I'm just a little uncomfortable," Sydney said in a half truth. "The law firm, Marcus and David. This game-playing is too weird to me. Everyone is acting so . . . civil. Like there's nothing going on."

"Par for the course for these folks," Kelly said. She paused, her expression changing to very serious. "Sydney, I was wondering if . . . I mean, you must think I'm awful—keeping my son away from his family."

"I'm not here to judge you," Sydney said, knowing full well why Kelly kept Jordan—and herself for that matter—away.

"I know. I just wanted to explain, even though I probably don't have to. You've lived at the house for a while."

Sydney smiled. "I have an idea. It's definitely an interesting setup there."

Kelly laughed. "Interesting? That's a fresh way of looking at it. Would the interesting setup have anything to do with why you push away from Marcus?"

Sydney's eyes shifted nervously. "What all is Bree telling you?"

"That both my brothers are developing a thing for you, but especially Marcus. You see, all Keith wants is to please Mother, so if Mother doesn't approve, you're probably safe from him. But Marcus, after the Celeste Johnson disaster, and the election, he doesn't care what either Mother or Daddy think. Kind of like me."

Sydney whispered, leaning in. "Bree told me about Celeste, but the election? That same year Celeste left, he lost the bid for Congress. What does that have to do with his relationship with your parents now?"

"He'll never admit it," Kelly said, "but Marcus lost that election on purpose. This was Daddy and Mother's dream, him becoming a state rep at thirty. He just stopped campaigning. Wouldn't talk to the press, nothing. Ironically he lost by only a little over two hundred and fifty votes. It was his way of getting back at them."

Sydney felt for him. "That was awful what they did, driving Celeste away. The poor girl. I know it hurt him. We've talked about it."

"The poor girl?" Kelly looked perplexed. "How much did he tell you?"

Sydney smiled nervously as she remembered the conversation that preceded their passionate kissing and embrace. They had come so close.

"He told me that your parents made it so hard for Celeste that she had to leave. Couldn't take it." Sydney thought. "Well, maybe Bree told me that. My information is a combination of the two of them."

"No, sweetie." Kelly's serious face held a hint of sadness. "Mother and Daddy did give her hell, but when Celeste left, she was very happy."

Sydney knew something bad was coming as the crowd roared at the opening pitch.

"When they realized," Kelly continued, "that Marcus was willing to take the struggle to marriage, they used Plan C."

Sydney felt an eerie chill at the familiar last words. "What were A and B?"

"A was to ignore her, B was to be mean to her. C was to offer her six figures to get out of town."

Sydney was shocked. "No."

"They took the nice little credit report they had a private investigator dredge up and found out Celeste was in serious, serious financial problems. That's what I heard."

"No," Sydney repeated. "Marcus didn't say that."

Kelly sighed. "Oh, Sydney. It killed him. She took the money and left. Mother and Daddy convinced her that this wedding, and therefore her access to Hart money, wasn't going to happen. So she took it."

Sydney felt weak and sick to her stomach as she looked at Marcus. Jordan was bouncing on his lap as they sat and watched the game. "I think Celeste sensed that he really didn't love her. She knew he wouldn't go all the way. So she'd get something out of this."

"Hey, girls." Mike approached them with a cautious frown. "You two look way too serious for a baseball game."

"Enough of the negative," Kelly said, wrapping her arms halfway around her husband. That was as far as they'd go. "Let's watch the game and pig out on some of these free eats."

Sydney forced a smile, but what she wanted to do was run to Marcus and wrap her arms around him. Why hadn't he said anything? She assumed it was still too painful. She could feel the pain this must've brought him as if it happened to her. Her compassion prevented her from turning away as he looked back at her.

Her eyes, her whole face was soft, serene and caring at the moment and Marcus felt a sense of bliss, untouchable satisfaction, and comfort wave over him. She was thinking, feeling something now that was stronger than those walls and she was looking at him. Marcus wondered if he was imagining it as Keith blocked his view approaching Sydney.

"What's wrong, Uncle Marcus?" Jordan gently slapped his uncle's cheeks with his open palms, his hands sticking to his face, squeezing it tight.

"Nothing, little man." Marcus winked, forcing a smile. "Nothing."

"Get it in gear, buddy." David was looking at him with all seriousness. "It looks like we're going to war. You gotta clear your mind. Are you here or not?"

Marcus nodded. "I'm here, man. No more distractions."

He didn't convince David. He didn't convince himself. For the rest of the night, his mind was scattered. He tried his best to enjoy the game and listen to David and the others on the community side of the issue. He cared about this, believed in this, but Sydney floated into every thought. He caught glimpses of her, laughing and eating, spending so much of her time with Keith. He knew he had to do something. He thought he'd be happier when she finally left, but after she was gone, all he wanted to do was leave.

Sydney avoided Marcus the rest of the evening, with the exception of stolen glances. Keith and Kelly kept her entertained with sibling banter. Even though she knew they were fraternal, she searched for twin similarities, but found none. She ate more than she should have and ignored the game after Chicago was down by eight runs in only the third inning. She was anxious to see if any arguments from opposing sides of the lawsuit would flare up, but none did. There was barely any interaction, and when there was, it was all generic politeness. Despite it all, her thoughts always veered to Marcus, as he all but stayed in his seat, keeping company with David and his wife. She was thrilled when Keith wanted to leave early to beat the after-game traffic.

"Am I boring you, darling?" May Hart leaned forward to pour herself a glass of iced tea.

Sydney shooed her hand away to pour it for her. "Not at all. I'm enjoying all these stories about the Hart kids."

They sat quietly in the Florida room of the Hart mansion, the sun reflecting through the glass doors. The intention was to learn of Hart ancestors, but the conversation quickly turned to stories of the Hart children. Sydney was torn, enjoying listening to stories of little Marcus, but also recalling her lonely painful childhood.

"Well, I'm done for now." She leaned back, smiling. "Dang-gone dog."

McKenzie was sniffing at her garden outside.

"I shouldn't hate him," she said. "At thirteen, he's probably as old as me. We old folks got to stick together."

Sydney stared at the woman, the soft lines of her face were comforting. She could sit with her all day and not be bored. How she wished she'd known May Hart in her childhood. Maybe she wouldn't have so much anger now.

"Back to business," May said gently slapping her thighs with both hands. "Now the Hart family is not great in numbers. We're quite easy to follow. Anthony had a little sister, Tracy. Beautiful girl. Born just a year after him. Didn't make it past ten. Multiple sclerosis struck her down. It left Anthony and his older brother by three years, Vincent. Vincent was designated as the leader, expected more of than even Anthony. He could handle it too. The Hart men are stubborn and strong, but World War Two took Vincent away, and the hopes the family had for him."

Sydney slid the tape recorder closer.

"So it was all left to Anthony. My young nephew. You see, Sydney, Hart women aren't let in on the important things. Now we are well educated, must be. Marry into good families, but the men control the Hart fortune and make the plans for the next generation."

"That was okay with you?" Sydney asked.

"What do you think?" May held her chin up high, stubborn. Now I was a big embarrassment, not married at twenty-one. Then by twenty-five, they gave up on me. No, I had other things in mind. I traveled and got my master's degree. It was fine. I wasn't the only Hart. There was

Kenneth, Anthony's father. He was three years my junior."

"Kenneth married . . ." Sydney knew she'd have a fairly easy time researching documents to back this up. Nothing complicated so far.

"Her name was Cleveland." May laughed. "Isn't that something? Of all the cities, Cleveland. Well bred like Daddy and Mama liked. Good family. I'd say, now don't quote me on this, she was twenty-two when Kenneth married her. Educated at Howard University. Kenneth was twenty-five. She was born in . . ."

"Cleveland, Ohio?"

"You'd think?" May laughed, shaking her head. "New York City."

"It was Kenneth who built the businesses our father started. The ones Anthony sold."

Sydney was impressed with the woman's sharpness.

"No." May's smile left, as a somber expression formed on her face. "Daddy built those businesses, Kenneth kept it growing, but Daddy really made them big. Daddy and his sister, my aunt Deborah, came to Baltimore in 19 . . . I think 1910. I'm not sure. He was only eighteen, she was twenty, but Daddy worked hard."

"What was his name?"

"Hugh Hart," she said with a nod.

"So Hugh wasn't wealthy when he came to Baltimore?"

"Oh, yes," she answered. "My grandfather, Reginald Hart, whom he never talked about, had much money. He never made it to Baltimore. Not sure what happened to him or my grandma on my father's side. My mother was Isabelle Montage, a fine, fine woman from a good family in Boston. Getting back to your point, my grandfather left most of the money to Daddy, some to Deborah."

"Getting back to Reginald," Sydney said. "You say he

and Isabelle never made it to Baltimore. Where was he? Was he a free man?"

May looked at her with confusion and hesitation. "It gets complicated there. I really can't remember. I do know my grandmother's name was Elizabeth Marie."

"Hugh and Deborah never talked about where they came to Baltimore from?"

Her eyes softened as she gazed out the glass doors. "It was so long ago. So many secrets. I remember the accent."

"African?"

"English, not American English. Old English. Daddy tried to hide it, and he did pretty good outside the house, but it slipped out when he was angry or had a little of the Satan sauce in him. Now . . . Aunt Deborah. She never let the accent out. I remember her practicing her American English all the time. Proper and perfect. When I asked her . . . Well, I stopped asking after a while."

"When did Deborah pass?" Sydney asked. "Did she marry? Did she leave behind any children?"

"I had a cousin, Edward Lansome. He headed West after Aunt Deborah and her husband, Samuel, were killed in a car crash. Never kept in touch, but I hear he does well. Samuel did well as an accountant. They left him a good deal."

Sydney noticed the great deal of untimely deaths in the Hart family. A lot of tragedy. She left this one alone, the Lansomes weren't Harts. She was sticking with the Harts now.

"Reginald and Elizabeth Marie," Sydney said. "We don't know where they're from, but it sounds like England. Do you think your father and aunt came to Baltimore from England? Or had Reginald and Elizabeth come to somewhere in the United States from England

and then Hugh and Deborah move to Baltimore from
there?"

May sighed, shaking her head. "I don't know. I'd never
heard of anywhere but Baltimore."

"You're getting tired, May." Sydney clicked off the recorder, noticing the woman's apprehension. "Let's stop
now."

"Yes," she whispered. "Let's."

Sydney was excited about what more she could learn
about the Harts. With English accents, this search was
going to take her out of the United States, which could
make this easier or harder. More interesting at least.

Dinner that night started as usual. Gabrielle pouted as
she always did, but more now that Gary was out of her
life. It was actually surprising to all that she even showed
up at the table. She usually had Laura send her food to
her room. Victoria shot hateful glances at Sydney, who
kept her eyes on her food. Keith tried to impress Victoria
with stories of his day. May's presence kept anyone from
shouting obscenities and everyone pretended as if they
weren't aware of the empty seat at the head of the table.
It wasn't until Laura began clearing off dessert that a
simple question began that night's drama.

"Now Aunt May," Victoria said as she waited for her
coffee to be poured. "I saw you and Sydney enjoying your-
selves in the Florida room today. I hope you didn't tire
yourself out."

This can't be good, Sydney thought. Any time Victoria
mentioned her name, an argument ensued. She watched
as Victoria's pasted smile turned to an impatient and annoyed frown as May rehashed the conversation she and
Sydney shared earlier that day.

"What was the purpose of that?" Victoria's tone was

controlled, yet high pitched. "Anthony said you'd given up this silly thing."

Before Sydney could respond to the insulting comments, Gabrielle spoke up.

"Don't you wish?" she asked, her angry eyes glaring. "But it's too late now."

Everyone's eyes were on Gabrielle, awaiting the storm.

"Bree," May admonished.

"What do you mean too late?" Keith asked.

Sydney turned to the girl sitting next to her. She was a loose cannon, her eyes like a bursting volcano.

"She already knows about you, Mother," Gabrielle answered, with a wicked smile on her face. "Does the name Merricka Tesler mean anything to you?"

Victoria's face went expressionless and lost a shade or two.

Gabrielle tore her leg away as Sydney grabbed it under the table. "No, Sydney. Why keep it quiet? You should be happy to know my mother, and the rest of us I guess, come from raping, murderous, slave masters. Our family came North with a secret—a horrible story. Old Sarah, she went willingly with the man who raped her mother!"

Keith dropped his fork and May gasped. Victoria's lips pursed, her chest was heaving as she shared icy stares between Sydney and Gabrielle. "How did you . . . Why . . . what do you . . ."

"That's why you've always been so secretive," Gabrielle spat out. "You didn't want anyone knowing the truth about the Halats. Oh, no! Daddy probably wouldn't have married you knowing where you came from. What would the ladies at the historical society say?"

Laura quickly exited the room without a word. Sydney would give anything to be her right now, but she was afraid to move.

Victoria looked as if she could slap her daughter. "You just shut your mouth, young lady. Not another word."

Sydney was stunned. "Bree. How did you know?" She whispered.

"You left all your notes on your bed," she answered. "You're a great note taker. It was a shock and a pleasure, putting two and two together."

"Gabrielle Marie Hart!" May spoke louder than Sydney had ever heard her.

It was loud enough to shut Gabrielle up. She leaned back in her chair for a second before pushing away from the table and storming out.

Sydney felt her entire body shaking as she looked around the table. May, Keith and Victoria were all staring at her.

"I . . ." She looked at each of them. "She's so angry about Gary. She . . ."

"She'll have to get over it," Keith said. Looking dazed, he stood up and walked behind his mother and began rubbing her arched, tense shoulders. "She knew I had to fire him."

"You fired the boy?" May asked. "It's bad enough you won't let her see him. You had to put him out of work, too?"

Victoria's eyes were set on Sydney. She'd be dead if looks could kill.

"It was her or him," Keith said.

"How much are they paying you, Sydney?" Victoria's words came out slowly, laced with hatred.

Sydney knew exactly what she meant, but only stared at her wide-eyed.

"How much?" Victoria repeated.

"She won't do it," Keith said nervously. "She won't do the project. Will you, Sydney?"

"It's not just money," Sydney finally said.

"This is ridiculous," May said.

"What else?" Victoria shrugged her son's hands from her shoulders.

"My tuition." Sydney couldn't believe she was answering, but she didn't feel she had a choice. She felt like a child.

"I'll double whatever you're getting." Victoria's eyes slanted.

Sydney envisioned this face directed at Celeste only a couple of years ago. She wanted to die. Everyone stared at Victoria as Sydney shook her head.

"I won't take your money," Sydney said.

"Victoria." May sat up straight, her chin lifting in an attempt to create order. "You stop this nonsense now."

Victoria ignored her. "Let's not waste time with pretenses of pride. You'll take it. Everyone takes money."

"Victoria," May said. "Remember where this got you the last time."

"I won't use it," Sydney said, standing up from the table. "I won't use the information."

"See," Keith quickly said. "She's not going to—"

"Why should I believe you?" Victoria asked. "I know you'd love to throw those dirty scandals out there."

"For Pete's sake, Victoria." May shook her head. "No one will look badly on you for this. It was generations ago. I don't know the whole story, but this type of . . . thing happened all the time."

"It's for your family," she explained to her aunt. "It needs to stay hidden for the Harts."

"Don't try to use my family to cover your embarrassment," May responded. "Keith, I've had enough of this. Help me to my room."

Reluctantly, slowly, Keith did as he was told. Sydney turned to walk out, only stopping as Victoria calmly called after her in just above a whisper. She turned around. Victoria was almost smiling, but it was such a cold smile, Sydney shivered. She was scared to death.

"How can I guarantee this?"

Sydney swallowed hard. "I'm not going to use any information on your family. I'll burn those notes tonight."

Victoria stood up and walked slowly to her. She was dressed all in white. She was almost always dressed in some shade of white.

"You'll burn them," she whispered, hands on hips. She was only a foot away. "But it's out now, isn't it? You've succeeded in making my daughter hate me even more."

"She'll get over this," Sydney said. "She's hurt and angry. She—"

"There you go again. Telling me about my children. For almost thirty, you're quite naive. You know nothing. There's a reason why some things are kept secret. You'll learn this."

Sydney stood defiant, alone in the dining room. She took only a moment to get ahold of herself. She'd been threatened before—by her own mother and stepfather, several times at that. She'd had no one to turn to then. She didn't need anyone now. So why now could she think only of Marcus, needing, wanting his arms around her? How could she possibly last this summer?

"Sydney! Come back, Sydney!"

Marcus awoke in the middle of the night, sitting up in his bed. He'd been dreaming of the day Celeste left him, but midway through the dream, she changed into Sydney. Sydney had taken the money and was leaving. He chased her, but he couldn't keep up. His mother held one arm, his father the other. He called her name over and over again. She never turned back.

Marcus threw the sheets off his sweating body. What was he going to do? He was becoming obsessed with thoughts of Sydney, wanting to touch her, kiss her, make love to her. He'd never felt this way about Celeste, about any woman.

Could he be so callous as not to care that his brother could be in love with her? Or she with him? He'd tried to be the peacekeeper so many times in this family, but war seemed inevitable. He'd wanted to walk away, like Kelly had, but he couldn't. With his father disappearing, Marcus knew he could never walk away. He loved his family, including his brother. Still his desire for Sydney was overcoming him, and he wanted to fight for her. But he was already fighting Keith too much.

"Damn!" Marcus's hands formed in fists.

In this bed alone. He was tired of this. He was tired of empty, superficial relationships that lasted only short months. Then alone again, waiting for someone to make him feel like . . . like he'd never felt before. Someone who wouldn't take any amount of money to leave him, no matter what. His mind kept wandering to Sydney. It was her.

Would it be Celeste all over again? No, he knew that Sydney was different. She was different than any woman he'd ever known and that was why he was falling in love with her. If she was with him, Marcus knew Sydney would never desert him. The problem was, how would he get her?

"Keith?"

Sydney knocked on the door to his office before entering. It was empty, and Ana was at lunch. Noon every day, she was gone. Most legal secretaries didn't get a break to breathe, but Ana wasn't playing that. Keith was on his own from noon to one, and he never handled it well.

"Be at my office twelve sharp," she repeated his phone message to herself. "We have a lunch meeting. Urgent."

She sat in his chair, swiveling around. He had a window, overlooking the Inner Harbor. Small, but still a window. Sydney looked out, letting her mind wander.

She was nervous, she hadn't spoken to Keith all week. Not since the scene at dinner. Sticking by his mother, which was occurring much more frequently lately, he'd ignored her out of respect to his mother. So, she wondered, what does he want now?

She heard Keith approaching and swung around in the chair. But when she saw who stood in the doorway, she lost the thought to stop her forward motion and went flying out the chair and onto the carpet.

Without hesitation, Marcus ran to her. "Are you all right?"

She let him help her up, her embarrassment flooding her face. Her head was swirling a bit, but she wasn't sure if it was from the fall or from Marcus's strong hands gripping her arms.

"I'm fine," she said, as she stood up straight. He was too close, his hands sending a quiver through her veins. "I'm fine. Thank you."

She wouldn't look at him, but he didn't care. Marcus could smell her fresh, unassuming scent, and that brought him more satisfaction than he'd had in a while.

"That was a pretty hard fall you took." Her skin felt like silk under his hands. He wanted her desperately. He was so happy to see her, at the same time wishing he hadn't. It only angered him to lay eyes on the woman he couldn't have.

"I'm fine," Sydney said. It was hard to breathe close to him. "Let me go."

Marcus hadn't realized how strong his hold on her was until her stinging words. He let go and she turned away. He refused to feel sorry for himself. He was a man, not a boy. He could handle this.

Sydney sensed how suddenly Marcus's mood had changed. She felt a chill as he walked past her to the window. She looked at his back, keeping one hand on the desk as her knees felt a little weak. He looked dashing as usual and time almost stood still when he was near.

"I heard about the chaos you've been causing at home." Marcus kept his voice in check, giving nothing away.

"The argument earlier this week," Sydney answered. "I've already—"

"Mother says you've been badgering Aunt May." He didn't believe that, but she was responding to him and that's all that mattered.

Sydney wasn't surprised. "I haven't at all. We've spoken a couple of times, but never too long."

He turned around, confident that he was under control. If she wasn't so horribly gorgeous . . . "Aunt May can be deceiving. She'll tell you she's fine, but she'll really be tired. She's a stubborn old woman."

"I know, Marcus." Sydney sat back in Keith's chair. He seemed effortlessly under control, while she had to clench her hands in fists to keep from shaking. "I've promised—"

"I know," Marcus said. "Mother appreciates that. You'll be leaving her family out. Although she'd be happy if you let it go altogether."

"It's not that simple." Sydney would give anything to let it, this, all go. She had no choice.

"I understand. You don't think anyone understands you, Sydney, but I do."

Sydney felt her insides melt all over as she looked at him. His words sounded so sincere, so soothing. His eyes, however, said nothing.

"I think Mother even respects your determination," he continued. "If only it was about something else."

"Let's be honest, Marcus. Your mother doesn't respect anything about me."

Marcus managed a sympathetic smile. "You're wrong. You're really the first person to enter her realm that didn't break under her scrutiny and bend over backward to please her."

Sydney wished she could only tell him how close she was to breaking, to losing it completely.

"All I ask," he said, "is that you take it easy on her."

Sydney's eyes widened. She was incredulous. "Look, Marcus. I know she's your mother, but . . ."

"But you don't know what she's going through," Marcus said. "Right now. She's devoted her life to being a good wife and mother. As wrong as her actions toward both goals have been, we are still everything to her. Bree is giving her hell, Kelly acts as if she's never known her. Then there's Keith and myself. This lawsuit, and what it's doing to us is ripping her apart. Not to mention Dad and his . . . other interests. He has no use for her now. It's tearing at her soul."

Sydney felt so much sympathy for him. She deeply respected him for standing up for Victoria after her part in the whole Celeste affair. Celeste. The name brought her back to reality. Sydney knew she couldn't afford to feel sympathy or anything else for him. It would only lead to . . .

"Marcus. What are you doing here?" Keith's eyes held mistrust and anxiety as he entered his office with Ana trailing behind.

Sydney jumped up from his chair, thankful for his arrival.

"We have a lunch date, remember?" He smiled at his brother's harried secretary. "Hi, Ana."

"Hello, Marcus." She blushed and blinked rapidly.

"He's aware of the meeting. I told him first thing this morning."

"Yeah. Yeah." Keith gave Ana a folder and she left promptly.

"I just came from visiting Mother at home. She's in bed with her fainting spells." Marcus's tone left a hint of disbelief, knowing her spells were a figment of her own imagination. "You and I need to call a truce."

"So we have lunch so we can say we like each other again." Keith's tone was sarcastic.

"Keith." Marcus's patience was thin, but he wanted this sincerely. "We can try."

Sydney started backing out of the room. "Then I'll just be . . ."

"No." Keith held up a hand to stop her. He walked to her, whispering in her ear. "You'll have to come to be a mediator. Otherwise, we'll kill each other."

Sydney sighed. How could she explain to Keith how every moment spent with Marcus tore her heart apart? She couldn't, so she nodded as her shoulders slumped.

Marcus held his envy in check as he watched them. Keith whispering in her ear, touching her shoulder. Anger singed at his nerves as she smiled and nodded. Would he ever come to accept this? He knew he wouldn't.

"Sydney's gonna join us," Keith exclaimed with a proud smile. "In her honor, I say we hit Morton's of Chicago. I feel like a good old-fashioned steak."

Marcus didn't bother to smile. He realized his hands were clenched in fists, and only let go when Keith took his hand off Sydney's shoulders.

Sydney was too embarrassed to admit that she'd never been to the famous steak house that originated in her hometown. She and Keith had taken the firm's car to the district, Marcus trailing behind. Sydney picked at her medium filet mignon and scalloped potatoes as the tension was twofold and thick as sin.

She felt Marcus's eyes on her, and sensed a hidden anger. To add to it all, every attempt at a civil conversation between Marcus and Keith turned cold or confrontational. When a final attempt brought the discussion to David's former mistress, Sydney had to step in and break it up before they almost came to blows. Dead silence followed for ten minutes. It wasn't until a middle-aged woman, heavy set and dressed all in banana yellow, approached.

"Mr. Hart," she said, with the most appreciative smile. "Congressman Marcus Hart!"

Marcus turned on the charm. He had no idea who she was, but he worked for her. He had to charm, no matter how he felt.

"You don't remember me," she said, taking his hand in hers and cupping it affectionately. "My name is Hazel Locks. I wrote you about my grandbaby, Luther."

Marcus's memory clicked. He was good at this. He did care. "Luther Locks. Yes, yes. Your poor grandson, wrongly arrested for mugging that woman at a gas station. The police coerced that confession."

Hazel held a hand to her heavy, heaving bosom. "Oh, Jesus Lord. No one believed us but you. You pursued the case and got those charges dropped, that false confession ripped up."

Sydney watched as Marcus empathized with the woman. He had a flair, a style, a way of consoling a person that locked up their trust. A smile that could sweep anyone off their feet didn't hurt either. Sydney could watch him for hours. No matter how much of this was predetermined by Anthony Hart, this was Marcus's destiny: to be a voice for the masses. A natural who wore his power, as if he'd had it since birth. Which was pretty much how it had been.

"You've fallen under his spell," Keith whispered in her ear. "You all do."

Sydney rolled her eyes, embarrassed by her obviousness. "Can you chill with the green monster for a while?"

He frowned at her.

"You asked me to come so I can keep peace." She shrugged. "So when play resumes, take it easy."

"You saw him," Keith said. "He pretended to want a truce for family harmony, but he's here only to convince me to lay off David Long."

"Laying off David Long would increase the peace between the two of you." Sydney spoke with a stern tone. "It's also a good idea."

Keith sighed. "Screw peace. I wanna win."

Sydney was surprised by the look of vengeful anger on Keith's face. It was new, at least for her. He was changing, becoming harder, colder.

"Tell me what Plan C is," she demanded. "What are you up to?"

"We," he corrected. "What are *we* up to? Don't worry, Sydney. We're holding off for Plan C. You just do your job and we'll back it up."

"What did I miss?"

Sydney's eyes lingered on Keith for a moment, as Marcus returned to their conversation. Recapturing his attention sent a satisfying and exciting chill through her, which Sydney did her best to dismiss.

"We were just admiring your performance." Keith leaned back. "Four stars. That senator seat is calling you, bro. Too bad about this lawsuit. When your guys lose, you can kiss it all good-bye."

Marcus grinned sarcastically as Sydney shot Keith a warning glare.

Marcus wanted Sydney's attention again. He felt his temperature rise every time she turned to Keith, and he sensed that Keith enjoyed it.

Keith glanced down at his watch. "If we leave before two, we'll get back by three and still keep the idea of a respectable day."

"Actually," Sydney said. "I'm staying down here."

Keith frowned.

"I have to do research, Keith." Sydney's stomach tightened, her eyes focusing on a morsel of potatoes. "I was going to do it tomorrow. I cleared the time off with Hillary, but since I'm here, it would be a waste to come back tomorrow."

Everyone at the table knew she wasn't talking about the lawsuit. Keith sighed and placed his napkin on the table.

"You're pretty stubborn." Marcus could tell she was anxious, and although he wished she'd give this up, he admired her persistence.

Sydney smiled, taking his compliment better than she usually took any compliment. "My next step is the Library of Congress."

"You can come with me," Marcus said, caring nothing for the vehement stare from his brother. "I can show you around."

"I've been there before." The concept of being alone with Marcus, even in public, concerned her. Sydney didn't trust herself. Already she felt herself getting tense at just the thought. No. No way. "I'm a student, remember."

"Then you have your registration card?" Marcus asked.

Sydney gritted her teeth. She'd forgotten it at the special reading rooms in the three-building library at the capitol. "I can get it easily. All I have to do is provide some identification and . . ."

"Regardless." Marcus felt his second wind come on after speaking with Mrs. Locks. She seemed resigned, but he was good at getting his way. Maybe Sydney wouldn't be his woman, but if he knew anything at all, he knew that maybe was just as much yes as it was no.

If it happened again, Sydney knew she'd lose her mind. Marcus was excruciatingly kind and tender as he joined her in the library's history and genealogy reading room. He was even flirtatious. She felt as if he was teasing her, daring her to give in to her attraction to him. It was working. Sydney counted. In the last fifteen minutes, he had touched her seven times. The accidental brushes were the worst. They sent her temperature soaring—the hair on her arm stood up. She felt beads of sweat on her brow when his hand trailed over hers as they reached simultaneously for the same catalogue.

Marcus swallowed hard. He was mustering every bit of strength he had as a man to keep from grabbing Sydney and making love to her right between the shelves. He could smell the flowery scent of her hair, and wanted to run his fingers through it. Her smile was so innocently seductive, and the swing of her curvaceous hips mind-blowingly subtle.

The conversation was infrequent and irrelevant as they searched among the 532 miles of shelves separated in three buildings on Independence Avenue. The genealogy room was in the Jefferson Building, the oldest of the three.

As the inadvertent touches mounted, so did the tension. Sydney was doing her best to keep control, but all her efforts were shot down as a couple of college-age girls rushing down the aisle, giggling, accidently forced her back out of the way and right into Marcus's arms.

As if on instinct, Marcus responded to his desire by

swinging her around him. Grabbing her arms, just under her shoulders, he pulled her to him. All of today had been building up to this.

"No." Sydney's words came as a whisper as she turned her head from his. "Marcus, don't."

"Sydney." The passion was threatening to take him over. He wanted to taste her lips again, have her hands on him. "I want you. I have to have . . ."

"We can't," she said, unable to let him finish. She couldn't bear to hear him talk like this, his voice deep and husky with longing. Her knees felt weak again. She wanted him to let her go, but feared she'd fall to the ground the second he did.

"We can, Sydney." He lifted one hand to caress her cheek. Her eyes closed for only a moment, and the movement pulled at the deepest part of him. "I know you feel this. I can't ignore it. I won't. I love my brother, but I can't think of anything but being with you. It's driving me insane."

Sydney was dumbstruck by his confession. No one. No one had ever said anything like that to her. Not even remotely close. She wanted to give in, give in now. But no, no, no. "Keith is not—"

"Do you love him?" Marcus asked.

"No." Sydney shook her head. "You don't understand."

"I do," he answered, having heard all he needed. "You don't love him, but I know you could love me. You could love me and I could love you completely."

Sydney felt tears coming on. Was he really saying this? Had she ever been so happy to hear any words, and so scared at the same time?

She held up a hand to stop him as he attempted to speak again. If she let him continue, she knew she'd betray herself. "It could never happen."

Her words slapped him in the face. She'd just admitted she didn't love Keith. She could let him go. She would. "I don't accept that."

"You have to," she said. "I won't deny this pull, this attraction. It's strong, but what would it cost me to go forward?"

He frowned, confused, until her expression changed. He understood now, and his heart fell with a thump. This woman, this young unassuming woman controlled his every emotion. "It wouldn't be that bad."

She raised a brow. "Victoria would make my life hell. You know its true. Anthony wouldn't accept me either—not ever."

"I'm my own man," he demanded. "I'm not a boy. My parents don't determine my life anymore."

"You're a Hart," she said. "You live in a world with a society that . . . I just couldn't deal with it."

"I wouldn't make you. I wouldn't be a man if I made you deal with my baggage. I'll handle them."

Sydney wished he would quit persisting. Her heart wanted to give in, but her mind, her memories, warned her. There was something else she had to do first. Love comes later. Love on a more even playing field. She had to get there on her own first. She couldn't romance her way there. It wouldn't count then. She pushed away.

"I could love you," she admitted. "Even maybe you could love me."

"Not maybe," he corrected. "I'm already falling . . ."

"But there are forces stronger than love." She couldn't bear to hear another word from him. "These forces are driving me, and they don't leave room for love."

"These forces are just walls. They're walls you've built up to protect you from something. You don't even know what."

"I do know what." Sydney fought back tears. "I know

exactly what. You'd never understand, but I can't do this. This can't happen."

Marcus hid his pain, his anger at her rejection. "What do you mean by *this*? You and I sharing with each other? Loving each other? Is that the *this* you say can't happen?"

Sydney let out a breath, her stomach tingling in anticipation of what he'd said actually happening. Oh, how she wanted it. But life wasn't about what she wanted. It was about what she had to do.

"Yes," she said. "*This* can't happen."

"Sydney Tanner," he whispered, leaning closer. His words affected her, he could tell. There was no way he'd give up. "*This* is inevitable. I don't see how either of us can stop *this*."

As he walked away, Sydney had to hold on to the shelf to keep from falling down. Did he intend to pursue her? How could she possibly fight that?

She couldn't. Sydney knew she wouldn't last long. Then everything would fall apart. Just as her mother had said it would.

TWELVE

Gabrielle entered the kitchen just as Sydney turned off the heat underneath her milk.

"Long time, no see." She watched as the thoroughly depressed girl sent her a bitter smirk.

Gabrielle had been in the worst mood since the blowup. She hadn't talked to Victoria or Keith in days except to insult them. She'd been all-around unpleasant, and Sydney thought it best to avoid talking to her about Marcus. It wasn't easy, being as he was absolutely the only thing on her mind.

"Cheer up, sweety." She stirred the chocolate in her cup and joined Gabrielle at the kitchen island. "The summer is almost over. Next thing you know, we'll be safe in D.C. again."

"I'm not going back to school." Gabrielle dug her hand in a box of crackers shaped like goldfish. "I'm not."

"You have to. Besides, it's the best way to be away from her."

"I'd be doing what they want," Gabrielle said, her voice full of disdain. "Why do they get to call all the shots? Do you realize what they've done? I love Gary!"

Sydney placed a hand over hers, squeezing. "I know. It's wrong. It's only wrong, nothing else."

"What's worse is I accepted it. I mean, I had to decide

that Gary wasn't worth being on my own. So they get that satisfaction, too. Me admitting I'm too damn scared and spoiled to be on my own at twenty-three. I hate them."

Sydney saw herself in Gabrielle's eyes. "Bree, no. Don't be that way. Use your anger to think positive. The best way to get back at them is to finish your education and make your own way in this world. Then you can live your life as you choose, with whom you choose. No matter what they think."

Gabrielle shrugged, rubbing red, tired eyes. "I just don't care."

"Well, you're dampening an already moody house, so start caring."

"What am I supposed to do?"

"Stop trying to start fights with everyone you come across. I'm doing my part. I'm throwing your mother's family out, and you're not going through my papers."

"I apologized for that," Gabrielle said. "So you're still doing the project? What have you gotten?"

"What did I just tell you?"

Gabrielle pouted. "I'll bet you're telling Marcus."

Sydney blushed, a smile a mile wide appearing on her face. "I'm keeping that to myself, too."

"Just tell me," Gabrielle said. "Is it juicy?"

Sydney couldn't tell her how X-rated her dreams of Marcus had been over the past week. She'd done a good job of avoiding him, but felt her resistance weakening. "I'm not gonna to get graphic, but I'll tell you that things have gotten hotter between us and I have to do something about it."

Gabrielle didn't crack a smile. "You do. I'd tell you to run as fast and far as you can. The last thing you want is to end up as a Hart."

Sydney wasn't going to argue that point, so she left it alone. "Look. You're going to come back to school with me. I'll drag you by your eyelashes if I have to. Just do your best to act like a human being in the meantime, and it'll all go by like a snap."

Gabrielle snapped her fingers. Sydney nodded reassuringly. Gabrielle smiled a genuine smile for the first time in what seemed like forever. They both laughed, neither aware of the person outside the kitchen listening to their every word and getting very angry.

In her room ready for bed, Sydney slowly undressed. She heard Gabrielle mulling around in the bathroom and wanted to give her some privacy. She wanted to take a shower and hope to think of nothing. She would settle for thinking of anything other than Marcus, but wasn't hopeful. She knew, being with Marcus would lead to disaster. At the same time, such sweet disaster. She'd been here since May and June was nearing its end. It felt more like a year than a month and a half. School started the last week in August.

She'd never make it.

As the noise ceased, Sydney grabbed her robe and walked naked into the bathroom. She was having a good body day, which didn't happen often. The sight of herself naked today didn't recall memories of name calling, endless diets, and romantic rejections. Today she loved her healthy glow, her hourglass figure. She thought of Marcus and wondered . . .

Sydney opened her mouth but couldn't even scream. She was so startled, her voice left her. She was frozen as Marcus lifted himself from the tub and took in a full view. The smile that formed on his lips brought her back to furious reality and she snatched the bathrobe that had fallen out of her hand and to the floor in her surprise. Covering herself, she ran out of the bathroom.

"That's just about the best way to end a day I've—"

Marcus was stopped cold as he entered the bedroom. A strong slap to the face sent a sliver of pain rushing through him.

"What in the hell are you doing?" Sydney was livid, humiliated. She wanted to die.

"I'm fixing the handle you broke." His hand rubbed his smarting cheek. "I thought you heard me."

"Get out!" She pointed her arm like an arrow to the door. This fix-it fetish he had was only causing her trouble. "Stay out of here."

Marcus couldn't hide his attraction. Didn't want to. "If it makes any difference, I think you're beautiful. You have a perfect body."

Sydney's arm lowered as she met eyes with him. He meant that. No one. No one had ever said that. Not even the few men who had seen her naked. Why did he have to be the one who said all the things she'd been waiting to hear her entire life?

Marcus saw his window. He didn't hesitate. "I'm sorry for the intrusion. I'd say I'll pretend I never saw anything, but I couldn't. The vision was too beautiful. And when you're mine . . ."

"When I'm yours?" She pulled tighter at her robe, feeling it wasn't nearly enough of a barrier between them. "Guarantees always get you politicians in trouble."

He loved her wit. "Not me. I never guarantee something unless I know it will happen. We *will* happen, and you *will* be mine."

"Good night, Marcus." She had to turn away to avoid him seeing the weakness of her armor in her eyes.

"It'll take more work than I anticipated," he said, slowly heading for the door. He'd enjoy the sweet torture of anticipation. "But I'll get ya. I'll get ya, and I'll keep ya for good."

Sydney waited until the door closed behind him before letting out an exhausted sigh. Don't fall for it, girl, she told herself. He's a charmer for a living. The price would be too high.

> Sydney heard her mother pacing back and forth in the hallway. David Williams had been gone for two weeks this time, matching his longest desertion. Sometimes it was a fight, other times another woman that temporarily caught his fancy.
>
> "Forget him" was all Linda Williams had to say.
>
> Sydney poked her head out her room. She'd never learn. "Mom, he'll come back. He always does."
>
> "Who cares?" she lied. "They all leave. Learn that now. They'll promise you, Syd. They'll charm your pants off. They'll say they love you forever, keep you forever. Means nothing. Not to women like us. Women like me and you. Men always leave us."

Sydney hadn't fallen for that. As she stepped into her warm, scented bath in the cool bathroom, she believed that when she was able to love after all other goals were achieved, she would find an everlasting love. Only it could never be with Marcus.

"There's no way." She spoke to herself, laughing sarcastically. "Falling for a Hart would be the worst possible predicament in the world."

Sydney leaned back, needing this break. She wanted to relax, but knew she never could while in the same house as Marcus.

As Sydney opened the door to her bedroom, the comfort of the bath was erased with a certain uneasiness. Her papers, all of the research she'd spent the afternoon at the library compiling, had been moved around. She'd remembered packing everything neatly in a folder in her knapsack, and closing the snap tightly before placing it all at the top, left edge of her bed near the headboard.

The knapsack was now at the center of her bed, with the snap closed, but loosely. It appeared as if everything had been hastily stuffed in there. Sydney felt an adrenaline rush as her heart started beating fast. She gripped the post of her bed, her knuckles turning white. She hadn't locked her door after Marcus . . .

Without thinking, Sydney threw on the shorts and T-shirt she'd been wearing earlier and stormed out of her room. She headed straight for Marcus's room, which was on the other side of the house, past the stairs. Just as she reached his door, he was coming out, a clean plate of what had been dinner leftovers in his hand.

His eyes met hers with surprise and he smiled widely. "Sydney—a change of heart?"

She hauled off and slapped him, but regretted it as soon as his face turned back to her.

Marcus tossed the plate on the table against the wall, fuming with anger. "What the . . ."

"Why did you do it?" she asked. "Did Mommy beg you to?"

"What are you talking about?" Marcus tried to control his anger. It was hard. The roller coasters this woman put him on.

"My papers! I know you took them out of my bag."

"You don't know what you're talking about." He saw her hands form in fists. "Don't even think about it. You've used up your strikes there. Hit again, and I'll hit back."

"It was all a game, wasn't it?" Sydney kept her hands down. She knew she was yelling, but she didn't care. "Pretending to help me with my research, pretending to care about me, want me. All a lie!"

"None of that was a lie." Marcus felt his pride take a blow, but he stood his ground. "Never. I meant every bit of that. Now tell me what you're talking about with these papers, and do it now. I'm not standing here one second longer for this nonsense."

"My research papers for my project were tampered with."

"When?"

He was confusing her with his empathetic tone. "I . . . I don't know. While I was in the bathtub or while I was downstairs with Bree. While you were supposed to be in the bathroom fixing the tub handle."

"So I did this?" he asked with sarcasm. "Since you know everything, can you tell me why?"

"Mommy asked you to. Keeping secrets secret. That's what you Harts are—"

Sydney hadn't even a second to think before his lips were on hers. Hungry and angry at the same time, his mouth ravaged hers. Immediately Sydney was aflame with desire, wanting nothing more than to melt into him.

Her hands, her body, never attempted to struggle, fight him away. He was in charge, or so Marcus thought as he kissed her. It was his intention to shut her up, control her rage somehow, but it had quickly turned on him. It was now about need. A dying need to satisfy his daily, nightly, constant yearning for this woman. He controlled nothing. She was his master, and he would be her willing slave. But first he had to earn her trust.

He grabbed her arms and held her away from him. Her eyes were hazy, she was weakening, but still trying so hard to hold up those walls. He loved her, and he knew it. He couldn't even pretend that was further down the line anymore.

"You tell me, Sydney." His voice broke with huskiness and passion. "What does that tell you? Did I do this?

Could I have? You don't need to ask, or speculate. You know. No more excuses or accusations to keep from caring. I won't let you fear me, fear us, anymore. I won't."

But she did fear. Sydney felt fear sweep over her. The fear that comes when you've lost control of not just your body, but your mind, your free will. She wasn't falling in love with Marcus Hart. She was already in love!

"No," she said, shaking her head violently. "I can't. Not now. I won't. Not yet."

She tore away from him, running down the hallway. She headed toward her room, but through tears she could see Gabrielle and Keith standing in the doorways to their rooms. They were both staring with confusion and concern was written on their faces.

Sydney averted them, heading down the wide staircase. She didn't know where she was going, but she had to go somewhere, breathe some fresh air and cry her eyes out. At the bottom of the stairs, she headed around the corner, toward the sitting room. She was stopped in her tracks as she was met by Victoria and Anthony. Both heads turned to her with alarm.

"What is it, girl?" Anthony asked, a hint of concern on his face.

Sydney wiped her tearing eyes, unable to speak. They'd been arguing, she could tell that much. They'd been arguing and Victoria wasn't at all happy to be interrupted.

As Marcus showed up in pursuit of Sydney, everyone's eyes set on him. It was obvious to his parents what was going on.

"What have you done, Marcus?" Anthony stepped forward, staring his son down.

"Stay out of this, Dad." Marcus had only Sydney on his mind. He hadn't meant to upset her so much. "Sydney, let's talk. Please."

"No." Sydney felt cornered. She couldn't even look

him in the face. She kept wrapping her hair behind her ears.

"You heard her, Marcus." Victoria sounded choked up—a rare sound for her voice. "Leave her alone. As a matter of fact, why don't you head on home? *With* your father!"

Anthony sighed. "Victoria, please."

Sydney was surprised to see tears in the eyes of the woman she thought had no real feelings.

"Don't please me," she snapped. "Marcus, your father has determined he must go back to D.C. tonight, even though he doesn't need to be there until Monday. A phone call created the urgency. Who was she, I wonder?"

"Victoria." Anthony seemed more annoyed than anything.

"Maybe he should leave," Marcus said, feeling nothing but disdain for the man standing before him. For so long, this man had been his idol. Now he was a stranger. "Excuse me, I need to talk to Sydney."

"You could keep an eye on him," Victoria continued. "Keep him out of trouble. Keep yourself out of trouble. The same kind, it seems."

Her eyes set on Sydney, who couldn't have cared less for her disapproval at the moment. Turning around she avoided Marcus's reach and headed back upstairs.

"Marcus!" Anthony called after his son, who had turned to follow Sydney.

"What?" He swung back around, staring with vehemence.

"You do *not* determine whether or not I should be in my house!" Anthony sneered.

Victoria let out a pain-filled laugh before falling into a chair and weeping uncontrollably.

"You leave that girl alone," Anthony continued. "She obviously doesn't want you. Your mother needs you now."

As Anthony walked past him, Marcus was consumed with anger. "She's your wife. She's crying her eyes out and you're walking away? Walking to some . . ."

"Watch your mouth, boy." He held up a warning hand. "She doesn't want me. She wants her boy. Her favorite Hart. Be that while you can. Very soon your younger brother will be replacing you—especially if you keep going after women like Sydney Tanner."

Marcus swallowed his words and went to his mother, who began shaking uncontrollably in his arms.

Late that night Sydney heard a knock at the bathroom door. She knew it was Gabrielle, but she ignored it. She had locked both doors to her room. Moments later she heard a knock on her bedroom door. She knew it was Marcus, but she ignored it, too, pulling her covers over her head.

Marcus left early the next morning for Georgetown. Sydney hated that he wasn't around, yet was grateful for that same fact. She loved him. She'd accepted that. She even accepted the possibility that despite Victoria's influence on him, he loved her, too—for now, at least. Only there was no way they could be together. Not with her goal just in sight. Not with him being a Hart. The two elements were too much to be chanced. Too much.

Sydney tried her best to function despite constant thoughts of Marcus. A visit to the National Archives and Records Administration on Pennsylvania Avenue with Professor Shue was a minor distraction, as she was able to make progress on her project.

The National Archives and Records Administration held everything possible related to family history. Most of its visitors were professional genealogists. In various forms such as microfiche, books, newspaper articles, one could find anything. Land contracts, census records, immigration and naturalization records, military service and war records, social security records, and information on every minority group in the United States.

With Maggie's help, Sydney found what she needed. The icing on the cake was finding the wedding announcements in an old black society newspaper. Young Isabelle Montage was a debutante in a small Maryland society of black elite. Her marriage to Hugh Hart, a dashing businessman new to Baltimore, was an event. Hugh Hart came from a fine family of store owners in London, England, where he was born in 1889 to Reginald and Elizabeth Hart, who had passed on in 1910 and 1908, respectively.

Sydney took this information to the Internet at various sites devoted to genealogy in England: Genealogy Gateway, Gendex, the Genealogy Home Page. With a stroke of genius, she found an article on Reginald Hart's death, which sent up several red flags.

"Reginald Hart," Sydney said, reading the article, "died of a heart attack in 1918."

Maggie spoke with a suspicious tone. "It would appear that Hugh Hart wanted everyone to believe his father was dead before he came to the United States."

"That's not all," Sydney said. "Elizabeth Hart did die in 1908 like the paper said. But listen. Reginald Hart left behind a son, Hugh, and a daughter, Deborah. Reginald's wife, Elizabeth Maric, died in 1908 from smoke inhalation as she was trapped in one of the Harts' neighborhood grocery stores, which burned down. The cause of the fire was never discovered."

"What a crazy turn." Maggie continued to search at her computer, right next to Sydney. "Anything else?"

Sydney shook her head. "I've hit a wall here. The search is bringing me nothing. I'm surprised I got what—"

"Bingo!" Maggie slapped her knee. "We have a link as to how the Harts got to England."

Sydney scooted closer. "That is unbelievable. That's too easy."

"It's too easy because there's a story tied to it," Maggie said. "Look at this."

Sydney did as she was told, waiting anxiously as the web site downloaded. Right in front of her, a barely visible copy of a freedom paper, declaring Reginald Hart a free man. Freed by his owner, Jonathan Hart, in 1830.

"Keep reading," Maggie said. "You picked a gem here. This guy Jonathan Hart is famous."

As Sydney read on, she found that Jonathan Hart was hated by English segregationists for his efforts to end slavery. He was best known for doing business with former slaves and African families who came to England after slavery was abolished in 1833. It was later found that he forged freedom papers for some of those Africans who had never been slaves between 1833 and 1840, placing his name as their former owner, which was how the name Hart came into play for Reginald. Jonathan Hart was killed by an angry white mob in 1840.

"I don't get it." Sydney reached for the printouts. "Why forge freedom papers after slavery was abolished?"

"To assimilate," Maggie answered. "This isn't unheard of, but it's rare. I'm assuming the Harts came to England from Africa of their own free will and with money of their own. Think of how they would've been accepted."

Sydney thought about it. "No one would question why or how they got what they got, came from where they came from. Just former slaves who prospered because of the white owner who helped them."

"What was important then," Maggie said, "was that white folks felt that everything blacks had, no matter how little or how much, they had only because white folks gave it to them, or made it possible for them to achieve."

Sydney shook her head. "Something's missing. Why would they risk the more racially hostile United States, even if it was the North?"

Maggie pulled back from the computer, standing to stretch. "That fire that killed Elizabeth Marie might not have been an accident. It could've been part of a campaign against Jonathan Hart and all the blacks he helped prosper. It happened in 1908. Maybe Reginald couldn't bear to go on. Maybe Hugh and Deborah wanted to cut their ties with their past to avoid repeating it. Maybe, maybe, maybe. Don't block yourself with questions that you can't answer. That's not very important. What do you have here that can help you?"

Sydney took her spot, pointing and clicking away. She linked here and there. "A list of names. It says these are some of the Africans Jonathan Hart did business with in England. It says most of these people came from Sierra Leone, after slavery was abolished in England in 1833, and he helped turn their African wealth into English pounds and prosperous companies. Many of these businesses were burned down by angry white mobs."

"You might've just answered your own question."

Sydney printed out the list.

Maggie shrugged. "Now what are you gonna do with those names?"

"Maybe one of these families is the Harts." Sydney folded the papers. "Somehow I've found the connection that ties Reginald Hart to Jonathan Hart in England. Now I've got to connect Sierra Leone to Reginald Hart, or whoever he used to be."

"I have a friend." Maggie took out a pen and paper. "Now mind you, this is the last favor I'm doing for you."

"I appreciate everything, you know that, Professor."

Sydney assumed Maggie's help was out of pity. Sydney felt her whole life losing direction and structure. Told-you-so's and hateful predictions spouted off by her parents all those years became louder and louder. Marcus Hart's face, smile, body, everything consumed her. Sadly even after years of practice, Sydney wasn't good at hiding it.

"Her name is Portia Webber. She's a historian on African cultures. Sierra Leone is one of her specialties. Make a copy of these names for me and I'll see what I can get for you."

Sydney cleared up her papers after saying good-bye to Maggie. It was five on a Friday, and she was reluctant to head home. Everyone had the day off because it was the Fourth of July weekend. Sydney hadn't driven, the train being a quicker ride. D.C. Metro traffic was nerve-racking beyond words. She thought to spend some time shopping at the quaint boutiques in Georgetown or Adams Morgan, but Gabrielle was expecting her for dinner at the Harborplace back home.

"Hart residence."

"Hi, Keith." Sydney recognized the voice right away. "It's Sydney."

"Hey, Syd."

Sydney cringed. She felt queasy for a moment, but calmed herself. It was natural for someone to call her Syd, after knowing her for a while. She'd never let many people know her for as long as a while, so this was rare. So much of what was happening to her now was rare.

"Sydney? Hello?"

"Sorry, Keith." She blinked, clearing her throat. "Is Bree home?"

He paused. "Sort of."

Sydney sighed. "What happened now."

"You don't want to know," he answered. "It'll calm down in an hour or two. Where are you?"

"D.C." Sydney scratched plans at Harborplace. "I think I'm staying down here for awhile. I just wanted to . . ."

"You fall perfectly within my master plan." Keith made a disturbingly exact impression of a sinister laugh.

Sydney knew she was about to be talked into something. She loved blues, and an invite to meet him at Blues Alley on Wisconsin Avenue—one of the most famous blues clubs, not just in D.C., but on the entire East Coast—Sydney couldn't resist. The music would fit her mood, the drinks would warm her body, and Keith, always the gentleman, would foot the bill.

Marcus had no intention of dropping by Blues Alley tonight, although he was a regular. He was leaving an early dinner, passing on drinks with fellow congressmen. He saw the funny looks they gave, but it was out of his hands. He was having a hard enough time carrying on an intelligent political conversation this week. Socializing was out of the question.

Sydney. Sydney. Sydney. He was becoming obsessed with thoughts of her. He'd tried to reach her at home, at work, but she always refused his calls. Marcus felt like he would go crazy if he didn't see her, talk to her.

Just by chance, he drove by the alley hiding off the busy Georgetown street and was drawn to it. He'd been there countless times, and the music soothed him. It wouldn't take the place of Sydney's full lips, her soft curving hips, but it would have to do. He parked his car at what seemed like a million miles away, and headed for the club. When he entered, the dark smokey, brick-walled room bought a sense of familiar comfort.

"Congressman Hart." Joe Davis, the host, smiled with excitement as he led Marcus into the dining area. "I can find a special table for you. Marsalis himself sat there last night in between sets."

Famous blues and jazz musicians did impromptu sets at Blues Alley all the time. They even recorded live albums here. Dizzy Gillespie, Ahmad Jamal, Wynton Marsalis, Mary Ann Redmond, even the great, late Charlie Byrd had been a member of the Blues Alley family.

Marcus froze in place when he saw them, his gut wrenching, jealousy and anger rushing through him.

At a round, romantic, candlelit corner table, Keith and Sydney drank and laughed. They were sitting right next to each other, so close to each other. Marcus wanted to explode, but he had years of experience keeping himself under control in public.

"Congressman?" Joe called. "This way."

"No, Joe." Marcus removed his tie. "I found my table. Bring me a gin and tonic."

Sydney dropped her glass when she saw Marcus. It was a good thing she had lifted it only an inch or two from the table, so nothing spilled. Once she got past how sexy he looked in the white, closely fitted button-down and neatly tailored pleated gray slacks, she noticed how angry he looked.

"Marcus." Keith leaned back, an accomplished smile on his face. "What a surprise. Come for another peace conference?"

Marcus helped himself to a chair and placed it next to Sydney. He leaned back, his eyes steady on Sydney. He knew Keith was reveling in his jealousy. Forget Keith. He ignored his brother.

"Hello, Sydney." He found her as usual, beautiful. She was dressed in jeans, short boots, and a ruby silk tank. She looked like the college kids who dropped by for the ten o'clock sets on the weekends. She looked more alive, more vibrant than anyone else in the room.

Sydney smiled shyly, then turned away. Her temperature soared at his closeness. She wanted him so bad, and hated herself for it.

Marcus was practically ignoring his brother's boastful rambling. As Keith went on about his impression of the progress of the lawsuit, Marcus kept his eyes on Sydney. He loved her, and even though she was here with his brother, he was happy to see her. She was afraid of loving completely, he understood that. Maybe she felt more for Keith than she was willing to admit. Not for long, he determined. If anything good came from being a Hart, he'd learned to be a winner.

As the lights dimmed and the first set began, a few couples scooted closer. Marcus was intoxicated watching Sydney as he sipped his drinks. Her eyes closed, her head swayed, she was a true blues fan. She felt it inside, he could see. She filled him with rich passion. He wanted to make love to her here and now. No one else existed.

Sydney knew he was watching her. The music felt so good, his eyes on her felt even better. She found an erotic pleasure in exciting him, against her better judgment. It was as if her body had a mind of its own. Forget what you know, forget what's best. Don't think. Don't worry. Feel, feel, feel. Let him watch you. Please him. Please yourself.

As the lights went up, and the applause of the room brought her back to reality, Sydney felt the disappointment. Her eyes met Marcus's. All she'd have to do was say the word. They could share . . . be . . .

"The Hart boys! The Hart boys!"

A tall, lanky woman with eyes as wide as saucers, and breasts much, much larger, sashayed her hips over to them. She was in her mid-twenties, with long, jet-black hair. She wore a lot of makeup, and her black dress was too short. It would be too tight if she had more than bones on her body.

She plopped herself right on Marcus's lap, hugged him tightly, and kissed his cheeks.

"Melissa," he said, nervously looking around. She was too young, too wild, and too scantily clad to be on his lap in public. "Let's have a seat."

She smacked her gum. "I forgot, big time politician. You already turned me down—add insult to injury."

"Hi, Missy." Keith sat up eagerly as the girl grabbed a chair and sat next to him. "Long time, no see."

"You boys"—she laughed, throwing back her head—"just beautiful specimens."

Sydney was already disgusted with this display.

"Haven't seen you two at the club lately," Missy said. "The Harts are such regulars with . . ."

Sydney shifted in her seat as the girl laid eyes on her. She was very thin. Sydney felt like a buffalo.

"Melissa"—Marcus took this opportunity to scoot closer to Sydney—"this is Sydney Tanner. A new family friend. Sydney, Melissa Beatty is an old family friend."

Both women nodded at each other. No need to pretend, but civility was expected.

"Jenna!" Melissa waved her hand in the air, her voice garnering stares. "Over here!"

She was Melissa's twin—not literally, but in every way that counts. Instead of black, she wore red, but Sydney could swear it was exactly the same dress. The breasts had to be fake. They were so perky, they almost blocked her vision.

Sydney watched with disgust as both women flirted and fawned over the boys. Apparently they were daughters of rich bankers, members of the D.C. Metro black elite and the Bethesda Country Club.

Melissa had Keith reeled in, and he followed her to

the dance floor as the second set, a lively set, got started. Sydney could only stare at them to keep her eyes off of Jenna as she toyed with Marcus's collar and shirt buttons while batting her eyes. She was jealous, and well aware of that. She was jealous of the size-two dress, although she'd never wear it even if she could fit into it. She was jealous of the country club background. No, Victoria wouldn't approve of this girl, she was too empty-headed, but she'd be better than Sydney. At least she came from class, even if she didn't appear to have any herself.

Marcus couldn't stand it. It bothered him to see Keith flirting with Missy in front of Sydney, although he knew his brother had had a crush on Melissa for over a year now. Maybe Keith and Sydney had an understanding, he thought. He was fine with that. It would only make it easier for him.

But now as he watched jealousy form in her posture and in the way she held her head up as she stared at Keith and Melissa, he knew it was something different. Melissa was glued to Keith as he danced without caution and control. Sydney was jealous. She was angry, and annoyed at the least. She cared for Keith more than he'd imagined. It was making him sick to watch, making his anger grow. He turned from Jenna, not having heard a word she'd been saying anyway.

"Sydney," he said, reaching for her arm. He wanted, needed her to look at him. "Sydney."

The room was closing in on her. His touch sent shock waves through her entire body. Sydney had never felt so out of control. She didn't even look at him as she leaped from the chair and ran out of the club.

It was pouring rain outside—like buckets, but Sydney didn't care. It was air. The stream invigorated her as she was drenched.

"Sydney!" Marcus found her in the alley, grabbed her

arm, turning her to him. "You don't need him. He doesn't love you."

"What are you talking about?" She could barely see through the shower. "Who?"

"Keith!"

Sydney pulled away from him. "You're drunk, Marcus. Go back to your friend."

"I've had a bit to drink," he said, "but I'm not drunk, and I won't go. I can't stand these rejections. I know you care about Keith, but I can—"

"Stop this, Marcus. Why do you insist on this fantasy relationship with Keith? I don't care about Keith that way. There is nothing going on between us. We work together, we're only friends."

Marcus was trying to understand through his liquor, the drops of rain. "Then . . . yes . . . then . . ."

"No," she said, although her body told her to say yes. "No, I can't. I can't do . . ."

His eyes shut her up. She couldn't fight him any longer. She couldn't.

"What in God's name?"

Keith walked up to them, holding his jacket over his head. "What is wrong with you two? It's raining buckets out here!"

Marcus pulled himself together. "Sydney isn't feeling well. I'm taking her home with me. When you're done partying, you can come and pick her up."

Sydney said nothing, letting the rain soak her.

Keith's eyes shifted to Sydney. He leaned over to Marcus. "Missy invited me home with her."

Marcus nodded. "Where does she live? Adams Morgan still? Fine. You can pick Sydney up in the morning."

"Sydney?" Keith asked. "Are you okay with this?"

Sydney nodded, not bothering to protest as Marcus took her arm and led her away.

"Hey! You've had more than a couple, bro," Keith called after them. "Sydney is driving."

With a little direction, Sydney found Marcus's neighborhood. She parked in his space in the back, and they went inside. Nothing personal had been spoken on the way. It continued as Marcus offered her towels to dry herself and an oversized T-shirt to wear.

As she dressed inside the second bedroom down the hall, Sydney could hear Marcus showering. The memories of the last time she'd been here raked her with desire.

Sydney tightened her still wet hair and braided it down the back. She slid under the sky-blue comforter, looking around the dimly lit room. It was pretty bare, and small. Blue and white everywhere. Sydney turned off the nightlight and listened to the rain, hitting the window with anger over her bed. It sounded like a storm, like more rain than . . . like that time . . .

"You've done it now!" Linda Williams threw her purse across the kitchen. It missed Sydney's ten-year-old head by a couple of feet.

Sydney jumped away. She regretted waiting until now to fix herself a fried bologna sandwich because she knew she wouldn't get to eat it now. She was so hungry.

"Can't I come home to peace for one day?" Linda raised her voice to compete with the thunder outside. It was a rainstorm. "Do you know how important David is to me? To us?"

Sydney said nothing. Stubbornly she didn't even nod. She knew her mother couldn't live a second without a man.

"I need this man," Linda said. "You don't understand how important having a man is. So when I come home to find my husband on his way out 'cause he can't take

my smart-ass kid nagging him and giving him attitude all day, we got a problem."

Thunder ripped through the sky, unnerving Sydney. "Well, if he got a job and wasn't home all day, it wouldn't happen."

"Look, little girl"—Linda pointed a finger in her voice—"it don't matter if he got a job. He brings money to this house."

"He nags me," Sydney said. "He makes me get stuff for him when it's right there next to him. He won't let me watch TV at all."

"I don't care." Linda looked at her as if she were crazy for even suggesting such behavior was unfair. "If David wants you to do something, you do it. You don't matter . . . he does. Without him, we're out on the street."

"I don't care." Sydney threw the bologna back in the refrigerator and slammed the door. "I hate him."

"That's it." Linda grabbed her by the arm, dragging her, fighting, to the back door.

"Stop it!" Sydney struggled. "Don't."

Linda opened the door that led to the back balcony. It was a five-by-five balcony, barely room for a chair.

"You don't care if we're on the street?" she asked, squeezing the little girl's wrist. "Well, let me show you what it's like. Then you'll shut your smart mouth."

Lightning lit up the sky. Sydney was crying, pleading. "No, Mama! It's raining!"

"It rains on homeless people." She pushed as Sydney gripped the doorway. "And if you start screaming, you'll be sorry . . . much sorrier than this."

Sydney banged on the door as the rain fell. The thunder made her jump high in the air. It was cold and she was soaked after only a minute. After a while, Sydney couldn't tell if she was crying. David and Linda only laughed when they visited the kitchen to grab dinner. She was shaking three hours later when Linda finally opened the door.

"Don't you trail water all through my place neither," was all she said.

Marcus heard her crying in the next room, and ran to her. Sobering up, his thoughts were clearer, still consumed with Sydney. From the first sniffle, holding her was all that he cared to do in life.

"Sydney." He wrapped his arms around, pulling her to the edge of the bed with him. "My poor Sydney. I've caused you so much stress and confusion."

"It's not you." Sydney felt years of lost comfort replaced with his arms around her. God, she loved him. She loved him more than she hated *them,* but she wasn't ready to give up her hate. It had been her life's purpose for almost two decades.

"Then who is it?" he asked, determined to get through to her and break those barriers to comfort her. "Who is it, and when was it?"

"Marcus." Her voice was a whisper, choked through tears. "They were awful. So awful. They stole so much from me. I hate them so much. I still hate them so much."

Marcus directed her head to his shoulder. "Tell me, baby. I'll make it better."

As he stroked her hair, her cheek, holding her in a loving, protective embrace as no man ever had, Sydney did just that. She told him everything. For over an hour, she talked, pausing to find more strength. It would take days to pinpoint every moment, so she condensed it all. Even then, with each word, she felt relief and understanding. It was as if she was letting go of a load she'd grown so used to carrying, she'd forgotten how heavy it was.

"Sydney," he said, his heart hurting at her painful

childhood. "Baby, you know it's time to let go. Let me help you let go."

She lifted her head, facing him. She saw the compassion, affection in his eyes. "I want to, but you couldn't understand."

"I can," he answered, shaking his head. "Now I won't even pretend to have suffered like you have, but I know what it's like to feel such anger at your parents. To want nothing more than revenge for the pain they caused you."

"Celeste?"

He blinked. She knew the truth. He saw it in her eyes. "How did you know?"

"Kelly told me. I'm sorry, I . . ."

He shook his head. "No, I'm glad you know. I was devastated. It wasn't so much because I loved her, because I don't know that I still did at that point. It was them: Mother, Dad. I couldn't believe . . . It was the beginning of the end."

"You stayed in politics, though."

He nodded. "I genuinely love it, but I knew it was their dream that year. It was going to be the pride of the Hart family that year. Then, when it happened, when I dropped out and lost, the sense of satisfaction didn't come. I just felt empty, wasted. In the end, because of my living for revenge, they won again."

He held her face, his hand covering each warm, tear-stained cheek. "I don't want you to feel empty, wasted like that. Don't let your parents win. They don't deserve it."

Sydney was drunk with love before his lips even touched hers. Her body tingled from the contact as he devoured the softness of her lips. His mouth melted into hers and Sydney responded with all willingness. She raised her arms, wrapping them around his neck as he pulled her closer.

Marcus was burning up. Her lips were like heaven to him. His love for this woman, his desire to protect her from all pain, was all that mattered. He was determined to finish what they had started the last time she was here.

His tongue entered Sydney's mouth. She tilted her head back to receive him, caressing the back of his head with her hands. She could never be close enough.

"Sydney." Marcus spoke in a jagged whisper. "I want you. Let me. Let me make it better. Let me make it all better."

"Yes," she said in almost a moan as his lips trailed her neck, her chin. "Yes, Marcus."

He caressed the sides of her waist as his tongue teased her neck and shoulders. Passion threatened him, but Marcus determined to make this last. Every second.

Gently, he slid the oversize T-shirt up, Sydney lifting herself up a bit so it could pass her waist. Their lips separated as Marcus lifted the shirt over her head.

Sydney felt only desire as he looked over her. She could see pure want in his eyes and she felt so proud of her body and its womanly curves.

Returning to her mouth, Marcus leaned Sydney back on the bed, moving the covers away from both of them. He took her hands and guided them to the bed post. As he trailed his hands down the underbelly of her arms slowly, caressingly, his mouth traveled to her breast.

Sydney let out an eager groan as he took one nipple in his mouth. So possessively he circled it with his tongue. Painfully teasing, he cupped the other breast with his hand, rubbing it softly. It felt like sparks of fire building and building for Sydney.

As she ran her fingers over his hair, Marcus was drowning in ecstasy—touching her, tasting her soft supple skin, caressing her devilishly feminine body. He could hear moaning, feel her body moving restlessly beneath him. He left his hands arousing her breast as his mouth laid shivering kisses over her abdomen.

Sydney called out his name. She had never felt such abandon. It was purely perfect torture as his tongue teased her belly button. She brought her hands to her head, grabbing at her hair in response to her welcomed insanity.

Marcus slid his hands under her soft buttocks and slid her panties down her legs. He returned his hands to her upper thighs. Gently he lifted her up slightly and kissed her inner thighs. Slow, pulsating, erotic kisses.

"Oh, God, Marcus." Sydney's entire body shivered. She bit her lower lip, aching all over. "Please."

When he kissed her in the most intimate part, Marcus felt her body shake and the movement threatened to send him spinning out of control. He knew there was one thing left to do before reason and thinking left entirely.

He lifted up, kissing her cheeks and whispering in her ear. "I have to get something, baby. Stay warm for me. I'll be only a second."

When he returned a few seconds later, the sight of her body squirming and moving with desire and anticipation delighted him beyond words.

They engulfed each other's lips as soon as Marcus was on the bed. Quickly he hurried his shirt and boxers off. He was already so aroused.

Sitting together on the bed, legs entwined, Marcus closed his eyes as Sydney touched him everywhere. She kissed his hard chest, his flat stomach, and caressed the rest of his body.

Sydney took the packet from him and Marcus left searing kisses on her forehead, running his fingers through her hair as she applied the protection to him.

When she was finished, Marcus laid her back and lowered himself into her. Sydney never wanted anything more in her life as she wrapped her legs around his muscled thighs. When he entered her, they both moaned in painful pleasure, each knowing that this was what they'd wanted since first laying eyes on each other.

As they made love to each other, Marcus whispered words of affection between kisses. Passion pounded in their hearts as slow intimate thrusts led to faster, carnal bursts of shuddering ecstasy. Their bodies moved to a tempo only they knew as they left reality and were absorbed in each other.

As she reached a mind-blowing climax, Sydney called out his name in sweet agony. Only moments later the world spun in Marcus's head as he shattered into a million peaks of sensation.

When he cradled her in his arms, Sydney had to fight back her tears of joy. Their sweating bodies molded into each other, as if they'd been crafted to fit this way.

"I love you, Sydney." Marcus kissed the palm of her hand and held it to his chest.

Sydney fell fast asleep with the storm raging outside her window.

The next morning Keith's abrupt ringing of the doorbell was all that separated Marcus and Sydney. Since making love again in the shower that morning, they'd been glued to each other, eating croissants and drinking coffee in the kitchen nook.

Sydney followed behind, her clothes dry but wrinkled. Keith looked like he hadn't gotten a wink of sleep. His eyes were barely open until Marcus flung his arm around Sydney's shoulders.

"I must've missed something," he said, a brow raised. "I thought Sydney wasn't feeling well."

"I'm better now." Nervous, she tried to slide away from Marcus, but he held her tightly.

"Sydney'll be out in a second," Marcus said. "Why don't you start the car?"

Keith blinked with a flicker of annoyance at being dismissed, but did as he was told.

"Marcus." Sydney playfully fought her way out of his grip. "He'll tell."

"So what?" Marcus fell back on the sofa. "I'm in love. I want the world to know!"

"I'm fine with the world knowing." She joined him. "It's Victoria Hart I'm concerned about."

"Look at it this way," he said. "Keith will get what he wants. Favored son status. He can have it. I don't want it. I have everything I want in you."

Sydney let his arms close around her, enveloping her in warmth and love. She had never, ever felt this way. "This could get ugly."

"Are you scared?"

She had to nod if she was going to be honest. She was scared of so much, not just Victoria.

"I'll be there for you," he said. "Don't be afraid of anything."

"One favor," she pleaded. "If they must know, let's at least not throw it in their faces. I have to live there."

"You don't have to anymore." Marcus knew what he was suggesting and there wasn't any hesitation. "You can live here with me."

Sydney had never lived with a man. It reminded her of her mother and David all those years before they were married. "Yeah, right. That's all I need. I'll look like a . . . No. I've been transient enough and you're a politician. It won't flow. Besides, I work in Baltimore. I'll stay there for now."

"Okay." He knew not to push. He'd have to be patient

with Sydney. She'd had it hard and needed to move slowly into a world of love and trust. She was worth the wait. "Then I'll come home every weekend to be with you."

"Sounds better." Actually Sydney thought it sounded perfect. "Of course, if Victoria kicks me out after finding out my low-class, gold-digging behind has stolen her prized possession . . ."

"Not gonna happen." He kissed her full, possessively on the lips. "I won't let it. I'm telling you now, you won't have to worry about where you'll live this summer."

Keith's horn honked for the second time.

Sydney kissed Marcus again before jumping up from the sofa and grabbing her purse. "When will I see you again?"

"I'll be down later today." He went to open the door for her, taking her hands in his. "Before the holiday dinner at least. Maybe you'll come to church with me tomorrow."

Sydney smiled and turned to head out before Marcus grabbed her one last time.

"Not another kiss," she pleaded, even though she loved it. "Keith will leave without me."

"Sydney." He looked with all seriousness into her eyes. "No matter what anyone says—not your mother or mine—you're not low class and you're not a gold digger. You're a survivor, a lady, and the best thing that ever happened to me."

Sydney felt the tears trail her cheeks. It was so hard for her to believe this, but she would. She would believe everything he said to her, because he loved her and she loved him.

It was a silent drive home and Sydney was grateful for that. She focused on her love, and Marcus's last words to her. She would force room in her life for him, for love. She had fought planting roots anywhere. Love was a distraction, a weakness that couldn't be afforded. Until today. Until last night. Love was Marcus, and it was strength. Her goal was still in sight. Sydney wasn't letting go of that. Only now she wouldn't be so lonely.

THIRTEEN

Sydney opened the door to her balcony. The smell of barbecue hit her nose, and the smile she'd had in her face all day widened. She could see Anthony dressed in the traditional garb for what she assumed was the one day he bothered to cook anything. Laura was beside him, holding an enormous plate of ribs, waiting for Anthony to add them to the steak, chicken, and turkey legs already on the grill.

They laughed and talked. Sydney found it ironic that Laura seemed more like Anthony's wife than the high-class Victoria. Observing them, she had to readjust her thinking. No, they didn't seem like a married couple. To Sydney, they seemed like old friends, who might have once, in a moment of weakness, been more than friends, but understood it was fruitless and returned to life as normal. At least Anthony might have. Laura was still holding on, Sydney saw it in her eyes every time she spoke of her boss.

Love. It would kill Sydney, waiting to see Marcus again. It was so foreign to her, feeling giddy in love, thinking romantic thoughts. She'd cared for the few lovers she'd had in the past, but never loved. Not like Marcus.

She laughed at the irony. Her parents had told her, warned her a man like Marcus would never want a woman like her. This would be the icing on the cake of sweet revenge.

Sydney thought of the possibilities with Marcus, promising herself not to let them get in the way of reaching her goal. Still she felt warm all over, contemplating a future with him. She wasn't going to be a dalliance, a distraction. No matter how much Victoria would try to make her so.

"You'll change of course."

Sydney jumped, swinging around. Speak of the devil— literally—Victoria stood in the balcony doorway, her face, her eyes as cold as ice.

"For our company," she continued. "We have several well-respected guests arriving for our Independence Day cookout tonight. Last night's clothes won't do."

Sydney stepped back, her eyes widening. Last night's clothes? She knew!

Victoria's lips formed a thin smile, seeming to find satisfaction in Sydney's embarrassment. "Yes, Ms. Tanner. I know where you were last night. My son wouldn't keep anything from me. Now let's not try to suggest it was all innocent. We both know you're anything but."

Sydney fumed. "You don't know anything about me. Not enough to determine—"

"That's where you're wrong." Victoria smoothed out one of a hundred silk pantsuits she seemed to own. "I know everything about you. It's my job to protect my children, and in doing so, I've done some research of my own."

Sydney knew what was coming. She'd expected as much. She gripped her hands in fists to brace herself. She had nothing to hide. Yes, she hated who she'd come from, but she was rising above it all now. Still there was no need to hide it.

"I know about your parents. Your father's a convict,

been in and out of jail his whole life. He's in San Quentin now for armed robbery. He'll be there for life now."

Sydney heard a whimper escape her involuntarily.

Victoria held up her chin. "Didn't know that, did you? I'm surprised, as inquisitive as you are about other people's family. Did you know your mother is still living in that run-down apartment? Still cleaning toilets in government buildings. She's still with your stepfather too. Only David Williams is in a wheelchair. Got shot in the back five years ago in a scuffle outside a liquor store."

Sydney turned away. She watched McKenzie chase his tail in the yard, feeling sick to her stomach. She hadn't bothered to check on them ever. She wasn't going to until she had it *all* to throw in their faces. Then she'd walk away and never, ever see or think of them again.

"You went to Chicago State," Victoria continued. "It took you six years, holding all types of odd jobs, menial jobs. All the while, I assume your objective was to escape that world. You've been waiting for one of my sons. Bree was your ticket in. You used her—"

"She did no such thing, and you know it!"

Gabrielle came from the bathroom, her eyes were red, no makeup was on her face. She looked tired, and so unhappy.

Gabrielle approached a mildly surprised Victoria. "Sydney ignored me. She ignored me all year. I had to practically beg for her friendship."

"It was all part of her game." Victoria's tone was very confident, very calm. "So she wouldn't seem obvious. So she could fool you all."

Sydney eyed the woman with disgust. No matter how this round ended, Victoria had won. Victoria knew this, which was why she wouldn't get upset at her daughter's protest. She'd gotten what she came for.

Victoria turned to her. "You remember, this is my house. My . . . house."

"I know that." Sydney spoke as calmly as she could.

"Nothing goes on in my house that I don't want to."

"Mother!" Gabrielle put her hands on her hips. "You can't kick her out. If she's out, I'm out. And you know where I'll go."

"Don't threaten me, Bree." She glanced impatiently at her daughter. "You wouldn't last a second and you know it."

Gabrielle's eyes tightened to slits. She pressed her lips together.

"Besides I wasn't going to kick her out." Victoria turned so slowly, heading for the door. "Marcus will have his fun for the summer. I learned with Celeste, my opposition only encourages him. It's probably the only reason he wants you now, but it won't last. I think you know that."

Gabrielle slammed the bedroom door behind her mother. She hurried to Sydney. Placing her arms around her, she led her larger, but at this moment, weaker frame to the bed.

"I'm sorry, Sydney." She rubbed her back. "She's such a . . ."

"Don't, Bree," Sydney said. "She's still your mother."

Gabrielle sighed. "Unfortunately. Don't listen to her. Marcus is not my mother or my father. Don't regret last night."

"How do you know about last night?"

"Mother headed straight for Keith's room after you two came home. I could hear her from the hallway. I'm surprised you didn't. Keith is an idiot, but he's no fool. He knows this news moves him up on the ladder of Mother's love."

"Marcus and I expected as much." Sydney grabbed a pillow, hugging it to her chest.

"Did Marcus tell you everything else to expect? I mean, I'm happy for you, but she's only just begun. Daddy is bound to get involved now."

Sydney sighed. She fought to stay positive. *Remember Marcus's words.* "If I can just see him . . . If I can be with him, everything will be fine."

Gabrielle clapped her hands, rubbing them together. "Now that that's out the way, I'd love details. Only they would be with my brother, which is kind of creepy."

"Very creepy." Sydney smiled. "I wouldn't give you any details anyway."

"Do I get anything?"

Sydney tilted her head. "Sorry. This is between me and Marcus. I wouldn't—"

The knock on the door caused Sydney to leap from her bed. It was intuition—she knew before she ran to the door, swinging it open. Marcus lifted her into the air, hugging her tightly. He assaulted her face with one hundred kisses.

"Okay, okay." Gabrielle sauntered toward the bathroom. "Save it for later. No affectionate displays allowed in the Hart home, remember?"

"Hush, little monster." He let Sydney down, winking at Gabrielle. In all his happiness, it didn't slip by him how miserable his baby sister looked. "Can we have some privacy?"

"Apparently not. Not in this family." She smiled before closing the bathroom door behind her.

"Marcus." Sydney led him to the bed. "Victoria knows. I think everyone does."

He ran the back of his hand down her soft cheek. The joy in his heart at seeing her, touching her again, couldn't be put into words. "Poor baby, you're so worried. Don't be. I'll shield you. I won't leave your side, not for a second."

And he didn't. The evening was bearable, kept civil because of the guests, a sample of the Baltimore area's finest. There were a few tense moments as, despite Sydney's pleading, Marcus was very demonstrative with his affection for her. Victoria sent eye shots like bullets at them throughout the night. When an inquisitive guest asked for an introduction, Marcus referred to Sydney as his girlfriend, which one time caused Victoria to almost choke on some barbecued chicken. She made every attempt to divert any conversation about the new couple, which Sydney decided to find amusing. Less amusing was her observation of Anthony's response to the new relationship. He seemed upset, distant, not even choosing to make eye contact with her. Marcus had told her that Anthony was receiving death threats at work again. Sydney was alarmed, but Marcus told her it happened often to government employees with his level of recognition and outside public exposure.

Marcus held Sydney's hand all night, stealing kisses and sending her temperature soaring. They ate much more than they should have and flirted shamelessly. They rocked on the swinging bench out back, kissing more passionately those few moments they were alone. It didn't happen too often. Sydney wasn't surprised that Marcus drew people to him all night. He was impressive, charming, and articulate. He seemed to relate to everyone, no matter what color, age, or sex.

After everyone finally left, Marcus and Sydney made their way to the kitchen, in search of her chocolate milk. Laura was cleaning up, May keeping her company. Sydney was impressed with the old lady. It had to be near midnight.

"It's got to be seventy-five degrees out right now," Marcus said, kissing his aunt on the forehead. "And Sydney wants hot chocolate."

"I'm making it cold," she said. "It'll take only a minute."

"Fine." Marcus attempted to help Laura, but she slapped his hand away. He couldn't tell if she was being playful or serious sometimes. She'd given him the cold shoulder all evening.

Sydney reached for the chocolate syrup and the carton of milk in the refrigerator. She noticed immediately that the syrup bottle was empty.

"Oh, darn," she said. "Laura, I forgot to tell you we were out of syrup. I can't believe I put it back in the fridge."

"We're out?" Laura asked, reaching for the bottle. She shook it, looking apologetic. "I'm sorry."

"Don't apologize," Sydney said. "It's me. I should've gotten some while I was out."

"So you won't have anything?" she asked. "I'll put the milk back."

"No." Sydney shrugged, reaching for a glass. "I'll just have some milk. That'll do."

Marcus wrapped his arms around her waist. "Me, too. I'm thirsty."

"No, you can't." Laura took the carton of milk from Sydney right after she poured. "There's only a little left, and I need it for Sunday morning muffins."

"Whatever," he said with a smile. "Let's just keep it moving. I'm getting tired."

"Wait a second," May interjected. "You're not suggesting . . . No, you won't."

"No, Aunt May." Marcus smiled at the thought of sneaking into Sydney's bed after everyone had gone to sleep. No, he couldn't chance it. "We just wanted to sit out on the balcony in her room. I was leaving right after."

"Don't tempt it," May said. "Your parents have acted civil so far tonight. You'd do best to say your good nights now."

"I agree." Laura shooed Marcus out of her way as she shoved a bowl of potato salad in the refrigerator.

Sydney placed the glass of milk down and put her hands to Marcus's chest. "As much as I was looking forward to spending more time with you, they're right. The guests are gone. There's nothing to keep things peaceful around here anymore."

Marcus frowned, He didn't like this at all, but he wouldn't say no to Sydney. Couldn't. He loved her too much.

In the entranceway to the kitchen, they said their good nights, then kissed their good nights, then hugged their good nights before kissing their good nights again before Marcus left for bed.

"Young love," May said with a memory-filled smile as Sydney returned. "Such a joy to watch."

"Too bad everyone doesn't agree with you," Sydney said.

May waved the air away with her hand. "Don't mind them. Victoria, you'll get used to. Anthony, well, he'll adjust. Won't he, Laura?"

Laura shrugged. Sydney had noticed her mood all evening and wondered if she was overworked or if it was something else. She was obviously on Anthony's side of every issue.

"I'll keep my opinion to myself," Laura said. "I think there are more than enough opinions floating around this house tonight. Sydney, I just hope you know what you're getting yourself into. Now I am tired, and the maid service is coming in the morning to finish this up. So I'm gonna take this last bag of garbage and head off to bed."

"I haven't seen you smiling like that since you've been here," May said. "Is it all because of my grandnephew?"

Sydney grabbed her glass, joining May at the table. "Mostly I'd have to admit—I feel like a schoolgirl."

"I watched you both tonight. Marcus seems alive again. For some time now, it seemed like he was just going through the motions coming here. Dating these women he knew weren't going to make him happy. That's all changed now."

Sydney placed her hand over May's. "I'm so glad I could be a part of that. It's not just Marcus. It's you and Bree. I'm letting people into my life, my heart. It's scary, but I'm happy."

Sydney held the cup of milk to her lips, but didn't sip it. She realized at that moment, she had no taste, no need for it. Not anymore.

"Something wrong?" May asked.

Sydney smiled as she stood up. "No, nothing at all. I think I'm going to head off to bed. How about you?"

"I'm right behind you."

Sydney's first intention was to put the milk back in the carton for Laura's muffins, but she couldn't remember if she'd sipped it or not. Instead, she noticed McKenzie's bowl was empty. She poured the cup into his bowl, realizing she'd even grown fond of the dog.

Sydney and Gabrielle were in their shared bathroom discussing last night's events while getting dressed when Marcus appeared in Gabrielle's doorway.

Sydney's heart leaped at the sight of him, but for only a second as she noticed the saddened expression on his face.

"I know we're late for breakfast," Gabrielle said, unplugging the curling iron. "Did you come to nag us? Don't tell me, Mother sent you."

"Bree." Marcus sighed. "I just want to prepare you."

Gabrielle's eyes widened. "What is it?"

Marcus put up a cautioning hand. "It's McKenzie. He's sick. He's very sick. Bree!"

Bree ran away from Marcus and past Sydney. She was headed downstairs with Sydney and Marcus close behind.

"What happened?" Sydney asked Marcus as they charged down the stairs.

"We don't know. Dad found him earlier this morning. He was staggering into the kitchen like he'd been shot. He was throwing up. Then he just dropped."

Gabrielle screamed out the dog's name as soon as she saw him on the kitchen floor. Sydney was shocked. He was lying on the floor, tongue hanging out, eyes barely open. The entire family, except May, stood around. Anthony held Gabrielle back as she wanted to touch the dog. Laura was near tears. Victoria appeared disgusted, and Keith was fervently on the phone.

With all that was going on, it didn't pass by Sydney that this was the most emotion she'd seen come from Anthony since she'd met him Over the dog?

"I can't believe it," Laura said, shaking her head. "He's never sick."

"I want him out of the house if he's going to die," Victoria said coldly. "He's already made enough of a mess. Laura, clean this . . ."

"Mother." Marcus silenced her with a glance. "Bree, calm down. Keith is talking to the vet now."

"We have to take him to the animal hospital." Gabrielle was sobbing, tears running. "Now."

Marcus, noticing Sydney's concern, held her arm tightly. "It'll be okay."

Keith held up a hand to silence them. "Okay. Okay then . . . Yeah." His eyes widened. He looked at the dog. He shook his head. "Fine. Okay."

He hung up, looking at Gabrielle. "Now, Bree, he'll be all right. The doctor says we have to get him to the animal hospital on South Ridge Road. They have an emergency room."

"What did he say it was?" Laura asked.

Keith shook his head, seeming perplexed. "I told him the symptoms and Dr. Sanger says he's almost certain McKenzie's been poisoned."

"Poisoned?" Gabrielle asked. "With what?"

Anthony gave an exasperated sigh. "We must have something poisonous in the yard."

"No, we don't," Keith said. "We had it checked out after those weird mushrooms started growing. It has to be something else."

"He didn't even get out last night," Gabrielle said. "We didn't want him getting into the garbage after the barbecue, because there were too many bags to fit in the cans. So we kept him inside, didn't we?"

"Are you all right?" Marcus made eye contact with Sydney as she seemed to shiver. He couldn't tell what she was feeling. Her eyes . . .

It hit Sydney like a tornado. She inhaled, stepping out of Marcus's grip. She looked at McKenzie, then at the people surrounding her. Everyone was looking at her. Sydney felt short of breath.

"Sydney," Marcus said. "What is it?"

Sydney could see McKenzie's bowl from where she stood. It was empty. She was overcome with panic.

"Who did it?" She looked around at everyone, no one. "Who tried to poison me?"

Victoria let out a laugh, Laura gasped. Everyone else was silently stunned.

"Sydney." Marcus walked to her, reached for her, but she stepped back. "What are you talking about?"

"My milk," she said in between deep breaths. "I

poured my milk in McKenzie's bowl. That's what hurt him!"

Everyone just stared. Marcus couldn't believe this.

"Where is it?" Sydney opened the refrigerator. "Where's the milk?"

Laura spoke cautiously. "I used the rest of it. This morning. I put it in the mix for the muffins."

"You're answering this girl?" Victoria asked incredulously. "She's mad."

"It was you!" Sydney's anger flared at the woman's condescending expression. "You did this."

"You're accusing my mother of trying to poison you?" Keith asked, his brows centering in anger.

"Calm down, Keith," Marcus said. "Sydney isn't accusing anyone of—"

"Someone poisoned my milk," she said. "Someone."

Laura turned to Anthony. "I drank that milk. What I didn't put in the mix, I put in my coffee.

"Don't panic, Laura," Marcus said. "We don't know."

"I don't care if you don't believe me," Sydney snapped at him.

"If you gave him chocolate," Gabrielle said, through tears, "of course it poisoned him."

Sydney shook her head. "No. It was regular milk. No chocolate. I've given him regular milk before—a couple of times and nothing happened."

"Can't be good for him either way," Victoria said. "Boys, take the dog."

"Sydney." Marcus held her arms. He needed to calm her. "You need to lie down. Keith, you and Dad take—"

She pulled away. "No! You won't dismiss this."

"Sydney." Anthony's tone was annoyed. "Laura drank the milk, she's fine."

"I do feel just fine," she added. "Just fine, Sydney. You drank some, didn't you?"

"No," she said. "None."

"This is ridiculous." Victoria threw her hands in the air. "Church starts at ten. We'll miss it with this nonsense. Poison. Please. Get the dog out of here."

"I'm going, too." Gabrielle leaned over McKenzie in a protective gesture, but Anthony pulled her back.

"Laura," Victoria said. "Get some blankets we can do without. I don't want him throwing up in any of my cars."

Sydney turned to Marcus, desperately looking for support. She could see he didn't believe her.

"Come on, Sydney," he said, concerned. How could she possibly think this? He wanted to get her out of here to talk to her. The stress was getting to her.

"Sydney." Anthony spoke calmly. "McKenzie gets into everything. It might not even be poison. It was a phone diagnosis."

A flicker of doubt hit Sydney. Still it was too much. It was all too much. She pushed Marcus aside and ran to her room.

"Marcus!" Anthony grabbed his son's arm as he passed. "Help get the dog in the car at least!"

"Keith can—" Marcus jerked free.

"Do what I told you, boy!"

"Marcus." Gabrielle stood up, wiping tears from her eyes. "I'll go to Sydney. I'll calm her down. Please don't fight anymore. Take care of McKenzie."

Marcus nodded reluctantly. "Tell her I'm coming right up. Come on Keith. Let's hurry."

Sydney grabbed her suitcase, flipped it open and started filling it. She fought the tears that wanted to come. Her conclusion had been an instinct. It seemed clear at the time, even though it was extreme. Her better sense told her she was being ridiculous. Still her gut told her she had pushed someone too far.

She laughed out loud. Her second suitcase was filled and she still had several items left. This was her problem. Never before, when it was time to leave and move on, did she have more than two suitcases and a backpack. Never got too attached. Letting her guard down—getting attached—was what had kept her from drinking the milk. The irony made her pity herself.

She sighed, thinking of Marcus. She loved him, but she couldn't disconnect him from the others. The ones she didn't trust. She had to get out of here, away from all of them. Away from the person she had become from living here.

She rarely had memories of home anymore. It was all from living here, loving these people. Some of them at least. She needed those memories, as painful as they were, to keep her strong, determined. To keep her goal first and foremost.

Sydney swung around as she heard her door open. Ready to tell whoever it was to get out, she said nothing when she saw Gabrielle and May.

"Sydney," Gabrielle started. "I told Aunt May. We came to—"

"Don't even try it." Sydney returned to packing, grabbing her large backpack. "I'm outta here."

Gabrielle tried to block her as she went for more clothes from the armoire. "Just think about what you're suggesting. Poison you? For what?"

"For going on with this project." Sydney pushed her aside. "For being with Marcus. Take your pick. Maybe what they chose only made McKenzie sick, but would've killed me."

May quietly sat on the bed, keeping a gentle smile on her face. Sydney was stuffing everything in that backpack, matting it down. It was all she had left. If she had to, she'd fill her purse, leaving anything else behind.

"You can't leave!" Gabrielle wrung her fingers together. "I'll just die if you go. You're the only—"

"Calm down Bree." May gestured to her grandniece.

"May"—Sydney stopped packing, giving the woman her full attention—"no offense to you. You've been loving and kind, but I don't belong here. I can't trust anyone or myself anymore."

May kept her smile calm, unfettered. "Where will you go?"

"You can't go!" Gabrielle began pacing.

Sydney wiped her tears as she sat on the bed. "I have no idea, but it doesn't matter. I can't stay here. So I'll have to figure something out. I always do."

"Bree," May called. "Bree, stop pacing. Listen to me. Leave us for now."

"You can't let her go, Aunt May." Gabrielle pouted, stamping her foot.

May's tone was stern. "Bree, you heard me."

Gabrielle hesitated for only a moment before leaving, closing the door behind her. Sydney started to protest any attempts to change her mind, but May headed her off. "You have nowhere to go, child. You've spent so much of your life keeping people at a distance. Yes, it might have been good to keep you from being distracted, but when the chips are down, it leaves you with no one to go to."

Sydney lowered her head. "I'll go to a motel."

"You can't afford that. What about Marcus? Under any other circumstances, I wouldn't approve. But now . . ."

Sydney's head shot up, her eyes widening. "You believe me?"

May looked away for only a moment, but long enough for Sydney to get her answer. "You have your own doubts, child. If you didn't, you would be calling the police right now."

"And I can't stay with Marcus. Not because of him." Sydney knew she was right, and it angered her. "I haven't made up my mind about that. I love him, but he doesn't believe me and I need distance. Distance from everyone."

"You can't afford a motel night after night, and the cheap ones are in dangerous neighborhoods, too dangerous for a young woman on her own. I can't have that. I forbid it."

Sydney smiled at the woman's possessiveness. "I'll think of something in the next few days."

May held out her hand, and Sydney accepted it. She felt something cold, stringy and hard. As May let go, Sydney brought her hand back.

"The key," May said, "is to an apartment in Bethesda. Fully furnished."

Sydney shook her head. "No, May, I can't. It's—"

"It's empty and you will. Now you call a cab to the station. There's a stop that connects to the Bethesda Metro. Take the downtown bus to Second Street. It's 7722 Second Street. It's only for a few days—while you figure something out."

"It belongs to them," Sydney said. "I can't take something from someone I think tried to poison me."

"It's mine. It's in my name. Now Anthony has used it in the past. Made himself a key and was holding his whores in there." She rolled her eyes in disgust. "No more of that. Now it's mine again. No one will bother you, I promise. I won't tell them you're there."

Sydney contemplated. "It'll be only a few days. I'll get a place soon."

Sydney held up the other item: a thin, gold chain with a quarter-size medallion hanging from it.

"This," May said with a proud, tender smile, "is a necklace that has been passed down in my family. My aunt Deborah gave it to me. She got it from my grandmother, Elizabeth. She never talked about its significance, but I saw how she treasured it. She never wore it, but took it out often and gazed at it. She told me it wasn't for wearing, but for treasuring. I never wear it, either, but its presence always made me feel safe."

"I . . ." Sydney was so touched. She'd grown weaker, easier over the past months. Usually she would've resisted further. But now . . . well, now she was giving in.

"You need to feel safe now," May interrupted. "You can give it back to me when you don't need it anymore."

Sydney hugged her tightly. She felt so warm in this woman's embrace, but the cold was all around them. She had to get out.

Marcus found Sydney sitting on the front steps of the house. He saw her suitcases, her bag, and assessed the situation as logically as he could.

He sat down next to her, his heart, his soul begging to understand her, believe her. But someone tried to poison her? He couldn't, and part of him hated himself for that.

She wouldn't look at him. He slid closer, but didn't touch her. She didn't want that, even if she needed it.

"Where are you going?" he asked. Take it easy, don't push.

Sydney sniffed back tears, hating and loving his closeness at the same time. "Somewhere. I can't tell you."

"That's not acceptable," he said. "Sydney, you know that's not okay. I'll go insane if I don't know where you are."

Sydney felt her anguish like a sword through her belly. "I'll call you."

"No."

She turned her head to him. "I'll call you. That will do, period. End of story."

He frowned. "Stay with me, please. In my guest room. Sydney, I'll give you all the space you need."

"You think I'm crazy," she said, eyes glinting. "Don't you?"

"No," he answered right away. "I think you're scared and nervous and stressed out. You're feeling things you haven't felt before and—"

"Shut up." She knew she caught him off guard with that and found a bitter satisfaction in it. "Don't patronize me, and don't tell me what I feel. I know someone tried to kill me. I think it was Vic—"

"No, Sydney." Marcus stood up, walking to the bottom of the steps.

Sydney knew he couldn't accept this. It stung at her heart. They could never be together after this. This fact hurt her even more than the idea that someone had tried to kill her.

"Keith still expects you at the office tomorrow." It sickened him, this polite, irrelevant banter. "He said so just before he, Laura, and Dad left for the vet hospital."

Sydney nodded. The cab had to come before Victoria came out for church. It had to.

"Bree is . . ."

"She'll get over it," Sydney said. "I'll keep in touch with her after . . . after all this."

The cab finally drove into the circling driveway. Marcus took Sydney's bags. She didn't protest. He handed them to the cabbie. Every awkward second seemed to last an hour.

"And me?" he asked, as she headed for the door held open by the cabdriver.

"You?" Sydney turned to him, biting her lip to avoid the tears.

"You said you'll keep in touch with Bree after this." He was laying his heart on his sleeve, in clear view. She could knock it off at will. He had no choice in the matter. "What about me?"

Sydney touched his cheek, reaching up her hand to kiss him. As soon as their lips touched, her heart turned over one hundred times. This was more painful than anything. Just twenty-four hours ago, she was so hopeful. Now she wasn't certain she would ever see him again.

Marcus felt the sorrow mixed with affection in her kiss. It hurt him, but he couldn't push away. When her lips left him, he saw the panic in her eyes and whispered her name. Sydney ignored his call, hurrying inside the car and closing the door behind her.

Marcus watched the car drive away. He wouldn't let her go. He couldn't. He'd figure out a way to fix this mess. He had to choose, take control, be a man.

He'd start with McKenzie.

Sydney was impressed. The building was a renovated hotel right in the middle of downtown Bethesda, a sophisticated trendy district. The apartment was a two-room suite. It had a responsible design with white walls, white carpeting, and oakwood furnishings. The paintings were generic, but welcoming and attractive. It was like a hotel room.

Sydney went straight for the bed. She wanted to break down, thinking of Marcus, but she knew she couldn't. She couldn't crumble. She had to keep her goal in sight. Keep it in front.

"Hello?" The voice sounded groggy over the receiver.

"Professor Shue? It's Sydney Tanner."

"Hello, Sydney. Sorry, I'm a little under the weather. I did tell you to call me today, didn't I?"

"Yes." Sydney tried to be polite, even though she wasn't

interested in small talk. She hadn't the stomach for it. "About your friend. The African historian?"

"Hold on." There was a short pause. "Professor Webber will see you tonight. She has a lecture at Georgetown at eight."

Sydney rubbed the necklace May had given her. Just hearing the name Georgetown—she was going insane. Had to be.

"She'll be in lecture hall 6 in the history building. Sydney? Are you there?"

"Yes, Professor," she answered. "Sorry, I'm a little under the weather myself. Thank you. Thank you so much. I promise I won't ask you for another thing."

"I don't mind. I shouldn't have helped you as much as I have, but I have an objective as well. You're a smart kid. I look forward to working with you."

Sydney tried to focus on the project, but Marcus was all she could think of. On the train to meet the professor, she considered stopping by his place. She wanted so badly to see him, touch him, let him hold her.

"No." Sydney whispered her resolve as the train stopped to pick up passengers. "You were right the first time. Love comes after. Not now."

She rubbed the medallion of her necklace between her fingers, not paying attention to how far into the aisle she was leaning. As a group of rowdy teenagers stumbled down the aisle, one bumped Sydney, jerking her hand back. She gasped as the necklace broke. Reaching for the chain, Sydney sat in horror. Her mind worked fast. There were plenty of places in D.C. that could fix it. It was after five on Sunday, so she'd have to wait until tomorrow. She didn't have the rental car anymore. Getting around would be—

Sydney was stopped in her tracks after turning the medallion around. May hadn't said anything and Sydney hadn't noticed it until now.

On the other side, which had been turned toward her chest the whole time, was a name. An African name: *Sesay.*

Sydney reached for the papers in her knapsack. She'd bought along everything she had. She found the list of names she'd printed out, the list Maggie had a copy of, connecting names to Jonathan Hart. Foda Sesay was the tenth name on that list.

Sydney's mind was off of Marcus and the disastrous events of that morning for once.

Portia Webber was a regal-looking woman. She was raisin brown with flawless skin. Her hair was cut short to her head and jet black. She was medium height, medium built. Her clothes were African, colorful, and wrapped perfectly around her.

"Sydney Tanner? I can tell from the excitement on your face. A student's face when they're excited about learning is a priceless thing."

"I know the name I'm after." Sydney laid her papers on the edge of the small stage. She was excited, breathing quickly.

"Sesay. That's the name. This is a necklace. See?"

"Calm down." Portia laughed as she accepted the broken necklace. She looked closely. "You're a very lucky girl."

Sydney followed her to the podium, where Portia handed her four manila folders.

"I could find information on only three of the names," she said. "The fourth folder was to help you work on finding the rest. It's exhilarating reading some of these stories. So many of our people don't know they even exist.

They think our history started with slavery and anything before that is a lost cause."

Sydney gasped at the third folder. "It's them!"

Portia nodded. "The Sesays were one of the three I could find. Is this . . ."

Sydney could see her hesitation, caution. "What?"

She coughed, her eyes shifting a little. "Is this your family? I don't remember Maggie clarifying that with me."

"No." Sydney found it ironic. At one point she had felt like a small part of this crazy family. "Then, well . . . It's just a project."

Portia sighed. "Well, you should know. It's juicy, but not pretty."

That sounded all too familiar to Sydney. She sat at the edge of the podium and read. As she did, her mouth dropped open.

"Yes," Portia said, sitting next to her. "The Sesays were infamous in western Sierra Leone. I'd actually used their family in one of my lectures on the topic. They acquired their wealth through the slave trade."

Sydney spoke as she read. "They sold prisoners they'd taken in their own wars to European and Latin American traders."

"That was standard," Portia said. "Many of those tribes kept their POWs as slaves or sold them all the time. You see, slavery in those terms was different than the atrocity of the Western culture. It was a kinder form of indentured servitude. Slaves in Africa were considered human beings. They were enslaved because they were prisoners of war, condemned criminals, condemned debtors, or accused of witchcraft. The Sesays came from the Bassa tribe. There was no natural harbor there, so slave trading didn't happen too often.

"Selling slaves gave the Sesays countless amounts of

money, rum, cloth, and guns. These were all sources of power and trade. Getting back to the point, African slaves in many tribes could work for their freedom, and marry out of slavery. It was a completely different concept. The Africans didn't know they were sending black people to . . . where they were. To live like that."

Sydney shook her head. "Some freed slaves that returned home told how they had been sold. The Sesays were run from their village, from Sierra Leone. They got greedy."

Portia nodded. "They started selling free persons, kidnaping them from other villages and tribes—then unforgivably, their own tribe. They had to leave. Their family name was so synonymous with betrayal that they were recorded in these tribal notes. There aren't many of them left that can be transcribed. This is precious."

"It says they came to England around 1840. At that time, slavery had been abolished in England. For some reason, they went there. There is no way to prove this, but I'm thinking that most of their cash was from English slave traders. So they went where they could use it."

Sydney contemplated their situation. "Did they have any idea what it would be like for blacks?"

"Some say, by that point, many of the Africans did know. Some of those slaves were returning home, told of the horrors."

"Where does Jonathan Hart come in? He was against slavery. Why would he help them?"

Portia shrugged. "Once the Sesays got to England, they had to live in the black community. There was nowhere else for them to go. This would make them determined to hide any connections to their past. He might not have known. Jonathan's purpose was to help any blacks prosper."

"So it was as simple as that?" Sydney asked, shaking her head. "He didn't ask for any explanations? When did Foda Sesay become Reginald Hart?"

"There's no way for us to know all that."

Sydney remembered Maggie's words that last day of class. Tracing a family tree can also bring grief, embarrassment, self-doubt, and more questions that can never be answered no matter how much you searched. Foda Sesay became Reginald Hart at some point, but had he come to England from Sierra Leone alone? Sydney shook her head, overwhelmed by it all. She tried to put together all she knew. Many of Jonathan Hart's business partners were run out of England by mobs, which is probably what happened to the Harts. But was it a white mob that didn't want to see blacks prosper, or a black mob, who found out who the Harts really were? In Sierra Leone they had sold their captives to England and Latin America, not North America. Maybe the Harts came to America, not because they thought it would be more prosperous or because the white community in England didn't want them, but because they were not going to run into their past. With Jonathan Hart's last name, they would fit right in. Former slaves, with no history beyond their bondage.

"No wonder they wanted to keep it a secret." She turned to Portia. "This family . . . today they represent the perfect black family. It's all on the outside, but still— this would . . ."

"It could destroy them," she said. "Not likely. They can't be held responsible for their ancestors. None of us can."

"No," Sydney agreed. "But how many of our ancestors did this? I know these people, the mother. She'll do anything to keep this history secret."

"Well"—Portia stood up as people were filtering into the small auditorium—"not anything. Let's be serious."

"I am." Sydney's face was stone as Portia looked down at her in surprise. "Now that I have this, I'm in danger."

FOURTEEN

Sydney wasn't in the office for ten minutes Monday morning before Ana phoned her desk, telling her Keith wanted to see her immediately. The usual five-minute walk to his office seemed to take a half hour.

It had taken enough courage for her to show up, but Sydney believed Marcus when he'd told her Keith expected her. A comforting call from May right before bed encouraged her to at least finish out the week. In the end Sydney needed the money—now more than ever.

Still she was scared. She didn't know if she could trust Keith. What part had he played in the attempted poisoning? Nothing could happen to her here, could it?

"I'm surprised you came." Keith's expression was unfriendly, almost as if he didn't know her.

"Marcus said"—Sydney swallowed nervously, staying in the open doorway—"he said you expected me."

"Come in." He leaned back in his chair. "Close the door."

Sydney hesitated.

Keith's laugh was laced with sarcasm. "What are you afraid of? I don't have any poisoned milk here."

Sydney sat across from his desk, doing her best to hide her emotions. "Thanks for the insult."

He shook his head. "Sydney, your idea . . ."

"Is this what you called me here for?" she asked. "To laugh at me? Call me crazy?"

"Mother is concerned," he said, returning to his serious self.

It was Sydney's turn to laugh. "Concerned about me?"

"You accused her of trying to kill you." Keith sighed. "She's concerned you'll go around telling people about this. She's afraid you'll call the police."

"Ah, yes, appearances again. Can't have any bad press."

Keith appeared to ignore her. "She's also concerned about Marcus."

Sydney stood up, her heart racing. "What's wrong with Marcus?"

"He had a fit after you left. Storming around, mumbling to himself. Wouldn't even respond to Aunt May. He didn't come to church. I guess he left soon after we did. Then late last night, he called the house, demanding that Aunt May tell him where you are."

Sydney's heart fluttered. She felt herself let out a soft breath. "Did she?"

He shook his head. "Mother thinks the longer you stay away, playing this victim role, the more he'll want to save you, protect you."

"Is that it?" she asked.

"No. There's Bree."

Sydney sighed. "I asked to speak with her when May called me last night. She said she'd already gone to sleep. She was so upset over McKenzie."

"Aunt May's a good liar," he said. "She didn't want to upset you. McKenzie is already recovering. Bree ran out last night, drove off. No one can find her."

Apprehension swept over her. "Did you try Gary's?"

"We did, this morning. Tried his home, his roommate said he left last night, never came back. He didn't show up for his morning shift at the zoo either."

"Try her friends. Her—"

"Mother blames me for some of this." He was angry now, his brows centering. "She blames Marcus for leading you on and me for giving you a job to keep you in Baltimore."

Sydney's concern was replaced by a now familiar fear. She was scared of Keith. He'd changed since she'd met him: darker, angrier, riskier. "I'm not responsible for your mother's perceptions. Besides, I'm out of the house now. I'm not even living in Baltimore."

"You think no one knows where you're at?" He leaned forward, over the desk. "You have to remember how old my aunt is. Besides, secrets have a way of coming out around you."

Sydney didn't respond. She left, heading straight for her desk. She ignored the concerned stares and questions of the other researchers as she grabbed her things. Her heart was pumping fast. She was tired of running, but knew she had to get out of there. Money or no money. Home or no home. She had to get her things out of that suite now.

"Sydney, stop!"

She turned around to the familiar voice. Marcus sped to her. He looked a mess, and it melted her heart. It tore at her to know she was causing this.

He grabbed her, embracing her tightly. He had to see her, hold her. He had to apologize for not having been there for her completely, for causing her even a moment of doubt.

"Baby." He kissed her cheek. "I can't think of anything but you. I've been going crazy."

"I'm fine," she said, even though it wasn't true. His

arms around her made her think she was. "I said I would call you."

"I couldn't wait." He led her to the marble bench in the lobby of the building. "I have to tell you—"

"I can't talk now." Sydney's eyes nervously roamed the lobby. "Keith could . . ."

"He's not here. I saw him leave just before you came out of the elevator. He didn't see me."

Sydney wondered where he was going. "He scared me, Marcus. He's very angry with me."

Marcus wouldn't blink. He'd made up his mind. "You think it's Keith? Is it Keith who tried to poison you?"

Sydney's eyes widened. "You . . . you believe me?"

He smiled, touching her cheek. "I believe you. I'm sorry I took so long. It was just so hard to believe . . . this is my family, with all its faults, but it's still my family. That's what I came to tell you."

Sydney felt herself floating. Happy couldn't describe what she felt.

"The doctor said McKenzie was definitely poisoned," he said. "He's going to be fine. We're still waiting to find out with what."

"When will we know?"

Marcus glanced at his watch. "We'll get the results in an hour."

She repeated their conversation, emphasizing the ending.

"Where are you staying?" he asked. Marcus wasn't certain Keith had the guts to go as far as trying to kill someone. Maybe he was doing it for Victoria. Was he really saying this to himself?

"May's suite in Bethesda."

Marcus knew his father's hideaway well. May wasn't aware, but everyone in the family except Bree was aware of this. "We have to get you and your stuff out of there."

* * *

"You'll stay with me now?" Marcus was driving 95 South fast.

"We talked about this," Sydney said. "You're a politician."

"That doesn't matter." He found it endearing that, even with her life in danger, she was concerned about his reputation. "Your safety is the most important issue now."

"I have a good prospect." She hadn't called Maggie yet, but was prepared to get on her knees and beg like nothing before. "I'm sure it'll pan out."

Marcus's cell phone range. He reached for it. "Might be about McKenzie."

Sydney's stomach was clenched tight until she heard Marcus greet David Long. She watched the scenic drive as he spoke and drove. How had this all happened? How had she gotten into all of this? All she'd wanted was enough money to pay for one more year of school. That was it. Now here she was, head over heels in love with a man she could see no sane future with and in fear for her life.

"You're not going to believe this," he said, hanging up the phone. "Or maybe you will."

"What?"

"David just got a call from Jesse Michaels at Preston. They want to settle."

Sydney was stunned. If her life wasn't one surprise after another. "That's good."

"Weren't you on Preston's side?"

"At first," she answered. "Fairview Hills reminded me so much of where I was from. I couldn't believe people would want to stay. It prejudiced me, but after interviewing those people, I could see it was still home, a neighborhood to them. Even with its faults, it held strength for them. Pride. It was all they had and it meant everything. Preston was wrong, whether it could be proven or not. I wasn't going to try and hide that."

"This is going to kill Keith." Marcus was more than worried about his family, which seemed to be falling apart at the seams, but Sydney was his priority now.

There was silence the rest of the way, the jazz station failing to soothe either of them. Neither had any idea what to expect next.

Marcus took her hand as they entered the building and rode the elevator. Sydney was tempted to tell him what she'd found out about his family, but decided against it. He didn't need any more bad news today. She understood how hard it must be for him to take her side against his entire family. She could never express in words what his support meant to her.

The elevator opened on the fifth floor and Sydney and Marcus stepped out. They both saw him standing just outside the door to her suite at the same time.

Marcus was stunned for only a moment. He'd never seen such hate in his brother's eyes. "What are you doing here, Keith?"

"You're in it together." Keith was sweating, nervous, and very angry. "I knew it."

"In what together?" Sydney stood halfway behind Marcus. Neither took a step forward.

"You're trying to destroy me," he answered. "You want Mother to hate me, and you, Syd, you're trying to destroy my career."

Sydney didn't even notice the nickname. "You know about the settlement."

"It's because of your reports. I wasn't monitoring them, because I trusted you. I believed you understood our objective."

"Keith," Marcus said, "calm down. Why don't you and I go for a drink?"

"They're gonna fire me because of you." Keith ignored his brother, focusing on Sydney. "This was the case of my career. Mother was right. You're a menace and you're out to destroy all of us. You're getting out of all our lives now!"

Marcus could see the shiny reflection of a key he was certain Keith had gotten from Victoria, who had spoken once of having one.

"Keith." Marcus started toward them. "Keith."

Sydney heard a click, then a flash of light illuminated the hallway. She heard herself scream and in an instant, she heard a booming sound. There was wood and smoke everywhere. She couldn't see either brother anymore. Then everything went black.

Victoria Hart burst into the private hospital room, frantic. She gasped at the sight of her son lying on the bed.

"Keith!" She ran to him, leaning over and kissing his bruised forehead. "My baby boy. Why won't he wake up. Oh, God! He's in a coma."

"No, Mother." Marcus, his arm tightly around Sydney, reached for her shoulder. "He's fine. He's just been given something to sleep."

"He suffered only a couple of cuts and bruises," Sydney said. "A few stitches and some rest is all the doctor said."

It had all happened so fast. Sydney only remembered regaining consciousness under the screaming sirens of an ambulance. Marcus was at her side, bleeding from the head. A paramedic was trying to help him, but he kept shrugging the woman away. Sydney had been groggy, but understood that Keith had been hurt.

Victoria turned to them. Her eyes held an honest look

that Sydney hadn't seen before. It was as if she was seeing a real person for the first time.

"What happened?" Affectionately she reached for the bandage on Marcus's forehead.

"I'm fine, Mother." He caught her hand, kissed it. "Just a little cut. The door exploded. Someone must've planted a bomb."

"But who?" Victoria turned back to Keith, gently rubbing his cheek.

There was a short silence before Victoria spoke again. "You think I did this, don't you, Sydney?"

She kept her back to them.

"No," Sydney answered. "You did send Keith to . . . see me."

Victoria took a deep breath. "I sent him to throw you out of that . . . that place. Fire you and throw you out."

"You wouldn't have put him in that kind of danger," Sydney said. "But someone did. Someone tried to kill me . . . again."

Victoria turned to her, using a handkerchief to wipe her own eyes. "Are you all right?"

Sydney nodded, surprised at the sincerity in the woman's eyes.

They all heard voices outside the room before the door swung open. Anthony burst in, his eyes connecting with the three before focusing on his youngest son.

"My boy!" Obviously stricken with grief, Anthony squeezed the sheets around Keith's chest.

"Let him rest, Anthony." Victoria motioned his hands away. "Let him sleep."

Anthony's eyes lowered, his shoulders deepening. He shook his head slowly. It was then, Sydney knew.

"It was you," she said, her tone surprising even her with its softness, quiet, and calm.

He looked at her, his face, his eyes completely void of any emotion.

Victoria gasped.

Marcus felt his chest tighten. "What?"

"It's always been our responsibility." Anthony's eyes looked to the ground. "The Hart men. We had to keep the secret. But first they had to tell us. You have to know a secret before you keep it."

Sydney felt chills run through her body.

"What secret?" Victoria asked.

"The Harts were slave traders," Sydney said, feeling weak in the pit of her stomach. "When they were the Sesays living in Sierra Leone, Africa. They made their wealth from kidnaping Africans and selling them into slavery."

"How do you know this?" Marcus asked, but Sydney wasn't listening. She was honed in on Anthony, anger seething from her.

She walked around the bed, standing only a few feet from him. "You tried to kill me to keep from being embarrassed about something your family did a couple of centuries ago?"

"Not embarrassed." He looked at her, cold eyes hiding feeling. "Destroyed. Everything we've tried to build up. Do you have any idea what this family means to Baltimore? To the black community? Could I be where I am? Could my father have been the prominent businessman he was in his day? What about Marcus? Could he have a chance at being governor? What about Keith? What about Jordan?"

"Jordan?" Marcus yelled. His mother held him back as he started for his father. "You're crazy. You want us to believe you're doing this for a four-year-old kid! That this thing that happened generations ago on another continent would've been a scarlet letter on him twenty years from now?"

"It will!" Anthony's hands clenched in fists. "All those people out there that hate for us to prosper, to do well. Oh, man, they'd love to throw this bone out there. You know how the society press types up every little thing we do. Just like my father and my grandfather. I was thinking of this family. Protecting my family."

"You haven't been a part of this family for years," Victoria said. "You were protecting yourself. I can't blame you, because I did the same thing. But murder? *Murder?*"

"What were you going to do?" Sydney asked. "Claim it was an accident? It was a bomb. There are bound to be questions."

Anthony showed a flicker of guilt. Only a flicker. "I've known what I would have to do for a while. I faked the death threats that I'd been getting recently. I would be believed, because I'd gotten real threats more than a few times. The police would think someone was trying to kill me. I used some connections and I had a bomb, a defective one, set at my apartment and one at the back entrance to the house. Those would both fail, not even make a sound, but the one at the apartment that I . . . occasionally go to . . . would. Only you would be there. They'd never assume it was meant for you. I'd found out from Laura that May sent you there. I had everything done last night and this morning."

Sydney reached out and slapped him across his face. He didn't move, only flinching a bit. Marcus stepped up and stood between them, daring his father with his eyes to retaliate.

Keith moaned and everyone turned to him. He moved his head, left to right. He moaned again.

"Moottheeerr."

"I'm here, baby." She leaned over him, squeezing his hand in hers.

"I never meant to hurt Keith," Anthony said. "I love my son."

"You don't love anyone but yourself." Marcus wanted to strangle him. This man, who used to be his father, had almost killed his brother and had tried to kill the woman he loved.

Anthony's eyes turned fiercely to Sydney. "You . . . you caused this. Everything was fine before you came."

"You're wrong." Sydney's eyes squinted, showing her anger. "Nothing was fine in this family, and you were mostly to blame for that. Then *you* made it worse. You're a sick man, and you're not getting away with it."

Sydney felt sick. This man tried to take her life, kill her—twice. She couldn't be in the same room with him. She freed herself from Marcus, and ran out of the hospital.

Marcus called after her, running into the hallway. She was going so fast. Behind him, he heard his mother call to him, heard Keith moan again. In front, two policemen were walking toward him.

"Mr. Hart." One of the officers held out a hand to stop him. "Mr. Hart, we're officers from the scene. We need to talk to you."

"Later." He pushed the officer's hand away. Sydney. He had to get to her.

The other officer grabbed his arm. "Now, Mr. Hart, not later. If you want to find out who set that bomb, we have to act fast. We're talking about attempted murder here."

Marcus felt the harsh reality tighten around him. The officer was right. This was the end and the beginning, and he had to stay. He had to take over now.

"Come with me," he said, turning back toward the

room. "I'll take you to the person responsible. You can arrest him. He won't fight you."

"Finally. You came back."

Sydney turned toward the newly constructed door to the Bethesda apartment. Gabrielle stood in the doorway.

"Bree!" She ran to her, hugging her tightly. She kissed her forehead. "Where were you?"

"Gary and I went to stay with his cousin in Owings Mill." She wrapped her arm around Sydney as they walked to the bed. "I just couldn't take it anymore."

It had been two weeks since the incident. Sydney was staying in Maggie's extra bedroom. She'd helped her find a job on campus a student quit just a few days before. It paid much less than the law firm, but still it was pay. Sydney had had no contact with the Harts, but thought of Marcus every day. She missed him with a pain. She loved him more than ever.

"What are you doing here?" Gabrielle asked. "Did you leave something?"

"No." Sydney sighed, looking around. "I was waiting for things to die down. I came to . . . see. To sort of end this for myself. It's still hard to believe."

"I know. I thought you would come back. I've been stopping by every couple of days, trying to find you."

It hit Sydney that Gabrielle had been missing when this all went down. "How did you find out?"

"The news." A single tear trailed her left cheek. "I came right away."

"I'm so sorry." Sydney couldn't imagine the pain the girl was feeling. The inability to keep it private only made the situation worse.

As soon as Anthony had been arrested, the news was out. It had been on TV and in the paper, local and national, every day. Sydney had been dying to go to Marcus, comfort him, but she couldn't. She wanted to, but simply couldn't.

"At least he confessed," Sydney said. "There won't be a hideous trial."

"Laura confessed to helping him." Gabrielle shook her head. "I always knew she was unusually loyal to him, but she did all the dirty work. She bought the poison, put it in your milk, and got rid of the evidence later that night. That whole scene about putting it in the muffins was a cover. Daddy used her as the middle man, finding someone to plant the phony bombs and the real one. They found him right away."

Sydney wasn't surprised. She believed Laura would do anything for Anthony Hart. Now she was going to jail for him.

"How is Marcus?" she asked desperately. "I have to know."

"He misses you. I know he's a mess inside, but he won't show it. He's too busy being there for everyone."

Sydney knew she had to see him against her own judgment. He needed her. "Keith is back to normal?"

Gabrielle shook her head. "It's a little weird. We all thought the firm was going to fire him over the Preston disaster, but they didn't. Not yet at least. I think Keith is going back next week, but he seems to think they're just waiting for the negative to die down."

Sydney couldn't believe all the damage her presence had caused this family. Anthony had been right in that at least. She didn't see a chance for her and Marcus being together. Still she had to see him.

Sydney sat up. "Where is Marcus? I'm going to see him."

"Actually," Gabrielle said, "he knows I'm here. This was his idea. He tried a couple of times himself, thinking you'd come to get your things, but I guess he missed you."

Sydney's heart melted. "I can't wait another second. Where is he?"

"The hospital."

"What?" Sydney froze, feeling panic set in. "What's wrong with him?"

"Marcus is fine." Gabrielle was already headed for the door. "It's Aunt May. He's there visiting her. All of . . . this. She had a panic attack."

"Oh, my God!" Sydney was horrified. "Let's go!"

Marcus wasn't there. May was sitting up in the hospital bed with Kelly on one side, and Victoria on the other. All eyes set on Sydney and Gabrielle as they entered.

"Sydney!" May cheerfully opened her arms. She was smiling, looking tired, but okay. "Come here, little girl."

Sydney sped to her, hugging her tightly. She was already crying. "I just heard. I'm so sorry. This is all my fault."

"You stop that," May said, her mouth tightening in a scornful scowl. "I'm fine now. A little tension is all. Victoria, Kelly, Gabrielle—can you leave us alone for a moment?"

The women did as told, no protest, no looks. Sydney pulled the repaired necklace over her head and let it fall from her hand to May's. "Thank you, May. It's time to give this back. You need it more than I do."

"I need to thank you." May covered Sydney's hand in hers. "For bringing out the truth. Now it's out there. No more Hart men will be burdened with this, losing their sense of reality, sense of right and wrong."

"No, May." Sydney's guilt was still heavy on her. "I destroyed this family. My coming here destroyed everything."

"Not much was together in this family long before you came here, child. This isn't the end. It's a hurdle, a chance for this family to rise above or fall apart. I'm already seeing signs of strength. I'm already seeing the will to survive and move on. You need to learn something from this."

Sydney looked confused. "What can I learn, except to stay out of people's business?"

"You have your own family secrets." May nodded. "I don't know what they are exactly, but you're not hard to read."

"It's not the same," she said.

"It's always the same. All families have problems, imperfections of some kind or other—some worse, but still everyone. The test is, can you rise above it, let it go, and stick together? What matters is now. Love holds us together when nothing else is there."

Sydney's eyes moved away, into space. She saw Linda and David Williams. "If I let go, they get away with it. I won't let them get away with it. I can't."

"Child." May cupped Sydney's chin with her hand, turning the girl's face to her. She looked sternly into her eyes. "Vengeance is the Lord's. No one gets away with anything. You . . . move . . . on. You . . . let . . . go. If you don't, you'll destroy yourself and you and Marcus will never be together."

Sydney sighed helplessly. She knew May was right. She had to let go, but could she? And Marcus. "We'll never be together anyway. I love him, May. God, I love him. But look at what's happened. It would be impossible for us to . . . to . . ."

"Be together?"

Sydney turned her head. Marcus was in the doorway, an endearing smile on his haggard, tired face. Her heart jumped, her soul warming. The sight of him sent her head reeling, as if she hadn't seen him in years.

"You're wrong, Sydney." As he approached her, he felt consumed with relief at laying eyes on her. He'd never let her out of his sight again. "We'll be together. I love you more than anyone in this world. You love me, too."

"More than life," she whispered, as his arms wrapped around her. The world was erased. "But all of this. Your family will never . . ."

He gently pressed his index finger to her lips. "My family will get through this. No one blames you for bringing to light what was already there. Even if you'd never been here, we wouldn't have made it through the summer without some of this ugliness coming out. You couldn't have possibly imagined it. Baby, I promise you, everything will be fine. You've found a new family. This one will love you and care for you."

"That's too much to ask." Sydney wanted to believe his every word. "For your family to accept me? Victoria? Keith? Wouldn't our dating just bring more press, more—"

"Forget the press," he said. "Forget appearances. As for Mother and Keith, they won't have to accept our dating, because we won't be. They'll have to accept my wife."

Sydney was speechless. She stared, stunned. Had he? Did he?

"Wife?" There went her knees again.

Marcus smiled. She was pleased. He felt lucky. He wouldn't have to beg, but he'd been prepared to do that. "If you'll have me. These past months, these past two weeks, my father going to jail. So much has been going on. It's brought the rest of us closer together. It's been a lesson in what counts: life, family, love. None of these exists without you anymore."

The joyful tears started down Sydney's cheeks. "You're all I've been able to think about."

"I felt guilty at first, feeling so sorry because I couldn't be with my love, but when you need someone, you need them. Now you won't be marrying into the Huxtables, but there are some pluses to joining this family."

"Name some, please." She smiled, teasing him. She already knew the pluses. Everyone she loved was in this family. Everyone.

Marcus bit his lower lip. "Well, I'll have to get back to you on that, but please say yes. Look, I'll pay off your student loans."

"Hmmm." She noddcd. "What else?"

Marcus smiled mischievously. "Well, I don't like to toot my own horn, but I'm a pretty talented young—"

"Marcus Kenneth Hart!" May folded her arms across her chest. "I hear you. You watch your mouth. You're not married yet."

Sydney was laughing and crying at the same time. She felt insane with love and contentment. This was the future and she was letting go of the past. Her new goal was to be happy with the man who held her in his hand. No more revenge. She'd have to learn to let go. She didn't doubt she could do it now, as she always had before. Not anymore.

Sydney wrapped her arms around his neck. "Can I have the student loan promise in writing?"

Marcus looked into her angel eyes, loving her completely. "I don't have a pen on me, but this should do."

His lips were on hers instantly. He devoured her, as if he hadn't tasted her sweet lips in years. This was joy, this was forever. This was his wife.

EPILOGUE

July Fourth at the Hart mansion was a joyous one. Only the family and a few close friends were there. Sydney was excited, nervous. She was the only one there that knew this was so much more than a holiday, a mere barbecue.

Marcus returned to his wife of six months with the lemonade she wanted. She was beautiful today, like every day. She glowed under the hot sun. Her hair fell carelessly around her face. She wore it like that for him. He loved it.

"You're too good to me." Sydney took a sip, smiling flirtatiously at the man she came to love more and more each day.

He kissed her, feeling a warmth inside of him that was hotter than the blazing sun. "No such thing."

Sydney's eyes twinkled. It had been like this all the time. Last July, when the disaster hit, their love for each other seemed to be the catalyst for the Hart family's recovery.

It hadn't been easy for any, but Sydney felt loved like she never had in her life. Victoria's turnaround was the most surprising. She had secluded herself at the family home in Vail, Colorado, as the media blitz hit. When she returned, she welcomed Sydney to the family. No one questioned why. Victoria was a different woman now. Not different in the sense that she welcomed Sydney with open arms, but in the sense that she was warmer, softer, humble, and real. Sydney was the one who needed some time to adjust. Her only idea of a mother, a family, had been Linda and David Williams. It took some time to trust, let her guard down again. A year later she and Victoria were getting along better than anyone could have expected.

"Marcus." Victoria's expression told of her displeasure as she approached her son. "Would you look at your sister? She's carrying on as bad as you two do. Only, she's not married to this Roger."

Gabrielle was sitting on her new boyfriend's lap and they were kissing, giggling, being young. McKenzie was lying at their feet, gnawing at a rawhide bone.

"It's Raymond," Marcus corrected. "And you should be happy. He's a lawyer."

"He's a law clerk." She shrugged. "He hasn't passed the bar yet. I guess if Keith hired him, he should have potential."

Sydney and Marcus had married in December. As lavish society weddings go, it was the midrange. Most people were simply interested in seeing the woman who had snagged one of the Hart bachelors. The negative press saturation of Anthony's crimes had died down, the real friends were still around. The disaster Anthony was ready to kill for never came. Instead, the story behind the story sparked a genealogy fever, with African Americans all over the area excited about finding out the good and bad about where they came from.

They spent their honeymoon over Sydney's holiday break, touring Africa. When they returned, Keith had left Panka, McDaniel, and Wagner and started his own practice. Six months later, he had more clients than he could handle.

Marcus waited until his mother had walked away. Sydney had that look. "Hey, baby. What are you hiding?"

He read her so well. The stubborn fighter in her didn't like that. The loving wife in her loved it. "I've made my decision about work."

"Let me guess." Marcus flipped up his sunglasses, looking into her mesmerizing eyes. "You accepted the consulting job."

"Which one?" Since graduating last month, Sydney had two lucrative job offers from the leading strategy consultant firms.

He leaned back, assessing her further. "Trick question. Neither. You're taking the corporate manager job."

She shook her head. She had two corporate offers from major D.C. area companies, one a major hotel chain, the other a telecommunications giant. A year ago these positions would've been her dream.

Marcus frowned, thinking hard. There was only one job left. "The nonprofit? Helping young parents from the ghetto? It's a small organization, pays next to nothing. It's not even full-time. What happened to my corporate raider?"

"That's the past," Sydney said. "At some moment in my teenage anger at my parents, I designed that as the best I could be. I know better now. I know I've really made it when I'm happy with what I do. This job lets me help our people. I'll be helping young mothers and fathers learn how to deal with the pressures of parenting, learn to nurture their children and develop strong relationships with them. Most importantly I'll have the free time I need."

"For what?" Marcus loved her for the progress she'd made. She taken several social work electives her second year at school and started seeing a psychiatrist to help deal with issues from her childhood. He saw the walls come down—the loving openness he had witnessed show itself to everyone.

"For my real job." Sydney slid her arm around his trim waist.

"As Mrs. Marcus Hart?" He was flattered and surprised. He'd been prepared to have a corporate wife. Loving her, he could be happy only if she was.

"No." Sydney looked lovingly into his eyes. "As a mommy."

Marcus's drink fell out of his hand onto the grass. Iced tea splattered all over their legs, making them jump high in the air. Sydney laughed out loud, everyone looking.

Marcus stuttered. "I-I'm g-gonna b-be a f-father?"

"Six and a half months from now." Sydney rubbed her stomach.

Marcus was overwhelmed. He hollered her name, lifting Sydney in the air. He brought her down, kissing her face everywhere.

Sydney took it in stride. She was getting used to being this happy all the time.

ABOUT THE AUTHOR

Angela Winters was born and raised in Evanston, Illinois, a suburb of Chicago. She is the youngest of Matthew and Merea Winters' six children. After graduating from Evanston Township High School, she majored in journalism at the University of Illinois at Urbana-Campaign and worked as a beat reporter for the Daily Ilini. She graduated in 1993, and worked in financial public relations, marketing, and executive search. She is currently a recruiter for a northern Virginia financial services company. She lives in Alexandria, VA with her 14-year-old cat, Jordan.

E-mail her at: angela_winters@yahoo.com

Or visit her Web site:

http://www.tlt.com/authors/awinters.htm

Coming in March from Arabesque Books . . .

__**FORBIDDEN HEART** by Felicia Mason
  1-58314-050-65 $5.99US/$7.99CAN
When savvy Mallory Heart needs someone to oversee construction of her
first boutique, she turns to Ellis Carson. Although he has little in common
with the college-educated men she's used to and he thinks she's a snob,
soon enough they start concentrating on their shared interest in each other.

__**PRECIOUS HEART** by Doris Johnson
  1-58314-083-2 $5.99US/$7.99CAN
Burned by love, Diamond Drew is determined never to trust another man
again. But after meeting handsome Dr. Steven Rumford, everything
changes. Since he comes with a disastrous past as well, the couple must
learn to trust each other if they can ever hope to find happiness together.

__**A BITTERSWEET LOVE** by Janice Sims
  1-58314-084-0 $5.99US/$7.99CAN
When Teddy Riley secures an interview with reclusive author Joachim West,
she never expects that a freak accident will lead to her being mistaken for
his wife . . . or that she might find an irresistible passion that promises
a future filled with a joyful, healing love.

__**MASQUERADE** by Crystal Wilson-Harris
  1-58314-101-4 $5.99US/$7.99CAN
Offered a chance to housesit in Miami, Madison Greer soon meets Clint
Santiago, the most handsome, mysterious man she's ever encountered.
But Clint is really a federal agent trying to bust a drug dealer and to do
that, he'll have to get close to Madison and risk losing his heart forever . . .

Call toll free **1-888-345-BOOK** to order by phone or use this
coupon to order by mail. *ALL BOOKS AVAILABLE MARCH 1, 2000.*
Name _____
Address _____
City _____ State _____ Zip _____
Please send me the books I have checked above.
I am enclosing $_____
Plus postage and handling* $_____
Sales tax (in NY, TN, and DC) $_____
Total amount enclosed $_____
*Add $2.50 for the first book and $.50 for each additional book.
Send check or money order (no cash or CODs) to: **Arabesque Books,
Dept. C.O., 850 Third Avenue, 16th Floor, New York, NY 10022**
Prices and numbers subject to change without notice.
All orders subject to availability.
Visit out our Web site at **www.arabesquebooks.com**